High school E
up with gorgeous assistant football coach.
But is the man what he seems to be? Skyler still has his
doubts when he spies Keith in some shady circumstances.
And there are still some unanswered questions as to what
exactly is going on at the high school. Who thought high
school could be so sinister? Meanwhile, Skyler's friends
from college have their own problems. Lovers and partners,
Evan and Jeff were kicked out of the Army for Don't Ask
Don't Tell, and the depressed Evan is found dead. Suicide,
says the police, but Skyler thinks otherwise. It's Skyler Foxe
on the hunt for a killer once more!

Featuring a roll call of some of the best writers of gay erotica and mysteries today!

Derek Adams	Z. Allora	Maura Anderson
Victor J. Banis	Jeanne Barrack	Laura Baumbach
Ally Blue	J.P. Bowie	Barry Brennessel
Michael Breyette	Nowell Briscoe	P.A. Brown
Jade Buchanan	James Buchanan	Charlie Cochrane
Karenna Colcroft	Jamie Craig	Kirby Crow
Ethan Day	Diana DeRicci	Jason Edding
Theo Fenraven	Angela Fiddler	S.J. Frost
Kimberly Gardner	Michael Gouda	Roland Graeme
Storm Grant	Amber Green	LB Gregg
Kaje Harper	Jan Irving	David Juhren
Kiernan Kelly	M. King	Matthew Lang
J.L. Langley	Josh Lanyon	Anna Lee
Elizabeth Lister	Clare London	William Maltese
Z.A. Maxfield	Timothy McGivney	Lloyd A. Meeker
Patric Michael	AKM Miles	Reiko Morgan
Jet Mykles	William Neale	Cherie Noel
Willa Okati	Neil S. Plakcy	Jordan Castillo Price
Luisa Prieto	Rick R. Reed	A.M. Riley
Rob Rosen	George Seaton	Jardonn Smith
Caro Soles	JoAnne Soper-Cook	Richard Stevenson
Liz Strange	Marshall Thornton	Lex Valentine
Maggie Veness	Haley Walsh	Missy Welsh
Stevie Woods	Lance Zarimba	

Check out titles, both available and forthcoming, at
www.mlrpress.com

FOXE HUNT

A Skyler Foxe Mystery

HALEY WALSH

mlrpress

www.mlrpress.com

Published by
MLR Press, LLC
3052 Gaines Waterport Rd.
Albion, NY 14411

Visit ManLoveRomance Press, LLC on the Internet:
www.mlrpress.com

Cover Art by Deana C. Jamroz
Editing by Neil Plakcy

Print format ISBN# 978-1-60820-423-6
ebook format ISBN#978-1-60820-424-3

Issued 2011

To L.S.H. You rock!

ACKNOWLEDGMENTS

A Big Thank You to my wonderful editor, Neil Plakcy, my publisher Laura Baumbach from MLR Press, and my cover artist Deana Jamroz, who listened to me change my mind over and over again. Another thank you goes to the kind people of Redlands, California, who let me poke around where I have no business doing so. I actually really love that town. I've got my eye on a couple of lovely Craftsman homes there, so watch out. Lastly, the biggest thank you goes out to L.S.H., who puts up with it all, God knows. As you can see, it takes a village rather than just one author sitting alone in a room typing on a keyboard. Thank you all.

"We'll make you some sport with the fox ere we case him."
—*All's Well That Ends Well*, William Shakespeare

From the bathroom, Skyler Foxe heard his friend Sidney enter his apartment. He was used to it. He took a long time to shower and primp, though he wouldn't admit that to her. But that was why he gave her a key. She could make herself at home while he finished his routine.

"Hi! I'll be out in a minute!" he called to the shuffling in the living room. "You know it takes a *lot* longer for bottoms to get ready. I don't know that tops truly appreciate that. There's extra stuff to take care of. Know what I mean?" But when he trotted into the living room for his wallet, wearing only a towel and dripping wet from the shower, the last person he expected to see was—

"*Mom!*"

Cynthia Foxe turned toward her son and seemed unruffled that he was half-naked and trying to cover himself.

Fifty years old and still trim, she was no taller than Skyler, who always said on a good day he was five foot five. The platinum blond hair had come from her side of the family, but hers was white-gray now and cut in a short though not quite chic style. She wore a slightly outdated Donna Karan dress in a salmon color that complemented her blue eyes. Skyler's eyes never quite made it to blue, but in the right light their gray was almost there. A Marc Jacobs handbag was slung over one shoulder and she clutched her wad of keys in one hand. She still wore her wedding ring though she had been divorced since Skyler was twelve.

She jangled the keys. She and Sidney were the only other people to have a key to his apartment. He had willingly given Sidney her key. His mother had demanded hers.

"Did I come at a bad time?"

"Uh…" When was ever a good time? He realized he hadn't called her in a while so that's what he got. No calls; you get a visit, usually unscheduled and at the worst possible time. He looked down at himself. "I just got out of the shower."

"Going out?"

He pushed his wet bangs off his forehead. "Yeah."

"With whom?"

He retreated into the bedroom and left the door ajar so he could be interrogated *and* get dressed at the same time. "Sidney."

"She's such a nice girl, even if she is a policeman."

"Police*woman*. And anyway she's a detective."

"When are you going to marry her, anyway?"

"*Mom!* In the first place we're just friends. And in the second place—" *She's a woman.* But he couldn't very well say that. With his mother, he was still firmly ensconced in the closet…and then he realized he was actually *standing* in his closet and repressed a laugh. "In the second place we aren't attracted to each other." There. That was no lie.

"That's not the vibe I get from her."

He poked his head out of the door, being still only dressed in his briefs. "*What?*"

"I've seen the way she looks at you sometimes. That isn't a just-a-friend look."

He shook his head. "You're nuts."

"So when were you going to tell me about that whole murder thing?"

He was so flummoxed he almost grabbed a striped shirt to go with his pin-striped pants. "Uh…" Dammit! She probably called Sidney first. "*Skyler never calls me. Is he dead or alive?*" He knew the drill.

"I didn't want to worry you." He stared at his clothes. How was he supposed to dress to pick up guys with his mother standing in the next room? He chose a champagne-colored silk shirt and figured it would have to do.

"Oh I don't worry," she said in that way of hers that meant "move over, here comes the guilt." "I know if something was truly important I'd hear it from you personally, instead of my having to call your friends."

"You could have called me."

"I don't like talking to your voice mail. Makes me think you're screening."

I am. "I'm sure Sidney told you it was nothing. I was perfectly okay." Sort of. If it hadn't been for the death threats and stuff.

"You find a dead person and a man beats up your car with a baseball bat. You call that nothing?"

"Well…it was. It's okay now. The car is fixed and the guy's my friend again."

"He's your *friend*?"

Oh shit! And he was coming over, too. "Yeah. Mom, I'm sort of on my way out. Was there something you wanted?" He came out of his room, tucking in his shirt.

"Does a mother need an excuse to see her son? I haven't heard from you in a long time and I worried about you and the car. I know how important that car is to you."

"It's fine. It's all fixed. The insurance covered it." Twice, but no need to go into that.

She buttoned the top button of his shirt and flattened the collar. "I just wish I could have bought it for you. I wish I could have done a lot of things."

Skyler recognized that strain in her voice. He undid the top button of his shirt again and hugged her. "You did quite a lot for me without buying me fancy cars. I was raised very well, in fact. I couldn't have been the proper gentleman otherwise." He smiled at her and then asked quietly, "Do you need any money?"

She blinked, turning her head to stare at the kitchen light. "Well, maybe a little, just to tide me over till the end of the month."

He reached into his wallet and took out a hundred. "This okay?"

She took it without looking and kissed his cheek again. "You're my sweetheart."

The doorbell chimed. Super. That would be either Sidney or Rodolfo. He opened the door.

Oh goody. It was both.

Rodolfo—dressed in a tight pink midriff top made out of some shimmery material with his trademark tight leather pants—pushed his way in and flounced down on the sofa. He was the spitting image of Antonio Banderas, and with the accent, too. "Skyler, *amante*, are you ready?" Then he spotted Mrs. Foxe and jumped to his feet. "Excuse me! We haven't met."

Skyler looked imploringly at Sidney but she wasn't getting it. "This is Rodolfo. Sidney's *date*."

Rodolfo laughed. "What?"

"Rodolfo, this is my *mother*."

Rodolfo clicked into suave-Latin-gigolo mode. His Ecuadorian accent grew thicker. He took Mrs. Foxe's hand and kissed it. "A pleasure to meet you, Mrs. Foxe," he purred.

Cynthia Foxe smiled. "Pleasure's mine. Sidney, you didn't tell me you were dating."

"Well, I wasn't at the time, Mrs. Foxe." She glared at Skyler as she slid past him.

"Well, Mom, we've got to run. I'll call you."

"Come over for dinner Sunday night."

"O-okay."

"Sidney, you come, too. Oh yes. And bring your boyfriend."

"He's not my boyfriend. And he's busy Sunday."

"I am?" He looked from Sidney to Skyler and they each shot him murderous expressions. "I am," he agreed sullenly.

"Okay. I won't keep you young people, then. Don't stay up

too late, Skyler." He escorted her to the door and she leaned into him, whispering confidentially. "I think you should tell Sidney to give up on this one. I think he's gay."

Skyler nearly choked. He looked back at Rodolfo, studying him judiciously, noticing how his ass conformed to the tight leather pants. "You think so?"

"Yes. I'm very good with that. I can always spot them."

Skyler smiled weakly and kissed his mother's cheek. "I love you, Mom."

She kissed his cheek and wiped off the lipstick with her thumb. "I love you, too, sweetie."

As soon as he closed the door, Sidney jabbed a finger in his direction. "Skyler. When are you going to *tell* her?"

"Not tonight, evidently." He crossed back to his room to grab a belt.

Rodolfo was laughing.

"This is not funny," she said to both of them. "Doesn't she think I have better taste than this guy?"

"Hey!" said Rodolfo, his laughter stopping abruptly.

"By the way," said Skyler, undoing another button on his shirt. "Mom says that she thinks Rodolfo's gay, so don't get too attached."

She slapped his shoulder.

"Ouch!"

♫ ♫ ♫

A short time later they drove in Skyler's white Bug to their local hangout, Trixx. When Sidney stepped out of the car and held the seat back for Rodolfo, he said to her, "You look very pretty tonight, Sidney."

She smiled at him. "Sorry about that remark earlier."

Rodolfo waived his hand at her. "Everyone gets nervous around mothers. But you really should tell her, Skyler."

"Have you told *your* mother?"

"Can't. She's passed on." He made the sign of the cross, kissed his fingers, and sent it skyward.

His friends were already at the bar: Jamie Ewing in blue hair and tight trousers, and Philip Price in square-framed glasses and his customary black T-shirt and jacket ensemble.

Rodolfo gave them a full grill smile. Philip still treated him with the usual indifference but Jamie gave him the works with squeal, hugs, and kisses. "I met Skyler's mother tonight," said Rodolfo.

Jamie giggled. "Oh man! How *was* that?"

Sidney, with margarita already in hand, gestured with her damp straw. "She thinks Rodolfo and I are dating, thanks to the Skyboy here."

Jaime laughed and spilled his mojito. The beer mat soaked up some of it. "So where's Hunk on a Stick?" he asked, looking around.

Skyler choked on his Grey Goose. "Who?" But he knew perfectly well who Jamie meant.

"You know! Your gorgeous boyfriend."

"He's not my boyfriend." Keith Fletcher. Hunk on a Stick. Walking Wet Dream. Any number of appellations that were apt to describe the sexy biology teacher and assistant football coach at James Polk High, the same school where Skyler taught English.

But boyfriend? Skyler had never had a boyfriend before and it didn't seem likely he'd have one in the near future. They'd only kissed, after all. He supposed they were considering the merits of starting a relationship when they worked at the same place and were both in the closet. There was also something odd about Keith that made Skyler just a bit leery. Nothing he could put his finger on, but he supposed there was a dark side to Keith. Maybe it was something in his past. Maybe it was something else. Or maybe it was just Skyler's imagination or insecurities.

"Skyler!"

"What?" He whipped his head toward Jamie. He had done it again. Zoned out. He did that a lot lately when thinking of Keith.

"He's dreaming about his Hunka Hunka Burnin' Love again," said Sidney.

"Am not," he said weakly. Though it was tough getting Keith off his mind. Keith had promised that they would "get together" soon. Skyler was hoping it would be *very* soon.

Sidney and Jamie moved to the crowded dance floor and began bumping and grinding to the beat of "I Love My Sex."

Philip sidled up to Skyler and adjusted his glasses. Rodolfo leaned on his other side. Rodolfo and Philip couldn't seem to get past their initial animosity for one another. Skyler hoped that they would get over themselves someday.

"Have you heard about Beat?" Philip shouted in his ear.

"What about it?" Skyler yelled back.

"Closed."

"Oh no!" Beat was a gay dance club in San Bernardino. The biggest county in southern California and there was only one gay dance club. And now it was closed. Riverside County had the only other one and that was some seventy miles away. "I suppose all that illegal stuff with their books did it, huh?"

"It would appear so. I read about it on the Inland Empire Business Blog. The murder in their back alley didn't help matters."

"Shit."

"You don't mean you would have gone back there? Not after all the trouble you had with the angry bartender and the murder investigation…"

"It was the closest place," Skyler whined.

Philip shook his head. "You sure are forgiving."

"Where dancing is concerned." He sighed and knocked back his drink and set it aside. "Dance with me and Rodolfo."

"What? That Latin gigolo?"

Rodolfo shot a glare at Philip. "I'm standing right here, you know!"

"I *know*."

"Guys, come on. Let's all try to get along. Dance!" He grabbed both their hands and pulled them toward the tiny dance floor. Both Philip and Rodolfo reluctantly allowed themselves to be dragged along.

Skyler draped his arms over their shoulders, drawing them all closer. "Love for the Weekend" cheered their spirits and Rodolfo was the first to let loose. Philip gave him an eye roll but started shifting into an energetic rhythm, and a smile even crept onto his face.

Much better. Skyler liked it when they got along, this loose association that Jamie teasingly called the Skyler Fuck Club, or S.F.C., since all his best friends used to be hook-ups. He closed his eyes and fell into the rhythm, swaying his hips and rolling his head on his neck. He was just getting into it when someone slammed into his shoulder, dislodging him from his friends and almost knocking him down.

"Oh shit! I'm sorry!" Hands reached for him and helped him up and he found himself looking into familiar soft brown eyes.

"Jeff?"

"Skyler?" The slender man looked around at Skyler's friends but didn't seem to recognize the faces of Philip or Rodolfo. Of course, he wouldn't. Skyler had known Jeff before he met Philip or even Jamie, and certainly before Rodolfo, whom Skyler had only met himself a month ago.

"Jeff." He looked the man over. Jeff Dwyer was even thinner than he remembered. He had that unhealthy look about him, drawn cheeks and skeletal arms, that made him wonder if Jeff didn't have AIDS. He took Jeff into a hug to prove that it didn't matter. "It's good to see you," he said to his cheek before pushing him back to look at him. He definitely didn't look good.

"It's been a long time, huh, Sky?" He glanced at Skyler's friends again and lowered his face. Skyler nodded to his friends and took Jeff aside.

"A long time," Skyler admitted. "What have you been doing with yourself?"

He gestured with hands that were each encumbered by full beer bottles. "Evan and I became officers and went overseas."

"No shit! You're kidding! You mean Iraq?"

Sweat sparkled off of Jeff's short hair when the lights caught it. "We sure did." His voice had a defeated tone to it.

Skyler had a sinking feeling when he asked, "W-where's Evan?"

"He's outside. He won't come in. Maybe if you talked to him. He'd love to see you. But Skyler. Things didn't go well in Iraq. Evan—"

"Let me just say hello." He signaled to his friends that he was going outside, and Jamie acknowledged with a wave. Anxiety squeezed his chest and he put his hand warmly on Jeff's back as he followed him out the door. Not only were these good friends of his, but they were also hook-ups at separate times in college, an early pre-cursor to the S.F.C. But they hadn't stayed in touch. He knew that Evan was quite the jock and very much into the military thing. He always suspected he'd join up, but he had hoped that Evan would be out of it when all this Middle East stuff started escalating.

All his fears were justified when they emerged and Skyler spotted the back of a guy in a wheelchair. *Please no.* But it *was* him.

Jeff scooted ahead and shoved the bottled beer forward. "Evan, guess who I ran into inside?"

Evan took the proffered beer and turned. His dark eyes held little emotion at first, but then they focused on Skyler, who was trying to keep the horror from his face. A small smile played at the edges of the man's mouth but got no further. "Skyler Foxe. Mmm. Mmm. You are still a tasty-looking morsel."

Skyler felt the vice grip on his heart ease somewhat. "Evan Fargo. You could always make me blush."

"I made you squeal as I recall."

Skyler's ears flushed hot.

Evan's face looked the same, though perhaps a little harder, and the fine lines at his eyes were etched a little deeper than he remembered. He had short brown hair, buzzed up the side, military style. But the significant difference was the pant leg folded up to the knee. Skyler grabbed one of the chairs from the outdoor tables and pulled it around in front of the wheelchair and sat. He tried not to look at the leg. "Jeff tells me you guys went to Iraq."

Evan's face clouded. "You mean it's not obvious?" He gestured toward his leg with the beer bottle. He took a swig. His arms were hairy and there was a nest of dark hair peeking out from the fatigue-green shirt collar. His uneven beard was unkempt and told of a certain disinterest in his looks, not at all like Keith Fletcher's carefully cultivated jaw stubble.

Skyler reached for him, fingers resting on the arm he had known so well. "I'm sorry, Evan."

"Everyone's sorry. Everyone but our commanding officers. Fags are immoral, didn't you know? Like adulterers. It's okay if we die or fucking lose our limbs fighting for freedom, but don't love your fellow man *that* way. Fucking generals." He took another long drink.

"We were in Fallujah," said Jeff, rolling his broad shoulders. The outside string of colored lights tinted the sharp planes of his high cheekbones. "And we were very good about not looking like we were together, you know? As far as anyone knew, we were just good buddies. We didn't even sleep together over there. Not once."

"Never touched, not even secretly," echoed Evan.

"We were good soldiers. We were heroes. Especially Evan." He laid his hand on Evan's shoulder, but Evan seemed to shrink from it. Jeff slowly withdrew his hand.

"Don't ask, don't tell…don't show," growled Evan. "And we didn't. We didn't deserve what they did to us. I gave my life to the army. I was an officer."

"We both were."

Skyler looked from one solemn face to the other. "What happened?"

"Shortly after Evan was wounded, I got leave to be with him at the Army hospital in Balad. That's when…when it fell apart." His long fingers wrapped around his beer bottle, moved restlessly, leaving smudges in the condensation.

"We were discreet. No one saw us. I know they didn't."

"Well someone did," said Jeff wearily. "We were both court-martialed. Evan got the better deal."

Evan snorted. "They allowed me to continue getting care at the VA hospital since I kind of left my leg in Iraq. At least they acknowledged that."

"They couldn't take that away," said Jeff. "Anyway, Evan got an honorable discharge. But I didn't. The goddamned snitch who told his tales managed to get me a dishonorable."

"Shit! Did you appeal?"

Jeff nodded. "Three times. No go. Do you know what a dishonorable does to your record? It's a felony, Skyler. That shit cans any chance for me to get a decent job."

Skyler didn't know what to say. It wasn't fair. The Army was all Evan had ever talked about, all he had wanted to do as long as Skyler had known him. It would be as bad as Skyler never being allowed to teach again.

"How long have you guys been out?"

"Three months," said Evan. "We've been fighting with the Army to change Jeff's dishonorable to honorable but it's all a pretty slow process. We contacted our Congressman and our lawyers keep telling us to wait. They were full of optimism when they took our first check. Of course *that* one didn't bounce."

"God, you guys. I'm so sorry."

Evan scowled and thrust his empty beer bottle at Jeff. "I

could use another."

Jeff took the empty and trudged back into the doorway. Skyler followed with a quick farewell kiss on Evan's cheek and a whispered goodbye. Evan gave him a brief smile. Once they got back inside Jeff put both bottles down on the first flat surface. He covered his face with his hand. "He's been like that ever since the leg and it's only gotten worse when they kicked us out. I don't know what to do about him anymore, Skyler. He's so depressed all the time. I'm worried he's going to do something."

Skyler grabbed his shoulders. "Like what? He wouldn't... wouldn't..."

Jeff shook his head. When he took his hand away his eyes were wet and red-rimmed. "I don't know. He's not like he was. But the Army turning its back on him like that. That was worse than losing the leg. I love him dearly, Skyler. I really do. But I'm afraid what he might do."

"What about you? You don't look so well."

"I'm all right. I'm just exhausted from this fight. I hold down two jobs so I don't lose the house. They're crap jobs but I've got them. And at least now we've got some pro bono lawyers from the LGBT center."

"Listen. Here's my number." Skyler reached in his pocket and took out a business card. "Call me anytime. I don't have much but I can bring over groceries or something—"

"Don't be ridiculous. We can't take your money. Just your friendship."

"Of course. I mean it. Call me anytime."

Jeff offered their number and Skyler took out his phone and entered it. After he stuffed the phone away in his pocket, they stood and looked at each other forlornly for a bit until Jeff patted Skyler's arm. Skyler dragged him into a hug. The man sighed tiredly. He pushed Skyler back and offered a brave smile. "Look, I've kept you away from your friends long enough. You go back to them. Evan and I will be all right. I'm going to take him home. This was the first time he would go out though he wouldn't come in. Too many people dancing. But I'm glad we came. I'm glad we ran into you."

"Me too. Take care of yourself and Evan, okay?"

He kissed Skyler's cheek. His lips felt dry and papery. "Thanks for being a friend, Skyler."

Skyler watched him walk away. He had been so full of energy and life when Skyler knew him in college. They had been a couple of years ahead of him and he knew they were both going places. He also remembered how burly and sexy Evan had been. Now the two of them looked worn out, empty shells of what they once were.

He'd call Jeff in a few days to see how everything was going. He didn't want to lose track of them again.

Jamie came alongside him and draped an arm over Skyler's shoulder. "I kind of heard," he said apologetically.

"Sucks, doesn't it?"

"Yeah, and not in a good way." Jamie turned him and steered him toward the doorway. "You're a good friend, Skyler."

"I try." Some things just shouldn't be. He hoped that all would turn out all right for his friends, but he couldn't help feeling a sense of unease for them, too.

CHAPTER TWO

On Friday morning, Skyler settled at his desk before his favorite sophomore class arrived. He logged onto his computer to check emails. Last week had been one hell of a week, what with murderers tracking him down, someone pushing one of the teachers down the stairs, and the delicious Keith Fletcher cornering him and kissing the daylights out of him.

Some weeks you just didn't know what to do with yourself.

There was an email about the injured teacher, Julia Meyers, and he quickly clicked it. It was from Mr. Sherman, the principal.

Fellow Faculty Members:

I have recently talked with hospital personnel and have the latest information regarding Julia Meyers. Unfortunately, I do not have good news to report. Ms. Meyers is currently under sedation while the doctors wait for the swelling in her brain to reduce. At this point, they don't know how well she will recover, whether there was damage to her brain and how severe it might be. And because this is still a police matter, her visitors have been curtailed except for family members. Please keep her in your prayers and best wishes. Detectives will continue to inquire next week.

Thank you for your patience and cooperation.

Wesley Sherman

That sucked. Poor Julia. Skyler hadn't forgotten that she had given him cryptic warnings about Keith and the football staff. But he had discovered why Keith was being so secretive. He, too, was a closeted teacher. And he needed to be especially careful working for Scott Carson, the homophobic football coach. Now *there* was a man Skyler didn't trust at all!

Skyler had promised Sidney to leave the police work to her, but after all, he *had* discovered the one who murdered Mr. Sherman's son, even caught him. Sort of. Who better to do some inside investigating than an inside man? Something was up with the football coach and Skyler wanted to be the one to get to the bottom of it.

The bell rang and there was the usual scramble in the corridor. Kids yapped on their cell phones as soon as they were through the doorways. iPod ear buds were suddenly back in ears, and the slouching masses headed to their destinations with all the enthusiasm of cattle to the slaughterhouse.

First to enter was, naturally, Amber Watson. Red-haired and wearing a pink hoodie, she was everyone's model student and leader. She also had a crush on Skyler and though flattered, it was really the last thing he needed.

Next was Amber's friend, Heather Munson. She couldn't be more opposite from her pink-trimmed friend. Heather was all Goth all the time, complete with dog collar and fingerless fishnet gloves. But Heather, even as emo as she liked to appear, had a desert-dry wit and was no slouch in the intelligence department.

Following her was blond football star Drew O'Connor who was walking in with—surprise!—Alex Ryan, newest football player and former angst-ridden teen. Skyler had gotten the square-faced boy on the team, knowing he needed some kind of outlet to bring him out of his slump, and it seemed to have worked. He hadn't known that Alex's other problem may have been more to the point; that he was gay and fighting it mighty hard.

But then Alex's secret boyfriend entered, class clown Rick Flores. Everyone loved the tall and lanky Rick, especially, so it seemed, Alex.

Rick owned the class. He high-fived the boys as he entered and smiled at the girls. He wore a crisp black shirt with his khakis hanging low enough to reveal a good slice of his striped boxers. He always wore his sunglasses on the back of his head and a heavy gold chain with a crucifix glazed against his tan skin.

Alex, alone in his back corner of the room, wore a blank and solemn face under a scalp of spiky hair, until Rick entered. His eyes lit up when the Hispanic boy took his seat in the front of the class. Rick gave a lazy look back towards Alex, and Alex ducked his head and grinned. It was a secret entrusted to Skyler alone, just as Skyler's secret had been entrusted to those two.

High school was still tricky, thought Skyler, even after having graduated eight years earlier.

"Okay, let's get settled down," Skyler said automatically. He raised a pile of papers in his hand. "This is the test on *Julius Caesar* from last week."

There were moans but mostly the class quieted. Heather had a smug look on her face, but Amber bit her lip. As if *she* had anything to worry about!

Skyler held them in suspense as he looked over all their faces. He smiled. "You all did pretty darned well. I must be an excellent teacher."

Breaths were released and a few spurts of laughter sprinkled about the room. Skyler presented the top sheet to Amber. "Amber got the top grade."

"Duh!" opined several students.

"Good job, Amber."

"Thank you, Mr. Foxe," she said, taking the paper with a deep blush.

He passed them out to each individual. "Those of you who didn't do so well, I jotted down some notes on your papers. If you want to improve this grade, see me after class."

He got to Alex and handed him the paper with a "C+" written on the top. "Good job, Alex. Maybe with a little more studying, you could bring that up."

"Are you kidding?" said Alex, staring at the paper in disbelief. "This is the best I've ever done!"

That was true. And the best overall in his other classes. Alex seemed to be trying harder for Skyler. No doubt he was grateful that a teacher stuck his neck out for him.

"Next week, we'll be starting on *The Great Gatsby* and I want you to do some preliminary work on that first. To that end, we will be taking a lighthearted look at the 1920s today by viewing *Some Like it Hot.*"

"We're watching a movie today, Mr. Foxe?" asked Rick, sitting up from his customary slouching position.

"Yes, Mr. Flores. A Friday treat. But I want you to take notes. We will see the second part of it Monday and we'll discuss certain aspects of the film."

"Will there be a test?" asked Drew.

"No, Drew. No test. Just discussion." He clicked on the television and DVD player and moved to an empty seat in the back so he could keep an eye on everyone.

When the title came up and the music began to play, there was bit of groaning. "Is this in black and white?" asked a sullen voice.

He rolled his eyes. "Yes. 'Fraid so. Bear with it."

Skyler leaned back. He had always liked this movie. He was sure they would, too, knowing that most of them if not all had never seen it. But even as the screen flickered with Tony Curtis and Jack Lemon hamming it up to each other, Skyler's thoughts drifted and he daydreamed about Keith.

They had hardly spoken to one another since that day last week when Keith dragged him into an unused classroom and kissed him, promising more. But "more" never came. Maybe the man didn't want to risk his job after all. And Skyler had been too much of a chicken to seek him out. This was unfamiliar territory. He was used to hooking up at bars and clubs and parting ways in the morning. He didn't know what he was supposed to do at this point. Pursue Keith or let it go? But one taste of the gorgeous assistant football coach was definitely not enough.

After forty minutes, Skyler aimed the remote and stopped the DVD player. He sauntered down the center aisle, asking the students questions about what they just saw. Amber always had her hand up, but Skyler picked the quieter ones, the ones studiously avoiding his gaze. They always knew more than they thought they did and Skyler was satisfied that they were at least getting the point.

Rick lost the luster in his eyes. "We can start one anyway," he said slowly. "Maybe Ms. Traeger will sponsor it."

"She's not a lesbian," said Skyler. He knew most of the school thought the girl's volleyball coach was a lesbian. But just because she was athletic didn't make it so. And Skyler had met her boyfriend and the man didn't seem like a beard to him.

Alex extricated himself from Rick, but Rick still held his hand. "That doesn't matter," said the dark-haired boy. "The charter says they don't have to be gay, just gay-friendly."

"Well, I'll help in any other way I can. You know I will. I just…just…"

"Leave him alone, Rick. It's his job, dude. Besides, there's no way I can join anyway. Football?"

Rick's smile was not as bright as it had been. "I know. Well. See you Monday, Mr. Foxe."

"See you guys." He watched them go. *You are such a coward, Skyler.* He felt like shit disappointing them, especially since they had come out to each other right in Skyler's classroom, but he had only gotten a full-time teaching job a few months ago. He'd hate to have to defend it now.

∫ ∫ ∫

In the parking lot, Skyler swung his leather satchel, glad that it was the weekend at last and wide open. Well, wide open except for Sunday night when he had to have dinner with his mother.

Coming from the opposite direction was the tall figure of Keith Fletcher, making long, purposeful strides toward him. Skyler's heart thumped. Standing over six feet tall, broad-shouldered, black hair in a tousled style, sporting a dusting of day-old beard stubble on his dimpled jaw, Keith made his pulse jump. And his eyes! They were ice blue like a husky's and always concentrated on Skyler in a most disarming manner.

The man was smiling, showing blindingly white, square teeth. "Hi," he said when he was standing right in front of Skyler.

Skyler's knees nearly buckled. "Hi."

He dismissed them a fraction before the bell, and they scrambled to their feet, back packs swinging over shoulders ar cell phones out and on.

"Have a good weekend, guys!" he called to their retreati backs. A few offered backward waves. Rick stood over Skyle desk with a bright smile while Alex hovered near the bac pretending to tie his shoe.

When the rest of the class had dispersed, Alex got close Rick and twined his stubby fingers with Rick's long, tan ones.

"Showing a movie about transvestites, Mr. Foxe?" said Ric still smiling and shaking his head. "Shame on you."

Skyler tried to hide his smile. "It's not about transvestites."

"Could have fooled me. That Tony Curtis is hot, though, or out of a dress."

Skyler made no comment. He glanced at Alex, who was but nuzzling Rick's shoulder.

"So what are you boys planning this weekend?"

"I have practice," said Alex, letting Rick's fingers go.

"Not *all* weekend, *mi pequeña*," said Rick, elbowing him.

"No, but you know."

"Besides." Rick turned to him and shocked Alex by taki him in his arms. Skyler shot a worried glance toward the op door and the windowed wall revealing the hallway. "I like it wh you're all sweaty."

"*Rick*!" he rasped, squirming out of his arms. "Not in fro of Mr. Foxe!"

Skyler laughed uncomfortably and rose. "Probably not a go idea in an open classroom, gentlemen."

Rick frowned. "Have you given any more thought to tl GSA thing, Mr. Foxe? James Polk High could use one."

"I know, Rick." Skyler felt horrible. He was the one w suggested beginning a Gay-Straight Alliance, and now he w backing out, afraid to be outed.

Keith scanned the parking lot and Skyler did too. No one was around.

"I'm sorry I haven't really gotten to talk to you since…you know."

"It's okay. I know you're busy with the team."

"And a science fair."

"Oh yeah. Right. You're doing double duty as biology teacher. It's no problem."

They both fell silent, merely staring at one another.

"Skyler, I was wondering if you wanted to go out."

On the one hand, Skyler was expecting something of the kind. But on the other, it was still a bit outside his comfort level.

Skyler blinked. "'Out'? What do you mean 'out'?"

"You know." Keith edged closer. "To dinner?"

Skyler's eyes automatically scanned the parking lot again. "You mean…like a *date*?"

Keith frowned. "It's not a dirty word. If you'd rather not, then forget it." He turned abruptly and headed for his oversized black truck.

Skyler's heart skipped a beat. He ran after him and grabbed his arm. "Wait. Wait. I'm…it's just…no one ever asked me out on a *date* before."

Keith stared at the ground and finally brought up those penetrating eyes again. "Well *I'm* asking," he said, his deep voice rumbling softly over Skyler's skin. That one stolen kiss they shared in the empty classroom had been *outstandingly* hot.

He had been focused on Keith's obvious physical attributes—which were many—and on his personality—still a puzzle. But now he pondered the whole dating scenario. What if they really had nothing to talk about after they exhausted the usual stuff about work? What if all they had was animal magnetism? He still wanted to sleep with the guy. But would Keith still want to if they didn't hit it off? Wasn't it better to fuck first and date later?

Skyler bit his lip. Well, you never knew until you tried.

"Okay. When?"

Keith's entire face brightened and his shapely lips opened into a megawatt smile. "I'm busy tonight with an away game. Last game of the season. What are you doing tomorrow night?"

"Saturday?" He had planned on calling his friends and maybe going to Trixx again. But the only reason to do that was to get laid, so... "Saturday night would be fine."

"Pick you up at eight?"

Skyler nodded and gave Keith his address. This felt weird. Was this what heteros felt before a first date? All fluttery inside? He watched Keith climb into his truck, then turned toward his white VW Bug and hit the button on his key to unlock it.

He got home fast. He speed-dialed Sidney to tell her and she squealed appropriately. He joked and laughed with her as he always did, but when he clicked off the phone, he chewed his lip. Pick-ups in bars didn't exactly prepare him for the subtlety of a date.

$$\int \int \int$$

Early Saturday evening, he showered. He chose his clothes carefully, going with a Hugo Boss gray sweater to match his eyes and khaki slacks, hoping that it wasn't a fancier place Keith had in mind. As he brushed his long platinum bangs off his face, he wondered if Keith planned on paying for dinner. If you asked, you paid, right? But that was weird, too. That wouldn't feel right. "What's the matter with me?" And why wasn't his hair cooperating? "Any red-blood American gay boy would love having a sugar daddy. Why *not* let him pay?"

Because it felt odd. He'd always paid his own way; helping to support his mom at home once he was of age and paying for his own schooling. It didn't feel right letting someone else foot the bill now. He'd just tell Keith. Yeah. They'd split the bill. That was only right.

Although it did feel nice that someone might want to do this for him.

The doorbell. He straightened his baby-fine hair one more time and went to the door. When he pulled it open, he remembered why he had first thought of Keith as a Walking Wet Dream.

He was wearing a maroon dress shirt under his black leather jacket. His shirt was open at the collar revealing a tan triangle of skin and curly dark hair. He still had that sexy one day of beard growth and he was looking at Skyler with those captivating eyes and smiling lips. And he smelled good, too. What was that? *Unforgivable?*

Keith measured Skyler up and down with a grin. "You look great."

"Thanks," he said a little breathlessly. "So do you."

It was then that Skyler noticed Keith was carrying a small bouquet of flowers. Skyler stared at the blossoms as Keith stretched his arm forward, offering them.

"You brought me flowers." He felt his face warming.

Keith's cheek dented with a smile. "Yeah. Corny, I know. But I wanted to."

Skyler took them since there didn't seem to be anything else he could do. He held them awkwardly in his hands, the cellophane crackling under his fingers.

Keith chuckled and walked in. "Got a vase?" He headed into the kitchen and began opening cupboards.

"Uh...top shelf above the fridge."

Keith reached it easily, something Skyler needed a step stool to do. He pulled out a vase and set it on the counter. He looked expectantly at Skyler before Skyler got the message and laid the flowers beside it, unwrapping the cellophane. He disassembled the bunch, trimmed the stems with scissors from a drawer, and arranged them in the vase. He took the whole thing to the sink, filled the vase with water and set it on his counter. He stared at it and wondered at the funny feeling in his stomach. No one had ever brought him flowers before. Not like this. His mother on occasion, and Jamie when he was sick, but not like this.

He turned to look at Keith.

The dark-haired man was scanning the room. "Nice place," he said, swiveling back to gaze at Skyler.

"Thank you for the flowers. They're…very nice."

That smile was back. "Not used to getting flowers, huh? Well maybe you should get used to it." He pushed a wisp of hair off of Skyler's forehead, trailing his finger down Skyler's face to his jaw. "Shall we go?"

∫ ∫ ∫

Skyler clambered into Keith's tall truck, but he had to admit it wasn't a bad or bumpy ride. Keith drove to a small Italian restaurant off of State tucked between a florist and a shoe shop. It was one of those pricey places Skyler had always wanted to try but could never find an excuse to spend the money.

When they were settled at their candlelit table, jackets draped over their chairs, Skyler edged forward. "Look, Keith. I think we should split the bill."

Keith scanned his menu, never bothering to glance at Skyler. "Nope."

Skyler laid his menu flat on the table. "W-what?"

"I said no. I asked *you* out. I want to buy."

"I know, but…"

The menu lowered and those ice blue eyes bored into his. "I'm paying. End of discussion." The menu rose and obscured him again.

Why don't you just hit me over the head with your club and drag me by the hair to your cave? Who did this guy think he was? So he was big and muscular. So what? So what if that image of him dragging Skyler to a cave suddenly turned him on.

Whoa. Wait.

He grabbed his water glass and drank half of it down. A little voice in his head that sounded remarkably like Sidney said, *Just relax, Skyler. Don't make a scene. Let the man pay.*

What the hell. He picked up his menu and decided on the shrimp scaloppini. And it was expensive, too. Ha!

They ate. They drank wine. They chatted. It was very easy to chat with Keith Fletcher. Skyler had had a taste of it here and there when Keith arrived at the high school to replace the pregnant biology teacher just a month ago. But so much else had been happening and Keith seemed odd at times, sometimes blowing up in a rage and at other times being a real sweet guy. The mood swings always seemed to have to do with football. Coach Scott Carson was a real hard ass and a homophobe of the first order. Not that Skyler had ever let on that he was gay. Only the principal knew that. But Coach Carson seemed to have exceptional gaydar about Skyler. Maybe he had an inkling about his assistant coach, too. Skyler decided to ask.

"Does Carson know you're gay?"

Keith choked a bit on his wine. "Uh...*no*. And I'd like to keep it that way."

"No sweat. Me too. Not particularly anxious for the Christian Coalition to picket outside my classroom."

"Amen," said Keith.

"Were you out at your other school? In Seattle?"

He nodded and placed his wine glass carefully above his plate. "It wasn't an issue. I mean there as well as in California, they can't legally fire anyone for their sexual orientation."

"Oh yeah. Except while they aren't doing that, they'll find some other way to get rid of you."

They fell silent for a moment. "You mean like starting something with a fellow employee?" said Keith quietly.

"Something like that."

Keith nodded and looked up. His eyes kept a rigid bead on Skyler's gray ones. "It's a risk I'm willing to take."

His intense gaze caused Skyler's breath to catch. "Oh," he

breathed.

Keith looked at both their empty dessert plates. "Ready to go?"

"Yeah. Uh…thanks for dinner. It was really nice."

"Yeah it was. The company made it that much better."

Skyler felt his face grow hot. He couldn't be blushing in front of this guy, could he? He hid it by reaching for his coat and slipping it on. It also helped to distract him as Keith laid the cash on the table.

They walked along State Street, looking into the darkened shop windows of antiques, fashionable eyewear, and books. The trees sported white twinkly lights wrapped around their trunks, giving the small street its own quaint ambience. Skyler suddenly wished he was some place like Palm Springs or San Francisco where he could take Keith's arm. He had to make do with walking as close to him as he could, brushing against him and inhaling whiffs of his cologne.

"I can see why you stayed in Redlands all your life," said Keith.

"Oh?" When he had first told Keith that, he got the impression that Keith was mocking him for never traveling further than his own backyard, even to attend college.

"Yeah. It's got a sort of small town feel. Streets like this. Museums. The arts. Old Victorian houses. The mountains in the background. I like it."

"It does have its high points."

They walked a long way, talking the whole time. This was the Keith Fletcher he liked. This introspective, intelligent, worldly man. Even if he did like football and drove a hetero truck. Skyler supposed dating wasn't so bad, except that he was getting a bit itchy to settle somewhere and kiss the daylights out of Keith. And then maybe go back to Skyler's place and have Keith pound him into the mattress. That would do just fine. He was getting a hard-on thinking about it.

Keith was apparently thinking about it, too, because he

suddenly looked up and said, "Where the hell did I park my truck?"

∫ ∫ ∫

They drove back to Skyler's place, one of Redland's many old Victorians converted into apartments. They climbed the outside staircase, and after Skyler unlocked his door he was suddenly surrounded by strong arms and overwhelmed by the hot press of Keith's lips on his. The man wasn't gentle. He all but slammed Skyler against the door. His tongue flicked once at Skyler's lips before plunging inside. Skyler groaned at the welcome intrusion and, tongues sliding together, he snaked his arms around the man's neck and clung tightly to him, chest to chest. A steely erection pressed to his, and Skyler unabashedly ground his hips into it.

Mmm! Skyler loved the feel of the man's scratchy cheek, loved the smell of him, the taste of his lips.

Keith broke away but kept his face close, breath gusting against Skyler's mouth. He pressed his forehead to Skyler's.

"Let's go in," whispered Skyler. His whole body was throbbing with anticipation and his dick was as hard as a rock, tightening his trousers. He opened the door, dragged Keith in, and kicked the door closed behind him.

There was some maneuvering of arms reaching and clutching, of fingers seizing buttons, and a general choreography toward the bedroom. Once they passed the threshold, they got serious about peeling off each other's clothes. Skyler delighted in each stretch of muscled skin revealed as he helped Keith quickly divest his shirt and trousers. Those legs were like hard columns of tan muscle, furred and sculpted. And his arms and chest were a delight of solid planes and wiry hair.

Skyler leaned forward and kissed the well-defined pecs, relishing the feel of the rough forest of hairs against his lips. His mouth fastened on a dusky nipple, sucking and teasing with his teeth, eliciting a moan from the larger man. Skyler whimpered when Keith pulled him back to yank Skyler's shirt off over his head. Keith bent to nuzzle his neck and, with a sigh, Skyler threw back his chin, giving Keith all the access he wanted.

The man's mouth was alive in uninhibited exploration. Nuzzling turned to nips and then lips covered the nuzzled bits, sucking gently. Skyler couldn't stand it and threw himself, skin to skin, against Keith's chest. He yanked a hunk of his hair and pulled his face down to kiss him again. With warm mouths and tongues locked together, they moved their way to the edge of the bed.

Underwear. Why are we still wearing underwear? Panting, Skyler reached for Keith's black briefs. There was a wet spot darkening the front where his cock was leaking, and Skyler quickly peeled it away.

Dayam! Keith was, indeed, a big man through and through.

Keith's hands reached for Skyler's briefs and made short work of them. When his underwear sat pooled around his ankles, Keith stared hungrily at Skyler's hard length.

Stepping out of his briefs and kicking them aside, he allowed Keith to get his fill of staring. A thrill of pure lust enveloped him, knowing that Keith was looking and drinking it in. He hadn't known he was such an exhibitionist, but he found he did a little posing, head tilted back, eyes drooping to slits.

Large hands came up and, despite their earlier haste, caressed his flanks with gentle slowness. Keith took his time. Bending forward, he started with lips and teeth nibbling on Skyler's collarbone before dragging his mouth down his body. He fastened on one tiny pink nipple, bringing it to a hard nub with licking and suction before working his way to the other one. Kisses and gentle bites feathered downward. Skyler whimpered. *God, he's good at this!* A tongue circled his naval and licked down the treasure trail of white blond hairs to his straining cock, where Keith gave it a hard lick from root to tip. Skyler hadn't even noticed when Keith laid him on the bed. But when he looked up with hazy eyes, the man was leaning over him with a feral expression that made his dick throb. Skyler reached up and pressed his fingers to the back of his neck, pulling him down for another kiss. He liked kissing and he just couldn't seem to get enough of the man's sensual lips and teasing tongue.

Keith leaned back again, eyes flicking over Skyler's heated form. Each pass of his fingers sent chills of delight over Skyler's pale, sensitive skin and he moaned and writhed.

"So responsive," Keith murmured.

"You have an amazing touch," whispered Skyler.

"So, Skyler." He licked his lips, reminding Skyler of a wolf looking over his dinner. "What are you up for?" His hands never stopped moving, caressing, squeezing. His hand dipped between Skyler's legs, teasing the soft skin of his inner thigh. His pupils were blown and he licked his lips again, moistened from Skyler's kiss.

"Anything and everything."

Keith's gaze flicked to the basket of condoms and the pump lube on Skyler's bedside table. "So I see. I have to tell you. I know this is a first date and all, but I really want to fuck you."

Skyler grinned. "Okay."

Keith rolled his eyes. "I forgot. You're the hook-up queen. It's always a first date with you."

He reached up and tweaked Keith's nipple. The man bit his lip and groaned.

"Are you going to talk or are you going to fuck?"

In answer, large hands grasped Skyler's hips and his thumbs traced down the hollows at Skyler's groin, just missing his pubic hair. Skyler's cock ached with need, bobbing and dripping a string of pre-cum that was pooling on his belly. His balls felt tight.

Lips touched Skyler's ear, sending more chills down his goose-fleshed skin. "What I'm going to do to you…" Keith rasped.

Skyler squeaked his reply. Keith slid his arm under Skyler's back, cradling him. He gathered Skyler in his arms and slowly drew him in for another kiss. It was soft and gentle, just lips teasing his mouth. A tongue poked at his teeth and Skyler parted his lips, allowing the intrusion. Keith's tongue just touched the tip of Skyler's and stayed there, breath tasting breath, before pushing forward. It gently explored, sliding over Skyler's teeth. Skyler's whole body throbbed. The gentler Keith was, the sexier it felt.

"Do you have any idea how long I've wanted to do this?" Keith asked.

Skyler could only squeak again.

Keith smiled. "I like that sound you make. I'm going to keep making you make that sound. Let's turn you over now. I want to see your beautiful ass."

Skyler didn't protest. Keith turned him and Skyler's cock pressed painfully into the mattress. Keith's hands never stopped; he smoothed them over Skyler's backside, cupping the underside of one cheek and lifting it. He wanted Keith inside him right now! But he didn't want Keith to stop touching him like this either. He spread his legs shamelessly. Those hands, those fingers, slowly explored, tracing imaginary lines down his butt, squeezing, tormenting.

At last, Skyler felt thumbs dipping into his crack and spreading his ass cheeks, holding them opened, exposing his pulsating hole. He felt the warm sensation of Keith's breath there and gasped loudly when the gentle flick of a wet tongue tested his furled entrance.

All his nerve endings concentrated on that sensitive spot and he waited, his hole twitching for Keith's tongue to continue.

The tongue returned with the flat pad sketching a long, firm lick upward. It repeated the gesture and then lanced at it, forcing it to open with whirling licks. Skyler tried to keep himself still, but it was a chore. He just wanted to shove his ass into Keith's face. He panted his frustration into his hands, his face hidden in the mattress.

Keith's tongue continued to slowly drill its way in, making little circles, pushing, forcing. Skyler felt himself open, felt the tongue, hot and wet, stab into him in its wicked pursuit. "Shit!" he groaned.

Keith kept stabbing his tongue into Skyler, fucking him with that wet muscle, changing occasionally to swirling his tongue all around the gasping entrance.

"K-Keith! Oh God!"

Keith sat up suddenly. He quickly grabbed a condom from the nightstand and tore it open. Skyler looked behind him over his shoulder but he was at the wrong angle to see the man slip it on his reddened cock, though he felt him gather a pump of lube and gently apply it to Skyler's crack, pushing Skyler's legs even further apart. He waited impatiently for the feel of the man's cock to kiss his entrance. He couldn't help wiggling his hips in anticipation until the tip of that dick pressed firmly to his loosened hole. Skyler spread himself as much as he could.

Pushing, Keith's thick cock forced open the tight rosette, spread it, as the shaft slid fully inside. He was still moving, still shoving in until Skyler felt the soft pat of Keith's sac rest against his wide-open ass.

Keith didn't move for a moment. He was allowing Skyler to get used to his girth and Skyler needed that moment. His sphincter clenched a few times involuntarily, until the muscle relaxed enough to expand and embrace.

It was then that Keith started to move. His cock slid outward, and Skyler's channel molded around the new sensations. And when Keith slammed back inside, Skyler clenched again. Keith fucked him slowly and changed angles. His cock glided over that sweet spot inside. It made Skyler suddenly tremble with unimaginable sensation and he groaned with pure pleasure. He angled his hips upward, rocking along with Keith's rhythm.

Keith hit that spot again and again as his thrusts sped up. Skyler pushed his groin into the bed and humped the duvet until he came seconds later with a stunted cry, clenching his ass tightly.

Keith madly pumped into him, grunting with each thrust until he, too, released inside, gasping and choking from the intense pleasure. His hips continued to fuck, but they were slowing, and they gradually came to a stop. He clutched at Skyler's hips for a long time and then slipped out of him. He crumpled beside him, arm thrown over the prone man.

Skyler felt a kiss land on his shoulder, felt a gentle nip and a few open-mouthed kisses speckling his back before they gradually trailed off. There was a pause before Skyler heard a soft snore behind him. Too spent to even look over his shoulder, Skyler closed his eyes and nestled down. They both slept for a bit, until a little while later roaming hands woke him and they started all over again.

∫ ∫ ∫

When Skyler finally awoke the next morning, it was to the strange sensation of his cheek pressed tight against a warm, hairy chest.

Momentarily startled, he suddenly remembered who lay beneath him. He hardly ever awoke to someone in his bed in the morning. Usually the trick left that same night.

Keith's arm curled protectively around him and Skyler smiled at that. He took a moment to savor the warm feel of it before slowly extricating himself and slipping out of bed. Pulling on his sweat pants, he looked over his shoulder at the slumbering man. Keith's dark, disorderly hair swept across the pillow and his plump lips hung open while he softly snored. He rolled sleepily to his back, legs splayed, looking perfectly content to stay there. Skyler felt an odd swoosh in his stomach as if he wouldn't particularly mind that either.

He scooped up the empty condom wrappers where they had fallen carelessly to the floor, tossed them in the trash bin, and shuffled to the kitchen to make coffee. He kneaded his lower back a bit, feeling the ache in his muscles from the acrobatics of last night. Keith was a big man in every sense of the word, and Skyler had been pushed, poked, prodded, and positioned in every which way. He rubbed his sore ass through the sweats.

Once the coffee was brewing, he returned to the bedroom and sat on the bed beside the sleeping man. He ran his hand down that furry chest and was rewarded when blue eyes snapped open and looked drowsily at him. And then that dimpled grin. "Good morning," Keith said in a bed-roughened voice.

Skyler felt unaccountably shy. "Good morning. Want coffee?"

"Sure."

"How do you take it?"

"Black, two sugars."

"Right."

Skyler quickly returned with two mugs and handed one to Keith. Wanting to acknowledge his enjoyment of the night before, Skyler could think of nothing better than leaning over and kissing him before ducking his head and sipping his own brew. They drank silently for a time before Skyler's gaze slid to the man who was watching him intently, fingers toying gently at Skyler's naked skin above his waistband. That gaze and those fingers made Skyler blurt, "Do you want breakfast?"

"Don't go to any trouble."

"It's no trouble. If...if you want to stay." A flutter in his chest accompanied his awaiting Keith's reply. He'd never had a trick to breakfast before.

"Can I use your shower?"

"Of course. There're towels in the bathroom and also a fresh toothbrush in the drawer." He got up to allow Keith room. The blankets fell away and Skyler gazed again at the trim form of a naked Keith Fletcher, only this time in sunlight. He stretched all six foot six of him. Skyler eyed the intriguing hollows and muscle, including that most important bit that was quite hefty even when semi-hard. He scooped Skyler into an embrace, kissed him soundly, slapped his sweatpants-covered butt, and meandered to the bathroom.

Skyler returned to the kitchen, switched on Diana Ross, who complained that "You Can't Hurry Love," and whipped up two egg white omelets with sliced kiwi and melon on the side. He was just arranging the plates on the small dining table when Keith emerged. Skyler thought the man would be dressed and ready to leave. He didn't expect he'd be wearing only a towel slung low around his waist.

Skyler swallowed and gestured toward the plates. "Omelet, Prince of Breakfast."

Keith smiled. "'Alas poor egg yolk. I knew him, Horatio.'"

Enchanted, Skyler lowered to his seat.

Keith dug into his plate eagerly. "This is delicious," he said, mouth full. "Do you do this for all your dates?"

"I don't date."

"Oh, that's right." He smiled at Skyler as he dipped his fork into the egg. "And why is that?"

Skyler ate without tasting. He didn't know why he felt so flummoxed. He was just eating a meal with the guy. No sense going to pieces. "I just never did, is all. When I came out in college I guess I went a little crazy. I never got around to dating and boyfriends and such."

"I see. Maybe it's an age thing. I mean, when I was in my early teens I was just figuring out who I was. Back then the AIDS crisis was pretty heavy. But I always dated. I was never one to jump in and out of bed with just anyone."

"Oh really?"

Keith smiled.

"Um…how old *are* you?"

"Thirty-five. How old are you?"

"Twenty-five."

"You're just a wee young lad, aren't you?"

"And you're an old geezer, in gay years." It was a joke, but the subtle change in Keith's expression said he didn't find it particularly funny. Skyler hastily added, "Did I mention that I happen to like older men?"

Keith finished and wiped his lips with his napkin. "Well," he said, tossing down the cloth. "I think it's time for dessert."

"Oh. Okay. I don't know what I've got. Some more fruit. Maybe granola and yogurt…"

"Skyler. I meant in the bedroom."

He looked up. Keith's eyes twinkled at him. "Oh!" He seemed to float up from his chair. Keith took him by the hand and escorted him back to the bed.

Keith was pressing him down into the mattress while sucking on Skyler's lips when the phone rang. He stopped and looked enquiringly at his bed mate. With a whimper, Skyler scooted to the edge of the bed, his sweat pants now dangling around his knees, and grabbed the phone.

"This better be good!" he growled into the mouthpiece.

"So?" said Sidney's voice. "How was the date?"

Skyler glanced at Keith before cupping the receiver in his other hand. "It's still going on—" he whispered desperately.

"It is? Oh shit. Dude! He's there with you right now, isn't he? Are you guys in bed? Are you doing it?"

"Sidney!"

"Well, usually the trick is gone by now—"

"He's not a trick!" he tried to say quietly, but Keith could hardly avoid hearing. "I'll call you later." He hung up. Sheepishly, he turned to Keith who was smiling broadly.

"Not a trick, huh? That means you had a good time and consider me more than a one night stand?"

"Um…I guess. Well…yeah. I like you."

"I like you, too. Frankly, I think you're adorable."

Skyler toed off his sweatpants and slid into Keith's arms again, stroking those hard biceps. "It's very mutual."

"So where were we?"

♪ ♪ ♪

It was a couple of hours and one more shower later that Keith finally went to the door. And after a lingering kiss in which

Skyler's toes curled and he had a hard time letting go, the man sauntered out, giving Skyler a long backwards glance. When Skyler couldn't see him anymore, he closed the door and leaned his face against it was a long sigh. "Holy fuck," he breathed. That had gone far better than he ever imagined. Maybe dating wasn't so bad, after all.

He pushed away from the door, switched on his iPod, and punched in *Dreamgirls* on the big speakers.

Who was he kidding? It was spectacular! Keith was not only a superb lover but someone easy to connect with. He loved talking to the guy, looking at him, being with him.

He pulled up short. Wait. This was going way too fast. Too much too soon. Had to pull back a bit before he got into trouble. He breathed out a long exhale. "Take it slow, Skyler," he told himself. "Give yourself a moment to breathe. Play it cool."

He grabbed his cell phone to call Sidney and noticed a message waiting for him from a number he didn't recognize. He punched it in and listened.

"Skyler, it's Evan," said the voice, "Evan Fargo." Skyler felt a jolt in his chest. He should have called them right away but had completely forgotten. Instead, he had gotten caught up in the drama of his own life. Evan and Jeff were having a *real* time of it.

"Anyway, I just wanted to say," said Evan, "that seeing you the other night really lifted my spirits. You always had that effect on me, Sky. I've been pretty low lately, as you probably imagined. But…well. Jeff is such a sweetheart. I know he's been running himself ragged doing the impossible. I know it's pretty hopeless, but I had to let him try. Let's get together soon, Skyler. Call me."

Skyler clicked his phone closed. Well, that was something good, at least. What happened to Jeff and Evan shouldn't happen to anyone.

While the phone was still in his hand, it suddenly rang. He opened it, assuming it was Sidney when a much deeper voice spoke. "I just wanted to hear your voice one more time."

Skyler felt his face flush and he sunk, jelly-legged, to the sofa arm. "Oh. Hi." So much for playing it cool.

"I'm trying not to be too presumptuous." Skyler could hear Keith's truck move into traffic in the background. "But I don't think I want to wait till next weekend to get together with you again. How do you feel about that?"

"Well, we have to be careful…"

"I know. But how do you feel about it?"

Skyler repressed a giggle. "That would be fine."

"Really? 'Cause I'm wracking my brain trying to come up with something we can do on a school night. You know. Other than…"

"As long as that's still on the menu."

"Definitely."

"I'll think of something. It *is* my town. I'll let you know when I see you tomorrow."

Skyler plainly heard the smile in the man's voice when he said, "Okay. See you, Skyler. Have a good day. What's left of it."

"Yeah. You too."

He waited until he heard the click from Keith's phone before he hung up and called Sidney.

"Well?" she said. "Hey, is that *Dreamgirls* on in the background? Someone's happy!"

"Someone is! Oh Sid. Where has this man been all my life!"

"Seattle, from what you were saying. So? Dish! Is he hung?"

"Why do you always ask that?"

"'Cause I'm living my sex life vicariously through you these days. Was he?"

"You know I'm not a size queen." Skyler paused for only a moment. "Oh my *God!* Like a horse! I am *so* sore."

"Poor Skyler. Want me to bring over some ice for your ass?"

"My ass is fine, thanks. But it was so much more than that. It was really…really…nice."

She snorted. "Some English teacher you are. One date with super hunk and your vocabulary goes to hell."

He fell backwards onto the sofa and stared at his ceiling. "But it was. It was so nice to connect with someone. To have a conversation. To...well...wake up to someone."

Sidney sighed. "Yeah. I miss that. So I guess I don't have to ask if you'll see him again."

"I will. But I think we should take it slow, you know. I don't want to go crazy after the first date."

"Yeah. Okay. I can see that... And this will last how long?"

"No, I mean it. I've never dated before and I don't want to make an ass of myself. Especially since we work together."

"You work at the same place. Not together."

"Whatever. It could get awkward. I want to keep it light."

There was a pause.

"Sid?"

"Skyler, this is the first time you've ever done anything like this. Caution is good, but too much caution might scare him off. And I don't want you to do that."

"*You're* telling me *not* to be cautious? Why detective, what gives with that?"

"Just have fun, for God's sake. And then promise me we'll make a short night of it."

"Short night of what?"

"Skyler! Have you already forgotten that in four brief hours you are taking me to your mother's for dinner?"

"Oh *shit!* Oh fuck. I did forget. Can't we get out of that?"

"No. She's *your* mother. See you at five." She hung up. There was no arguing there. And she was right. He hadn't seen his mother in a while and it was time to make the pilgrimage.

Chapter Three

Sidney arrived promptly at five, and Skyler drove her the few blocks to his childhood home. It was a small bungalow cottage from 1919, and though it was looking a little rundown these days, Cynthia Foxe kept the cottage garden impeccable. Wisteria vines grew over the front porch but the blossoms were beginning to drop. Even with the onset of November, the weather was still hot as the Inland Empire's perpetual Indian summer invaded fall.

They walked up the flagstone walkway that Skyler and Sidney had installed his senior year of high school, and Sidney quirked a grin at Skyler. "Someone's walking funny," she said.

"Shut up."

"Seriously, Skyler. You are *glowing*. She's going to want to know what's up. Wouldn't this be a good time to tell her?"

They made it to the steps and climbed to the covered porch. "Tell her that her only son sucks cock with the same mouth he kisses her with?" he whispered. "That he takes it up the ass? I don't think so."

"Skyler, you—"

The door swung open and Cynthia Foxe stood in the doorway. "Sidney! Skyler! Right on time." She kissed them both on the cheek. Skyler handed his mother a bouquet of orange chrysanthemums and Asiatic lilies, but he couldn't stop thinking of the flowers Keith brought him. "This will be perfect for the table! Thank you, Skyler."

Cynthia wore a pair of tan slacks that hugged a figure still toned from a daily routine at the gym. She adjusted her lavender sweater over her hips and cocked her head at her son, smiling with the Dior "Rose Panorama" lipstick she always wore.

"Sidney dear," she said. "You are looking lovelier all the time."

Skyler turned his head to look at his friend. And he noticed... that she was. Her face was long and angular with a thin, straight nose and shapely lips. Her make-up was subtle—just a bronzer for her cheeks, a dark, natural tone for her lips, and a little liner for her eyes. Her dark hair hung in corkscrewed locks just to her shoulders. If he had been straight, he would definitely have made a move—and then that thought gave him pause. One day, his Sidney wouldn't be his anymore. A pang of jealousy warmed his chest. Silly really. She'd always be his Sidney. She'd just belong to some other guy, too.

"And Skyler." His mother cupped his cheek. "Sweetie. You look positively radiant."

"Must be someone he's seeing," said Sidney.

Skyler shot her a murderous glance.

Cynthia Foxe broke into a smile. "Skyler! You're seeing someone? You should have brought her."

"I…we…only went out once."

"What's her name?"

"I don't know if this will turn into anything. No sense in getting your hopes up." He retreated through the dining room and pushed open the kitchen door. Footsteps followed him. Cynthia was there when he closed the refrigerator door.

"So who is she?"

"Just…someone."

"A fellow teacher," Sidney interjected.

He was going to kill her so much! He gripped the iced tea pitcher hard and set it down, afraid it would shatter. He reached into the cupboard for a glass and set it beside the pitcher.

"Oh, a teacher." She folded her arms. "Is that wise dating someone from work? Do they allow that?"

"The district frowns on it but it isn't disallowed." He poured the liquid into his glass and gulped it down. Mmm. No one made it like his mother. "Anyway, who knows? Can we talk about something else?"

"Well, I just don't want to be too old for grandchildren."

She had no idea how comments like that made his heart hurt. What could he possibly say to her? *You'll never get grandchildren, Mom. It's just not ever going to happen.* He couldn't say it.

"Do you have anything stronger than iced tea, Mom?"

♪ ♪ ♪

"It's just that you never brought home any girlfriends."

It was turning into a nightmare, what with Sidney's sly innuendos and his mother's complaining, the night was stretching longer and longer with no end in sight.

He spooned more pasta onto his plate. "I don't have girlfriends. I don't really date."

Cynthia Foxe shook her head. "I'm no prude, you know." She always said that right before she launched into a prude-ridden diatribe. "But with all the diseases out there a young man your age shouldn't be hopping into bed all the time."

"Mom!"

"I'm just saying it isn't safe. And I don't think it's good for your psyche. You're twenty-five, Skyler. I was married at that age."

"And look how well that turned out." It was out of his mouth before he could stop himself. His glance darted toward her stony face. She readjusted her cloth napkin in her lap without looking up.

"By the way. I ran into a couple of your friends the other day," she went on.

The change of subject was expected. Cynthia Foxe dodged personal issues, especially having to do with Dale Foxe, Skyler's dad.

But then Skyler pulled up short. Friends? Which ones? God, not Jamie!

"I was in the supermarket and Vanessa the cashier was talking to me and I guess she must have said my name, and the boys behind me asked if I was related to you. You knew them in college, apparently."

Skyler wracked his brain. That could have been anyone.

"That poor boy," she said, manicured fingers delicately holding the stem of her wine glass. "I didn't ask, but they looked like vets. Probably lost the leg in Iraq."

"Jeff and Evan?"

"Yes, I think that's what they said." She sipped her wine. "We chatted a little about you."

The back of his neck broke out in a sweat. "What did you say? What did *they* say?"

"That they knew you in college and you were all friends—" She set the glass down. "You never introduce me to your friends, Skyler."

"Well…there's a lot of them out there."

"I'm glad you're so popular."

Sidney choked on her drink.

Skyler spared her a glance before he asked, "Did they say anything else?"

"Only to tell you hello and it was nice seeing you the other day. That sort of thing."

He relaxed. Well. That was okay then. When he turned to Sidney she wore that *just tell her* look again.

"So," said Cynthia Foxe. "What about this girl you're seeing?"

§ § §

Managing to skirt the issue once again, Skyler and Sidney took the dish-washing duties while Cynthia took the linens to the service porch. "Will you stop trying to egg my mother on!" he rasped out of the side of his mouth. "It isn't your responsibility to out me, you know."

"What are you waiting for, your death bed? What if you find Mr. Right? What if you *have* found him? Don't you think she'd want to know that her only son is happy?"

He scrubbed angrily at the plate before rinsing it and thrusting it into the dishwasher. "She sees that I'm happy. I don't have to shove my lifestyle down her throat."

"She already knows you sleep around."

"Yeah. And where did she get that tidbit of news, huh? Have you been talking to her again?"

She shrugged. "She asks me stuff. I answer. I'm a public servant. I find it hard to lie."

"Well you'd better get used to it. I don't want her to know and that's final!"

"Don't want who to know what?" asked Cynthia, returning to the kitchen.

"It's nothing. It's just Sidney poking her *yiddishe* nose where it doesn't belong."

"*Goyishe kop*," she said, slapping him upside the head.

Cynthia chuckled. "Honestly. You two. You might as well be married the way you carry on."

She rearranged the plates Skyler had already placed into the dishwasher and poured in the soap. Skyler wiped his hands on the towel, relieved that the evening was almost over. What he really wanted to do was go home and have a nice, long masturbatory session thinking about Keith Fletcher.

Sidney left the kitchen chatting with Cynthia when her cell phone rang. Sidney looked at it, clicked it open, and said, "Feldman."

She listened intently for a moment before her eyes widened and her glance darted toward Skyler. She nodded again and made writing motions toward him. Cynthia stepped forward and handed her a notepad and pen. Sidney wrote, nodded, wrote, before she hung up.

She stared at the note for a long time before she slowly stripped the top sheet off the pad. She held it in her hand and swiveled toward Skyler.

"I have to go," she told him. She looked at Cynthia and offered a perfunctory smile. "It was a very lovely dinner, Mrs. Foxe. I'm sorry we have to cut the evening short. But my car is at Skyler's."

"Sidney?" He touched her arm. It was obviously about a case but he'd known her long enough to realize there was more to it than that. "What's going on?"

She stared at him and took a deep breath. "Skyler, sweetie. I hate to be the one to tell you this, but…it's Evan Fargo."

Skyler's breath seized just as his mother gasped behind him. His chest felt a flush of heat. "What?"

She shook her head. "Skyler, I'm really sorry. But it looks like…he committed suicide."

CHAPTER FOUR

Skyler let Sidney drive. He was too upset to take the wheel.

"Take me there."

"No, Skyler. Absolutely not! It's a crime scene."

"But it's Jeff's house. He'll need someone."

"You're not going."

"Fine. As soon as you drop me off, I'll go anyway."

"I'll take your keys."

"I'll get a taxi."

She gripped the steering wheel, her arms rigid. Skyler felt the car accelerate through traffic. Horns honked as she cut off cars, slipping in front of them with ease. She accelerated around a corner with squealing tires. The little Bug clunked and bounced. He grasped the seat and held on.

"You don't touch anything and you don't ask anyone anything."

"Why would I do that?"

"He used a gun, you know. Are you sure you want to go?"

Skyler felt a squeamish wriggle in his stomach. He wished he hadn't had dessert now. "It's for Jeff."

"Skyler. He used a gun," she said enunciating each word. "*In his mouth*. Do you know what that means?"

He closed his eyes, trying to keep his stomach contents where they were. "Jesus. Okay, okay. Just…get us there in one piece."

Sidney dodged the traffic and managed to skim through every yellow light. Both Skyler's feet were jammed to the floor on imaginary brakes. He flopped to the side, first at the window and then almost into Sidney as she wheeled around trucks and over the curb a few times.

"Jesus!" he squealed, but she ignored him. When they turned

the corner, it was obvious which house it was. There was an ambulance and two black and whites with red and blue lights flickering. They were parked in front of a modest white stucco house from the sixties, a small boxy one with square hedges. Cops were standing on the lawn talking to neighbors and a horrible sense of déjà vu welled in Skyler again. It was like that first murder scene, that one where he found his principal's son, Wes Sherman Jr., so many weeks ago. But that had been in an alley behind a dance club and so much had happened since because of it.

Sidney was out and standing by his car door. He emerged slowly and glanced up at her stern glare. She was clipping her badge to the waistband of her jeans. "You stay outside. I'll come get you. Do you understand me?"

"You'll get Jeff?"

"Yes." She put a reassuring hand on his shoulder. "Trust me, Sky. You don't want to go in there."

"Okay." She hurried ahead and Skyler walked across the lawn in slow motion. People bustled beside him, some going in, some coming out. The ambulance doors were open, but he knew there was no need for them to hurry. It was only to take the body away to a local mortuary.

Skyler milled, looking for familiar faces but not finding any. Was Jeff inside? Did he find Evan? How horrible! Skyler's stomach still felt funny—fluttery and kind of sick. He couldn't believe it. He had just seen them this last weekend. And Jeff had been so worried.

Skyler moved between the porch and the sidewalk. Uniformed police looked his way but didn't stop him. There was a bit of police tape in a square in the flower bed on the side of the house. When Skyler drew closer it looked like a footprint but he couldn't see any details. Some criminalists crouching beside it were mixing what looked like plaster in a plastic container.

He glanced at the house again. What was taking so long? Was Jeff even in there? Had Sidney forgotten about him?

He needed to decide. Dare he go in? If Jeff was there he'd need Skyler's support. He doubted that Jeff had any friends inside. He *had* to chance it.

Skyler approached the porch cautiously, eyeing the cops taking notes. No one made a move to stop him as his trembling hand touched the doorknob. He twisted it slowly and eased the door opened. The hinges whispered and he poked his head in the foyer. A latticework divider blocked some of the living room from view. Men and women with gloves and shoes covered in blue scrubs crossed before him.

The first thing that assaulted him was the sight of two men in EMT uniforms tightening the straps over the unmistakable shape of a body in a zipped-up body bag, lying on a stretcher in the hallway. Skyler swallowed past a lump in his throat and turned away.

On a card table against the divider, but on the living room side, sat a box of ammunition, some thin metal tubes the length of bamboo skewers, a can of oil, a bottle of something called Hoppe's Nitro Powder Solvent, and some tiny squares of blackened, oily-looking cloth.

In front of the sofa sat an empty wheelchair.

But when he looked up, he saw the wall beyond it.

A splatter of slick material and blood fanned across the wall. It could only be one thing.

Not going to get sick. Not going to get sick. Lightheaded, Skyler wondered as his stomach warred within if the mantra would work.

"*Skyler!* Dammit!"

Sidney grabbed his arm and dug in with her fingernails. It hurt, even though she was wearing gloves. She yanked him out the door and hurled him onto the porch. "What the fuck do you think you're doing? Didn't I tell you to stay outside?"

He swallowed a few times, not yet trusting himself to speak. He ducked his head and leaned over on his thighs, breathing evenly.

Sidney motioned to a plainclothes detective. "You see this man?" and she pointed at Skyler. "*Do not* let him inside again."

She whirled away and entered the house once more, leaving Skyler alone with the detective. He frowned at Skyler. He seemed about Keith's age with a slim build. A little taller than Skyler which put him at about medium height. He had a high forehead, dark short-cropped hair, and tanned skin with Asian features. His badge clipped to his russet suit said "De Guzman."

Skyler felt the need to apologize. "I know them," he said weakly, gesturing toward the door.

De Guzman's frown vanished. "I'm sorry," he said.

Skyler shook his head and leaned against the wrought-iron porch railing. "I haven't seen them in years, you know? And I ran into them just last weekend. This is so awful."

"Detective Feldman is very good at what she does. She'll see that everything will be in order."

"I know. She's my best friend."

De Guzman brightened. "Are you Skyler?"

Skyler looked up. The man's dark eyes were studying him with renewed interest. "Uh…yeah."

"She talks about you all the time. I'm Mike de Guzman." He said it as if Skyler were supposed to recognize it. But when he didn't, the man's features darkened. "So she's never mentioned me."

Something he was missing? "She hardly mentions anyone she works with by name," he said quickly. "I'm sure she must have talked about you…" But by the look on the man's face, he wasn't pleased to hear this half-truth.

"Great," said the detective under his breath.

Someone stumbled out of the door. It was Jeff, red-faced with tears streaming unabated down his face. A uniformed female officer was holding his arm when he looked up and spotted

Skyler.

"Skyler!" He fell forward into Skyler's arms. Skyler held fast, just clutching him. The tears started to flow down his own cheeks.

Skyler led Jeff down the steps and sat him down. He never let go of the man's shoulders, gripping tightly. He wanted to say something, some sort of comforting words, but the warm lump in his throat wouldn't allow it.

Jeff's arms were streaked with red scratches and his wrists were bruised, but he didn't seem to bother about them in his grief.

"Skyler," Jeff choked. "My God. What am I going to do? What am I going to do without him?"

Skyler rocked him, rubbing his back soothingly. They sat that way for a while until the paramedics wheeled out the stretcher.

Skyler pulled Jeff out of the way and tried to turn his face into his shoulder, but Jeff pulled away.

"Evan!" he cried, sinking to his knees on the lawn. "Why did you *do* it! Why!"

So many thoughts spun through Skyler's head as he watched his friend fall to pieces on the front lawn. Besides the horror of losing one's partner this way, there were going to be those inevitable legal problems Jeff was soon to encounter. For one, they had no legal standing with one another. They might have been partners for years, but if Evan had a family, *they* would likely be notified for funeral arrangements. Was the house in both Evan and Jeff's name? Their bank accounts? What about VA benefits? Jeff was going to be quickly cut out of the picture.

It was going to be twice as bad as it was now.

Skyler knelt beside Jeff and pulled him to his feet. "I'm going to get you out of here, Jeff."

"No! No! I can't. I can't!"

"Jeff! We've got to get out of here. There's nothing more we can do right now."

"But what about… Skyler, I don't know what I'm supposed to do now."

"It's okay. Remember that friend I told you about in college? Sidney? She's a police detective. She's in there right now. She'll tell us. I'm taking you to my place."

Jeff said nothing more as Skyler ushered him to his car. He opened the passenger door for him, gently coaxed him inside, and even seatbelted him in.

He trotted to the other side and slid into the driver's seat. After readjusting it from Sidney, he started it up. But de Guzman was at his window.

"Where are you taking him?" he asked.

"I'm taking him to my place, detective. Sidney knows where that is. She has to pick up her car there, anyway. She can check on things."

"Mike. You can call me Mike."

"O-okay. Mike. Do you want my phone number?"

"No. Sid has it, as you said." He gave the window sill a few pats and stepped back so Skyler could pull away from the curb.

They drove to Skyler's place in silence. The autumn evening had cooled considerably from the warmth of the day. Street lights offered dispirited pools of white along the sleepy neighborhood streets. The wind was picking up, and the canopies of giant ancient date palm trees danced over the sidewalks, flickering the streetlights and appearing as sinister fingers clawing towards the parked cars.

Skyler pulled into a space near his front stoop and shut off the engine. He glanced at Jeff, but the man didn't move. He merely stared into his lap. Skyler got out and came around. He opened the door, grabbed his arm, and hauled.

Jeff complied and Skyler took him up the dark front walk between the dwarf orange trees, up the dim staircase to his front door. He opened with his key, flipped on a light by reaching through the doorway, and urged Jeff in ahead of him.

He sat Jeff on the sofa. He left him for only a moment to get an extra pillow and blanket from his bedroom closet. He tucked them into the sofa's arm and sat beside his friend, clutching his shoulders again. Jeff sunk his head against Skyler's chest and pulled a trembling breath. "Would you rather sleep in my bed with me?" Skyler asked softly.

Jeff didn't answer, but after a while, he slowly nodded. Skyler lifted him and took him to the bedroom, sitting him on the bed. He got out a pair of sweats and an extra-large T-shirt Sidney left at his place to sleep in, and proceeded to undress his guest and redress him in the T-shirt and sweats. He pulled gingerly on one of his wrists and looked down at his arms. "Should we do something about this?" he asked, wondering if he had any antiseptic. Jeff shook his head and Skyler tucked him into bed. He stripped off his own clothes and pulled on his drawstring sleep pants and a T-shirt. Lifting the blanket, he doused the light, then pulled Jeff into an embrace.

Over the long night, they both slept on and off, with morning still far away.

§ § §

Skyler rolled over and found the bed empty. Bleary-eyed, he stumbled into the living room and found Jeff dazed and sitting on the sofa watching the muted TV.

Skyler trudged to the kitchen and made coffee. He supposed he should call into work and tell them he wouldn't be in. As he picked up the phone to do that, Jeff finally spoke.

"I called the number the detective gave me," he said.

Skyler put the receiver down and leaned back against the cold tile counter. The world outside his tall front window showed a gray, foggy morning, almost too early for the sun to glaze the fog white.

Jeff toyed with something. A wallet. "He said that I had to make some decisions about Evan. He has no family, so it's up to me." He hacked a dry imitation of a laugh. "Who else would it be up to?"

"I'll take you anywhere you need to go."

"Thanks, Skyler. You're a real friend. But you have a life. A job. I called our LGBT Center counselor and he's coming to pick me up."

"Jeff... It doesn't matter. I'm here."

"I appreciate it, Skyler. I do. But there's a lot to do right now."

He moved closer in emphasis. "But if you need me—"

"I know where to come. You know, I almost thought that seeing you again gave Evan a new lease on life. He talked of nothing but you since we saw you."

Skyler stared at him. Something was scratching at the backdoor of his thoughts.

"He was almost normal for the first time in weeks," Jeff went on. "I just...I just..." He sighed deeply and leaned back. He opened the wallet and looked in it.

Skyler sat beside him.

"I forgot I had this," he said, gesturing with the camo nylon wallet. "It's Evan's. I always carried his wallet since the leg. He just didn't want to." He laid it on the coffee table and began pulling things out; pictures, credit cards, business cards.

He showed Skyler the pictures, some of the two of them in Iraq before Evan's injuries. They had their arms around each other, just two buddies in desert fatigues on patrol. Jeff flipped through the gas credit cards, his VA ID, his ATM card. "I guess I'll have to cancel these."

"Don't do anything today, Jeff. Give yourself some time."

"For what? You know they trained us for this. What to do when a buddy gets killed. But it isn't the same as the training. This is different. He wasn't just my buddy. I loved him, Skyler." He sniffed. It seemed all the tears had been pulled out of him last night. He turned and looked at Skyler with red-rimmed eyes. "Do you have someone, Sky? You were always so full of life back in college. But you were always on to the next guy. Do you have a boyfriend now? Someone that cares about you?"

A flash of dark hair and ice-blue eyes flickered through his thoughts. He shook his head and then shrugged. "No. I...I don't know."

Jeff gave a half-smile. "Still playing the field. Such a loverboy." He spread the business cards on the table. There was one for Studs, a leather bar on Redlands Boulevard; Alonzo's, an Italian restaurant in San Bernardino; Skyler's card with his phone number; a well-worn lawyer's card; a card for Redlands Orchid Farm; the LGBT Center card; and half a Veteran's Administration card, with "James Fis—" cut in half.

Skyler said nothing. And then a hint of...*something*...finally filtered through his thoughts. Evan's phone message on Skyler's cell. Evan hadn't seemed depressed on that. He seemed hopeful and said as much. When was that? Skyler excused himself to the bedroom and grabbed his cell, calling up the messages. There it was. Evan had called only hours before he and Sidney went to his mother's for dinner, probably while Skyler had been in the shower. What could have happened in those brief hours to have changed his disposition so drastically?

Unless...

Skyler looked through his bedroom doorway to his desolate friend sitting on his sofa. No, it wouldn't help matters to tell Jeff that Evan may not have committed suicide at all.

CHAPTER FIVE

As it happened, Sidney already knew. "He had scratched at someone awfully hard. There was blood under his nails and a bruise on his wrist. Someone forced that gun into his mouth."

"Oh my God!" He swerved. Never have a phone conversation while driving, he admonished himself, especially when it involved a conversation about murder. He straightened the car and turned the corner for the high school.

She sighed. "I'm sorry, Skyler. I keep forgetting you two were...close."

"Was it...was it his gun?"

"Yes. A Berretta M9. He had a few. Standard Army issue. We don't know what happened yet. We're trying to piece it together."

"Have you told Jeff?"

"Yes. He seems to be taking this news better. It's easier when there's someone to blame and it isn't the deceased."

"What about his house? Does he have to clean that up himself?"

"No. I gave him a card for a company that does that sort of thing after a crime."

"Jeez. There's a business for everything."

"I gotta go, Skyler. Call me tonight if you need to."

"Okay. Thank you for helping him, Sid."

"Yeah. I'll call you."

She hung up and he pulled the Bluetooth from his ear just as he pulled into the faculty parking lot. He parked and hurried up the steps to his second floor classroom. No time for coffee in the staff lounge. He'd have to go without until break at ten. The door to his room was open, probably left that way by the janitor. He slipped inside but as he turned toward his desk, he froze.

A large bouquet of exotic flowers was sitting on his desk in a glass vase. He set his leather satchel down next to his chair and reached for the FTD card. Someone sent flowers?

Looking forward to another wonderful night out.

K

He stared at it a long time before a warm feeling thawed the rawness that had settled in his chest from the past few hours' events. Had it only been yesterday that he had bid a long and sensuous farewell to his "date" on Sunday afternoon? He couldn't stop the smile that crept over his face and looked at the card once more before slipping it into his shirt pocket.

He checked his emails and tried to ready himself for class, but thoughts of Jeff intruded, keeping an edge on his already tender emotions. When it got a little overwhelming, he glanced up at the bouquet and smiled. He so wanted to do something with Keith tonight, but he wanted to keep his schedule open in case Jeff called him. He hoped Keith would understand.

As it was, he became too busy to leave his classroom. He ate a power bar for lunch that he kept in his satchel for emergencies and tried to catch up. He called Jeff several more times between classes but always got his voice mail. He thought of calling Sidney but he knew she'd call him if she could.

The bell rang for the last class of the day, and the sounds of many feet followed it. Laughing students pushed into the room and settled at their desks, tucking away backpacks and cell phones.

Heather, her raccoon eyeliner making her eyes appear brighter, stopped dead before his desk. "Ooh. Mr. Foxe! Who gave you the flowers?"

The rest of the class made catcalls and whistles.

Skyler felt his face redden and he ducked his head behind the computer screen, checking for emails. "What makes you think anyone *gave* me those?" he asked innocently.

Rick Flores sauntered in and stared at the flowers as he slid into his front row seat. "Whoo hoo. Check out the flowers. A secret admirer?" He looked toward Alex at the back of the class and winked.

Heather sat as Amber joined her and pouted, looking at the spray of anthuriums, birds of paradise, orchids, and harakeke. "He won't say. The man is being coy. I wonder if it's a teacher here."

Another round of "oohs" and whistles accompanied that and Skyler, unable to stop blushing, launched himself from his chair and headed for the front of his desk, ostensibly to begin teaching but hoping to hide the large bouquet from view.

"Enough speculation. Just leave my personal life out of it."

Amber nodded her head with finality and glared at everyone in the room. Of course he knew she didn't want to own up to the fact staring her in the face that Skyler had interests elsewhere.

"We're going to see the second half of *Some Like it Hot* today, remember?" He wheeled the TV into position and slipped in the DVD. With the remote he found the place they left off Friday and started the movie.

He snuck to the back of the class and noticed Keith walking by the windows in the corridor, peeking in. Skyler slipped out the backdoor and caught Keith by the sleeve. The taller man turned a brilliant smile on him. "Hey, Skyler."

His stomach gave a little swoop and he smiled up at Keith. "Hi. Thanks for the flowers."

"You're welcome." He stepped closer but seemed to catch himself. He glanced back at the class through the window. Skyler looked too but they all seemed enthralled by the glow of the TV. "So have you thought about getting together tonight?"

His spirits plummeted. God how he wanted to! "Oh... A friend had a really awful thing happen and I think I have to be available to him."

Keith's face fell. "Oh. Well...naturally you have to be available. To him."

There was a hint in his tone that Skyler chose to ignore.

"Maybe tomorrow night?" Skyler suggested.

"That might work out. I'll let you know."

They stood awkwardly for another moment, Keith leaning toward him seeming to want to touch. But Keith finally turned, and with a little embarrassed wave, left.

Skyler watched him go, wondering for the umpteenth time if his seeing another teacher on the sly was such a good idea. *Take it slow*, he told himself. *Play it cool.*

♪ ♪ ♪

When Skyler got home after class he set the delivered flowers from Keith beside the other flowers the man had brought for their date, then kicked off his shoes. He tried to call Jeff one more time but got his voice mail yet again.

Sighing, he fixed himself a dinner of pasta with fresh tomato, garlic, and basil. He washed it down with a little Pinot Grigio and took a full wine glass with him to his desk and began reading and correcting essays.

The phone rang. Relieved, Skyler dived for it, but it wasn't Jeff. It was Philip. "Oh. It's you."

"Well thanks a lot," said Philip.

"No, I'm sorry. I thought it was Jeff." And he told the whole terrible story.

"My God, Skyler. That's horrible."

"Yeah. I was sort of hanging around keeping the evening open in case Jeff called me. I feel so bad for him. For both of them."

"Well, it's about ten now. Do you think he's going to call?"

"I don't know."

"Want me to come over and keep you company?"

Skyler looked around the lonely apartment and decided that company was a good idea. "Yeah. Come on up."

Philip arrived not too long after. The large exotic spray of flowers sitting next to the smaller arrangement on the kitchen counter dominated the room. "I didn't know I was supposed to bring flowers."

"Oh," Skyler said, toying with the petals on the small autumn bouquet. "Keith brought this on Saturday. For our date."

"And this one?"

"Um…Keith sent those today."

"Sooo. How *was* that date? Jamie didn't call me so I assumed the worst."

"I didn't call Jamie." Skyler wandered into the living room and sat on the sofa. Philip made himself at home, poured some wine, and joined him.

"So what's up, Sky?"

"I don't know. I don't know how I feel about the whole dating thing. I don't know how I *should* feel."

"Was the date that bad?"

"Bad? No. It was that good!" He snatched up his wine glass and knocked it back.

Philip frowned and pushed his glasses up his nose. "Wait a minute. The date was good… and that's bad?"

"No. Yes. Well, not really. I mean, the guy's a spectacular lover. He is the poster child for stamina. We were at it half the night and a good portion of the next day. So that was great."

"Uh huh. I'm failing to see—"

"But what does it all mean? Where does it all go? Is it just a reflection of a heterosexual lifestyle? Am I trying to emulate something I'm not?"

"Whoa, whoa there, dude. Just hold on. You're getting way ahead of yourself. Let me see if I can put this in some sort of perspective. You had a spectacular first date with a guy you've been crushing on, he brings you flowers—"

"He bought me dinner."

"He bought you— Ah shit, Skyler. You're just being an idiot."

He glared at Philip and threw himself into the sofa cushion. "Gee, thanks, Philip!"

"No, I really mean it. This man is perfect and you are fucking it up because you are afraid of commitment. It's a classic case, really."

"I'm not afraid of commitment," he muttered, still crunched up tightly against the sofa, arms clenched over his chest.

"Yes, you are. Of all the members of the S.F.C., you and I were the closest to becoming boyfriends. Am I right?"

Skyler cocked his head and glanced at Philip. He was still quite attractive even with his bland brown hair and honey-colored eyes. "Yes."

"And why didn't we?"

He shrugged, feeling a bit cornered.

"We liked each other, we have the same taste in things— except for your unnatural obsession with Motown music, which I will never understand—and we were pretty darned good in bed, as I recall."

Skyler nodded, loosening his arms a little.

"So why didn't we?"

He stared hard at his friend, trying to recall what did happen to their love affair two years ago. They'd fucked almost nonstop for a week. The following week Skyler began stopping by The Bean. The week after that they started to do other things and never slept together again. They'd never had what one would consider a date. Not like he and Keith had done Saturday night.

"I honestly don't know, Philip," he said seriously.

"You wouldn't commit!" he said, finger pointing at Skyler's chest. "It was one or the other with you. I wanted to stay all night, you wanted to kick me out. You wanted to come to The Bean and hang out but then you wouldn't come home with me. It seemed like as soon as you got to know someone or was on the cusp of knowing them, you'd back away. Not that I mind just being your friend. I love you, dude, you know that. But it could have been more. You just wouldn't let it. Are you going to do the same thing with Keith?"

It was as if Philip was someone he'd never met before. He stared at his friend anew. No one had ever put it to him like that. Maybe Sidney tried but it never sunk in as it was doing now.

"Jesus," he whispered. "Is that what I did? Really?"

Philip bobbed his head and drank his wine. He scooted toward Skyler and more gently, he asked, "How do you really feel about Keith?"

He dredged up a deep sigh and did his best to contemplate Keith Fletcher objectively. "He's...gorgeous."

"Yeah, I got that part. But what do you *feel* about him?"

"Well...I like him. I do. He makes me feel...special. I feel more differently about him than I have for other tricks. I mean... he's not a trick."

"Hmm." Philip silently drank his wine.

Skyler jumped on the comment. "'Hmm'? 'Hmm' what? What do you mean?"

"Well, I've never before heard you say that anyone you brought home wasn't a trick."

"He didn't feel like one. He felt more important than a trick. But maybe it was the whole date thing."

"Maybe. Or *maybe*," he said, gesturing with wine glass, "it's something about *him*."

Thinking about it, Keith did seem different. His being a teacher might have had something to do with it. His sensitivity. His good looks. He seemed a little domineering but that was okay. It was probably the jock in him. And that was a bit appealing, too, he had to admit.

They talked a bit more, and Skyler ended up turning on the TV and flipping off the lights. Sitting comfortably on the sofa sipping wine with Philip was very nice for a change. It had seemed like ages since he and Philip had a chance to be alone without the rest of the S.F.C. being there.

The doorbell. Skyler glanced at Philip and then the clock. It was 11:15. He rose and opened the door never expecting to see Keith standing there.

"I took a chance that you'd be up." Mute, Skyler stepped aside to let him in. "I thought maybe you wanted some company while you waited for your friend to call…"

Philip switched on a light and Keith whipped his head toward the source. His eyes homed in on Philip. "I see you *have* company," he said tightly.

"Hi there!" said Philip, waving like an idiot. He slid his shoes on and stumbled toward Keith offering his hand. "I'm Philip Price, Skyler's friend."

Keith took his hand warily and shook it once. "Keith Fletcher."

Philip's brows disappeared into his hairline. His lips mouthed "holy shit" and his eyes did a quick appraisal of the taller man. Everyone stared wordlessly at one another for a moment, before Keith broke the silence. "Well I guess I should go. You and your…friend…seem to be busy."

Philip waved his arms. "Oh no! I was just going. It's late. You stay."

"No, maybe I shouldn't—"

"Look, Keith. I'm sure Skyler would prefer your company—"

"Are you sure?"

"Oh, yes. Must be off. Thanks for the wine, Skyler." He passed Keith and behind his back made a "call me" gesture to Skyler before he was gone.

Skyler watched him depart and slowly closed the door. He turned and smiled wanly. "That was Philip."

"So I gathered. Sorry to interrupt what was evidently an intimate moment."

There was that tone again that so irked Skyler. "Well, it wasn't an 'intimate' moment. We were just watching TV."

"In the dark."

"It's *my place*," he said, voice getting a bit louder. "I like watching TV in the dark."

"Far be it from me to tell you how to watch TV in your own place. I just thought you said you needed to be there for a friend. If you're seeing other people then I'd appreciate a heads up, that's all."

"Philip is not other people. He's one of my best friends. And he *was* just keeping me company in case *Jeff*, my friend in *need*, called. Which he didn't. So chill."

Keith's lips were pressed tightly into a thin line. "I see. Sorry. Maybe I should go."

"Maybe you should."

Keith gave Skyler what he could only describe as a hurt-puppy-dog face. But it didn't matter. Skyler was royally pissed off. This jealous attitude was one thing that did *not* work for him. He went to the door and pulled it open. With shoulders slumped, Keith passed over the threshold. He stopped in the doorway and turned. "See you tomorrow."

"Yeah. Right." He made sure he didn't slam it in Keith's face but he closed it with a certain flourish and threw the deadbolt.

He listened as Keith thumped down the stairs and seethed, his back to the door. "Couldn't commit, huh? *That's* my problem? I think Keith Fletcher has far more problems than I do."

♬ ♬ ♬

The next day, Skyler studiously avoided anyone that even remotely looked like Keith Fletcher, including being more than unusually rude to Ben Fontana, the art teacher. He was tall and broad-shouldered, too, except he had a rather dumb sheepdog aura about him.

Skyler scrambled to his classroom through the throng of students after break, waving his hello's to those who shouted greetings to him.

Sitting at the computer, he checked the emails and found one with the subject line "Sorry again for being an a-hole." Checking the source he saw it came from kfletcher.

Skyler sighed and opened it.

Skyler,

I'm sorry about last night. I don't know why I was acting that way. It certainly was uncalled for. Please accept my apology here and in person. I have to run the boys through practice all afternoon, but I could get away for a few minutes. Would you meet me at the boy's locker room after 3 today? Please?

Keith

Well, he supposed it was the polite thing to do. He'd gotten a call at lunchtime from Philip asking how it went last night after he left and Skyler told him.

"I never thought I'd say this, but don't be too hard on the guy," Philip had said.

"He was being a complete jerk. Jealousy is not my thing. If he can't listen to me when I'm telling him something—"

"There's those walls again."

"What walls?"

"Those commitment walls. The least little excuse and they're up again. I'm telling you, Skyler. Don't fuck it up!"

"*Goodbye*, Philip!"

He'd hung up abruptly on his friend and didn't feel the least bit guilty about it. Relationships were too complicated. Why shouldn't he find excuses to get out of them?

But thinking of Keith, how sweet he was in bringing those flowers, taking him to dinner, their conversation that never had a lull until, it felt right to just *be* with him without saying a word. Wasn't that worth fighting for? Is that what Philip meant? He supposed he'd find out at three o'clock.

The rest of the afternoon dragged. When it got to the last

class of the day, Skyler felt a sense of relief wash over him. The class had started reading *The Great Gatsby* and though Skyler was supposed to be discussing it, he found himself getting distracted. Someone tall with dark hair would walk by the windows and his eyes would snap to the corridor, zipping away again when it turned out to be a teen. This was getting ridiculous. He was watching the clock just as much as his students.

When the clock hands hit two-fifty, the bell rang and the students did not wait for any formal dismissal in order to rise from their desks and collect their things. Amber tried to get Skyler into a conversation about the Daisy Buchanan character, but Heather pulled her friend away, smiling back at Skyler with her black painted lips as if to say to him "You're welcome."

Skyler took his time. He scanned the emails to see if he needed to reply to anything, shut down the computer, and stuffed homework assignments into his satchel. He didn't know what he was going to say to Keith as he walked slowly through the emptying corridors and down the stairwell. He'd be polite and listen to what the man had to say. That was the very least he could do. But he'd seen Keith's temper and once you added jealousy into the mix it made for a losing combination.

It always amazed Skyler how quickly the school emptied after the last bell. Of course there were still many stragglers. Some of them were in band, some in the school play and were headed to the auditorium for rehearsals, and some were in sports, mostly football. The season was over but the team still had to meet for exercising and, he supposed, strategy sessions and practice.

Passing the field as he walked, Skyler could see the team doing laps. He thought he could just make out number forty-nine, Alex Ryan, making his way around the far side of the oval. He searched the bleachers and sure enough, Rick Flores lounged across two rows, pretending to read his homework. These were heady days for those two. Their coming out, the first flush of love. How would it turn out for them? Could they overcome the obstacles of homophobia? They both had two more years of high school. Rick might go to college. He was certainly smart enough. Alex on the other hand wasn't likely to go. If he only applied himself, he could surely go to community college and then maybe get the confidence to go on to a university. It was so hard when one didn't have the support at home, something Skyler suspected of Alex's family. He wondered what Alex's aspirations were and decided he'd try to get a chance to talk to the boy's guidance counselor.

He reached the boys' gym, with its art deco entrance arch and clerestory windows. Up the brick-red-painted steps and he was inside. There were a few lights on at the far end of the locker room, a towel lying on the floor near one of the benches, but no one else. Except.

Up the metal catwalk staircase to Coach Carson's office, Skyler saw the light on and Carson, Ed Fallows, and Mac Simpson, two of the assistant coaches, speaking loudly.

Mac was a broad beefy guy with no neck and a shaved head. Either some of the kids took to emulating his haircut or half the football team were really skinheads. There were rumors, of course, but Skyler didn't like to believe it, even though they gave every indication of acting just like goosesteppers.

Ed, on the other hand, was a tall man, too thin for his bones which stuck out in lumps at his knees, shoulders, and elbows. His dark hair was cropped short to his round head. It was strange that he had a sallow complexion since he spent a lot of time outdoors.

But right now, his sallow face was burnished red. Carson kept telling him to calm down, that everything would be fine. Uh oh. Was the district making budget cuts? Also being at the bottom of the food chain at the school, Skyler worried that he could get the ax, though he knew he had the support of Mr. Sherman and most of the staff. They all seemed to like him, especially the secretaries. They were the ones who made sure all the paperwork was in, after all. But last hired, first fired.

Mac stood by, saying nothing. His arms were firmly folded over his broad chest, crushing the whistle hanging from a lanyard around his neck.

Skyler stepped back into the shadows. The situation didn't look as if Carson would want company right now, especially Skyler's. They didn't get along, what with Carson's general animosity toward Skyler. The coach seemed to know that he was gay and liked to taunt him about it with sly asides attempting to humiliate Skyler at every turn.

Carson managed to get Ed settled down and they continued to talk quietly for a time in a low tone Skyler couldn't decipher. The scenario made him think about poor Julia and who it might have been that shoved her down the math building stairwell. Skyler had been certain it was Carson but Sidney had maintained he had had an alibi. But was it ironclad?

And what about Ed? Wasn't he one of "Carson's flunkies," the very type Julia had warned Skyler about? Did *he* have an alibi? And what about Mac, Mr. Skinhead? Did he have a penchant for mayhem, as well?

And of course, she had warned him about Keith, too.

The light switched off suddenly. Ed opened the door to the glass office and Carson, Mac, and Ed headed down the metal steps. Panicked, Skyler looked around for a hiding place and finally had to settle for ducking into the showers behind the tiled wall. It was damp and smelled of mildew and feet. Just the smell of it sent him into unwilling memories of his days in gym class. His eyes moved unbidden to his old locker. Number 323. Three separate times he had been stuffed in there wearing only his underwear. Not a pretty thing when the coach had to get him out and blamed Skyler for it!

"What are you doing in the shower?"

Skyler's heart jumped into his throat and he spun around, facing Keith. Embarrassment took over and he felt his face warm as he stepped out. "You know, they could stand to re-grout that," he muttered, trying to recover his lost dignity.

Keith looked at him steadily and when Skyler gazed up into those forlorn eyes all his arguments for putting Keith in his place melted away. The man was really too good-looking for himself.

"I'm here," he managed to say.

Keith smiled warmly. "Thanks for coming. I thought you might not show. I got a little carried away at your place the other night. I'm sorry. Really. I just saw this other guy there and I thought maybe you ditched me for him and I...well. I guess I was a little...jealous." He grimaced. "That's not a very attractive trait, I know. But I can't help it. When I'm really interested in someone that's how I get. This wasn't just a hook-up to me, you know?"

"I know. It wasn't to me either. But I'm not used to this. I'm more used to hooking up."

"So I gathered." Keith worried the handle of his gym bag. He seemed anxious, a new look for the normally confident man. "Look, Skyler, I have to be here for a few more hours, but could we do something tonight? I want to see you."

His gaze was unnervingly intent on Skyler's. It was hard to look away. And when all was said and done, Skyler didn't want to. "I want to see you, too," he heard himself say quietly. He laughed, suddenly finding all his earlier intentions flying out the window. "Come over when you're done. I'll cook dinner. A quiet evening at home. We can talk."

Keith's smile was positively radiant. "A home-cooked meal? Great! I can be there around seven."

Skyler left the locker room feeling light on his feet. He swung his satchel and if he weren't afraid of someone seeing him, he would have kicked up his heels.

♫ ♫ ♫

At his apartment, Skyler chopped the peeled blood oranges into small pieces and mixed them with red onions, strips of red bell pepper, and balsamic vinegar. The zucchini was quartered into bite-sized pieces and steaming on the stove, and the sea bass was broiling nicely, almost ready to come out.

He had just put the butter in a heated pan when the doorbell rang. Flinging open the door he smiled on seeing Keith standing there.

Before he could even think about it, he reached up to the taller man and kissed him on the lips. Keith was almost as surprised as Skyler. Feeling himself blush at his audacity, Skyler gestured for the man to come in. He poured him some white wine, and Keith sat on one of the stools at the breakfast bar, watching Skyler in the kitchen.

"You really can cook, can't you?"

Skyler preened. He had changed into the tightest jeans he had, with his favorite champagne-colored silk T-shirt. He slung a towel over his shoulder. "I do like to. Not as much fun cooking for one, though."

Keith glanced at the small dining table where they had shared breakfast last weekend. Skyler had rearranged the tropical bouquet Keith had given him into a shorter and smaller decoration between two squat candles. The table was set with his Mikasa Global china.

"This is just spur of the moment cooking?" asked Keith, clearly a little taken aback.

"Well, yes. I was going to make the sea bass this way anyway. And there was enough for two. I hope you like fish."

"I think I'd like anything you made."

He warmed at that. "Do you cook?"

"I can throw a steak on the barbecue and make grilled cheese sandwiches. That is the extent of my gourmet abilities. But I enjoy good food."

"Well, I hope you like this."

The fish was ready and he placed a filet on each bed of zucchini. Finally, he spooned some of the blood orange relish on top and brought it to the table. "Dinner is served."

"Smells wonderful." Keith took the seat he'd taken last time and after placing the cloth napkin in his lap, took a forkful of fish.

Skyler waited. He had cooked for Sidney plenty of times, and even made Thai for Philip and Jamie, but this was the first time he really wanted to please someone.

Keith chewed with a barely concealed smile. He glanced up at Skyler and grinned. "It's great."

Skyler drank his wine, relieved. "So what's new in the world of biology?" he asked, tucking into his dinner.

Keith pushed the zucchini around with his fork and finally speared a chunk. "Well, nothing so startling that we need to alert the Nobel committee, but the kids are developing proposals for the upcoming county science fair."

"Lots of baking soda volcanoes and dissected frogs?"

"I'm encouraging some more thoughtful projects. Some of the kids are really getting into it. Heather Munson—I think she's in your class—had a very interesting green energy proposal."

"That's my Heather. She's a pretty smart one. She might just solve the world's fossil fuel problems and still look Goth doing it."

Keith smiled. "I wouldn't be surprised." He took a sip of wine and set the glass down at the top of his plate. "Sort of makes me look forward to having my own kids someday."

Skyler choked on a bit on fish and coughed into his napkin.

"You all right?" asked Keith, reaching over and pounding on his back.

Skyler held up a hand. "I'm fine," he sputtered. "So. You...w-want your own kids?"

"Yeah. Someday. How about you?"

His fork trailed languid circles in the fruit relish. "I really like kids. Wouldn't be teaching if I didn't, but...my own? I don't know."

Keith set his fork down. "Why not?"

"I don't know. Raising kids. Alone. My mom raised me by herself and it was such a struggle. I barely saw her because she was working so much."

"What happened to your dad?"

"They divorced when I was twelve."

"Does he live nearby?"

"Haven't a clue. Last time I talked to him was in 2001."

Keith said nothing, but when Skyler looked up his face wore a soft expression. "Your mom must be quite a special person."

"She is. I really respect her for the sacrifices she made."

"Skyler, I don't suppose it occurred to you that you wouldn't have to raise a child alone. You might..." Keith kept his eyes down and toyed with the napkin in his lap. "You might find a partner someday. Maybe even get married if it ever becomes legal here."

Skyler froze and stared at Keith. "Marriage?"

Keith poured Skyler and then himself more wine, his mouth firming into a straight line. "It has been known to happen."

"I've seen how marriage works. No thanks."

"Just because your family—"

"What about *your* family," he said quickly. "Folks still married?"

Keith corked the bottle and set it down. "Yes, as a matter of fact. Forty years. My older brother has been married for twenty and my younger sister has been with her husband for fifteen. No divorces."

Skyler took a hasty gulp of wine. "I guess some people still do stay married." He dipped his fork into the last of his vegetables while Keith quietly ate, watching Skyler with a hooded expression. Finally, Keith took a deep breath, smiled, and with his glass in his hand, asked, "So how's English Lit going?"

Relieved the conversation had shifted, Skyler relaxed. He hadn't realized how tense his shoulders had become. "It's a good blend of history and lit. The dialogue has been great in all the classes. Right now the freshmen are doing *To Kill a Mockingbird*, the sophomores are getting into *The Great Gatsby*, the juniors are starting *Ragtime*, and the seniors have completely lost the plot."

"It's a little early for senioritis, isn't it?"

"We're a progressive school."

Keith chuckled, a pleasant rumble that Skyler felt deep in his chest. He appreciated that Keith had dropped the subject of kids and marriage when Skyler was obviously uncomfortable with it. He hadn't realized himself how much the subject bothered him. *Freud would have a field day.* Fortunately, there was plenty to distract him. Keith himself was a pretty good distraction. Skyler watched the man talk, followed the curve of his lips and the white flash of teeth. And every now and then, Skyler shivered pleasantly from the reverberation of Keith's renewed laughter.

They continued to talk and finished everything, including the bottle of wine, in short order.

Keith wiped his mouth with his napkin and set it aside. The conversation had abruptly come to a halt. Those blue eyes rose and nailed Skyler to the spot. "It's a school night," said Keith, rising.

"Yeah." Skyler rose, too.

"It's getting late."

"Yeah."

"Maybe I should…"

Skyler moved around the table and stood before him. He really was the handsomest thing. His cologne was Skyler's downfall. He loved a man who smelled good. Reaching up, Skyler touched Keith's scratchy jaw with his fingertips and leaned closer.

Keith bent forward and before Skyler knew it, he was met with warm lips and a wet, curious tongue. Their bodies melted together. Skyler's long fingers closed around those hard biceps, but only managed to circumnavigate them halfway around.

Keith's large hands skimmed down Skyler's back, dropping lower, until they reached his bottom and squeezed a handful of each cheek.

They made their way to the sofa, and even before they reached it, Skyler's shirt was up and off. He worked on Keith's buttons, mouth never tearing away from the man. Trousers and underwear were soon discarded and, naked, Skyler straddled his hairy thighs, writhing in his lap. Keith's fist wrapped around both their cocks, squeezing them together, as he slowly stroked. He smeared his palm over the heads of both reddened crowns, blending their pre-cum and using it as lube. The stroking became intense and Skyler arched back, letting the feeling overwhelm him.

The phone rang. *Let it ring*, Skyler thought dreamily, pleasure coiling deep in his gut and traveling lower. When the machine switched on, he heard Sidney's urgent voice.

"Skyler. Skyler! Pick up the goddamned phone! It's Sidney. Skyler. Ah fuck. Okay. I hate to be the one tell you this and on your machine, and all, but... Look, Skyler, we had no choice. The evidence... The thing of it is, we had to arrest your friend Jeff...for the murder of Evan Fargo."

CHAPTER SIX

Skyler hopped off of Keith's lap and fell on the floor, nearly hitting his head on the coffee table. The news was enough to wilt his erection, and he began grabbing his clothes from the floor. "Keith, I'm so sorry, but I have to go."

"Skyler," said Keith, looking dazed. "What's going on?"

"Evan and Jeff are partners and they were just kicked out of the Army for Don't Ask Don't Tell," he said, pulling up his trousers and zipping the fly. Keith was slowly gathering his own clothes, though his cock was still mouthwateringly stiff. Skyler looked away and grabbed his shirt where it had been discarded. "Evan was wounded and lost a leg. He was really depressed and it looked like he killed himself."

Keith gasped and froze.

"Yeah, but then it came out that he was murdered."

"*That's* the friend you were waiting around for? That's not the guy I met the other night, is it?"

"No, you met Philip. He's a friend. Well…" He pulled his shirt over his head and tugged it down in place. "Jeff is an old friend, too. So is Evan. The d-deceased. This is really awful. Sid's made a terrible mistake and I've got to sort this out."

"Of course. Sidney's your friend…the detective."

"Yeah. This sucks so much." He sat on the sofa, pulling on his shoes.

Keith dressed quickly and offered to go with Skyler to the police station, but Skyler declined, thinking how sweet it was of him to even say. They kissed lingeringly at the door with promises of getting together again soon. With a wave, Keith was gone and Skyler was left to grab his wallet and trot down the stairs.

He probably broke a few speed laws getting to the police station but he was thankful to make it there quickly. Tired women with drawn faces sat on the uncomfortable seats in the lobby. Children were sleeping on their laps or tugging at their skirts. The harsh fluorescent lighting cast no shadows over the line of people snaking toward the front counter. Skyler got in line and followed the roped barrier until he reached the policewoman sitting behind a wide sheet of bulletproof glass. She was a little older than Sidney and had her brown hair pulled back in a severe ponytail. "Can I help you?" she repeated, her voice muffled by the glass.

"A friend of mine was arrested and I don't know if I can bail him out or what I'm supposed to do."

"Name?"

"Mine or—"

"The one arrested."

"Oh. Jeff Dwyer."

She typed it into her computer and shook her head. "I don't have that name. Could be he wasn't processed yet."

"My friend is the detective on the case. Sidney Feldman."

She typed something else in and then looked up. "Detective Feldman appears to be in interrogation right now. If you want to talk to her you'll have to wait."

Interrogation? Was she in there interrogating Jeff right now?

"Can I leave a message for her? Let her know I'm here?"

She pulled over a yellow pad, held her pen, and looked up expectantly.

"Um...tell her Skyler Foxe is here in the lobby."

He spelled his name for her and she wrote it down, then tore off the top sheet.

He didn't see what she did with it but he thought it best to get out of the way. "Thank you," he said and shuffled out of line, found an empty chair, and slid into it. He stared at the big institutional clock on the wall, not unlike the clocks they had at school. It read nine-fifteen.

The minutes crawled by. Skyler found himself stealing surreptitious glances at the others. Some of the children were running around loose, while some were hugged by anxious women. An old man with gray stubble who smelled like cigarettes sat beside Skyler, thumbing the corner of a black leather-bound Bible. A young man, a little younger than Skyler, sat opposite him, and was staring openly. He was Caucasian with a shaved head and wearing a dirty T-shirt and wide-legged jeans, with a silver-studded black belt threaded through the belt loops. He looked like the type to carry a switchblade or gun. He kept staring at Skyler and Skyler kept glancing nervously at him. Was he coming to bail out one of his gang member friends or was he here to be arrested?

Skyler couldn't stand it anymore and jumped out of his seat.

It was too cold to stand outside so he lingered at the door, stepping aside when a cop or civilian entered or exited. It seemed that few people were leaving. Instead, they were waiting, all waiting for something.

An hour and a half went by before his cell rang. He looked at the number with relief. "Sidney?"

"Are you still at the station?"

"Yeah, I've been hanging out in the lobby for over an hour. What's going on?"

"Jeff is going to be here a while."

"What? Sidney, you've made a mistake. Jeff would never do this."

"Skyler, I'm not going to argue with you. Your friend says he needs some medication at home. Will you go get it for him?"

"Yes, of course. What—"

"I wouldn't ordinarily do this but since he has no family to do it for him and you guys are friends, I'm bending the rules. It's for high blood pressure. Here's the name of the stuff." Sidney rattled off the name on the bottle. "Bring that and only that. I'm sending someone out to you with the key. Don't dawdle. Just do this, okay, Skyler."

"Yeah, all right. Sidney, can I bail him out tonight?"

"Not until tomorrow. Bring back the meds and I'll call you later tonight. Very late."

Before he could ask anything else, the call clicked off.

"Jeez." He stuffed the phone in his pocket and looked up just in time as a skinny young cop stepped through the heavy metal door. "Skyler Foxe?" he called to the room. People looked up but no one moved.

Skyler ticked a glance at the skinhead and waved at the policeman. "Hi, um, yes, I'm Skyler Foxe." The policeman looked at Skyler and took him over to the counter. He took out a paper and put it down on the counter along with a pen from his breast pocket. "Could you sign here?"

As soon as Skyler did, the cop handed over a small manila envelope. Skyler felt the shape of a metal key inside. "Thanks."

The officer said nothing but as Skyler was walking out, the skinhead smiled at him and mouthed "Skyler."

$$\int \int \int$$

"I'm never going there again," he told himself in the car, but then realized he'd be returning there just as soon as he completed his mission to secure Jeff's meds.

"Jesus Christ. How can she work in such a depressing place?" At least Sidney wasn't the officer sitting at the counter. No wonder she worked hard to get a detective badge. She was the youngest on the force to get one, too. Not only because she was smart, but she well knew it was due to the fact that they had no female detectives and there was pressure to promote. Sidney was pragmatic and took it all in stride. She knew she would prove herself and Skyler knew it, too.

He pulled the car over next to the curb in front of Jeff's house and looked out the passenger window. The house was dark except for a weak porch light that only illuminated the front stoop. The long concrete walkway that cut the lawn in two was a dark gray under a night sky and the shadows cast by the giant umbrella shapes of date palm trees.

Skyler got out of the car and headed up the walk, key in hand. He cringed going up the steps, thinking about the last time he had been here, when Evan was wheeled away in a body bag. Jeff, with all those scratches up and down his arms. Sidney said the killer had forced the gun in Evan's mouth and he had fought.

No! No, he refused to believe his friend was a killer. Absolutely not. And why would he? Jeff loved Evan.

He stood on the porch and stared at the front door. But Jeff was working two jobs and having to deal with Evan's depression and who knew what else. Maybe he was just tired of it. He had been a grunt. He certainly knew how to use a gun.

His chest panged with painful heat. "Oh God. It can't be possible, could it?" He shook his head. *Stop thinking, Skyler. Just get the meds.* He fit the key in the lock and opened the door.

Half expecting to see that splatter on the wall, his tense muscles relaxed when he saw a perfectly normal living room in the dark. He timidly switched on a lamp and breathed deep. No splatter on the wall. No empty wheelchair. No bridge table with gun cleaning supplies. Just a normal living room that smelled of normal air freshener. Those crime scene clean up guys were miracle workers.

He headed down the dark, narrow hall and stuck his head in each room. Bedroom. Pretty plain. Pictures on the walls, a king size bed, a desk. Not much else. Another bedroom. Big American flag on the wall, another desk, some chairs. Bathroom. *Finally.*

Skyler turned on the light and headed for the medicine cabinet. Lots of pill bottles. Percocet, antibiotics. He read labels and finally found the Ziac. He pocketed it, closed the cabinet, and switched off the lights. He headed down the darkened hall and almost made it to the living room when he heard a rustling.

He stopped, ears pricked. Another rustle. Definitely coming from the living room. He hadn't locked the front door behind him and someone was in the house!

He tiptoed backward until he reached the bathroom and crept inside, closing himself in the room and locking the door. He stood in the dark, breathing in quickened rasps against the bathroom door, afraid to move.

Think, Skyler. Cell phone! He thrust his hand in his pocket and fumbled getting it out. It slipped through his fingers and clattered loudly on the tile floor. "Shit!" he hissed and groped around. "Dammit!" Now on all fours he scrambled around, fingers searching. Where the hell was it? He was tempted to turn on a light but he didn't want the intruder knowing where he was. *Of course with all the noise and the swearing he'd have to be deaf and stupid not to know.*

Stretching around the toilet with his cheek resting against the cold porcelain, Skyler's fingers touched something plastic and square-shaped. *Got it!*

He grabbed it, sat on the floor, and opened the phone. The little tune began to play, sounding much too loud in the little space. He pressed it tight to his chest to muffle it.

Someone knocked on the bathroom door and Skyler made a very unmanly shriek.

"Hey. You in there," said a man's voice. "How'd you get in here?"

"I could say the same for you. I'm calling 911."

"Don't do that. I'm a friend of Jeff and Evan's."

Finger poised over the nine, Skyler paused. "Wh-who are you?"

"I'm from the VA Center. I was an adviser."

Skyler got to his feet, and still holding the phone, he took hold of the doorknob. "What's your name?" he called through the door.

"James Fischer. Wouldn't you rather come out and talk instead of standing there in the dark?"

"You snuck in after me."

"Sorry. This whole thing is pretty upsetting."

Skyler waited for his heart to slow a bit and he carefully unlocked the door and opened it a crack. A man in a plain T-shirt and black jeans was standing in the darkened hall. He looked like the kind of guy you'd see on an army recruiting poster, square jawed and rather handsome. Skyler clicked his phone off and came out into the hall. "You scared the shit out of me."

"Sorry. You kind of scared the shit out of me, too." He reached for a pocket and Skyler jumped back. "Easy. I'm just getting my wallet." He slipped his wallet from his pocket, opened it, and pulled out a business card. He handed it to Skyler. Skyler used the light from his cell phone to read it. "And who might you be?" said Fischer.

"I'm a friend, too. My name is Skyler Foxe. I went to college with them." Skyler rummaged for his wallet and took out his business card with the school address and phone.

"No kidding." Fischer blinked and looked down at the card. He stuffed it in one of the pockets in his pants. "Well, this is all a helluva thing." He relaxed against the wall and ticked his head. "Happens more often than you think, though. Guys leave the service and come home with PTSD and no one knows it or they look the other way."

"Evan had more than post traumatic stress disorder. He lost a leg. And anyway it wasn't suicide."

Those eyes stared at Skyler steadily. "What do you mean? I read about it in the paper. The police say it was a suicide."

"It's not. Someone killed him."

"Wow," said Fischer. He spun in a tight circle in the narrow hall. "No shit. Fuck."

"Yeah. So what are you doing here?"

"I came to talk to Jeff, to give my condolences, but then I saw you coming in here and I didn't know what you were up to."

"Oh. I'm picking up meds for Jeff. He's—" He didn't want to say arrested. That was none of this guy's business, so he said,

"Out of town."

"I can understand that." He stood for a moment, staring at the carpet, before he turned abruptly and headed for the living room.

"So, um, I'll tell Jeff you stopped by," said Skyler, trailing after him.

"Oh that's all right," he said over his shoulder. "I'll shoot him an email."

"I'm sure he'd want to talk to you."

He turned to Skyler and looked him evenly in the eye. "I said that was all right. He'll hear from me."

He strode quickly toward the door and pulled it open. Skyler stood there slightly stunned but followed after. He watched the man head down the walkway and pivot right at the sidewalk. But he didn't see a car. The man kept walking until he turned the corner.

Freaked out, Skyler quickly closed and locked the door and escaped into the safety of his own car.

CHAPTER SEVEN

Mr. Skinhead was, thankfully, absent from the police station lobby when Skyler dropped off the meds. Sidney called him later that night, saying he could bail out Jeff first thing in the morning after his arraignment. "You're making a mistake, Sidney," he insisted, though he wasn't sure how he felt. He didn't want his friend to be guilty, couldn't quite believe it.

"I'll talk to you later, Skyler."

"Sidney—" A click. "Bitch hung up. Dammit."

He was certainly going to tell her a thing or two about her phone manners.

After a bad night where his sleep was disturbed by harrying dreams, Skyler first called in to let them know at school that he would be late. It was likely he would miss the first two classes of the day. He certainly didn't tell the secretaries why he would be late. Sidney had told him that he'd probably have to go to the courthouse in San Bernardino and when he got down there, it was another long wait with bad coffee until Jeff's case came up and he could finally post bail, depleting his savings.

Jeff looked dazed when Skyler took hold of him. He was clutching a little plastic bag with his wallet, his meds, keys, and phone. They got to the car and Jeff looked over at Skyler with a hollow look in his eyes. "Why, Skyler? Wasn't it enough that Evan is dead? Do I have to continue through this nightmare and go to prison for it?"

He was dry-eyed. Skyler supposed there weren't any more tears left in him. They were silent on the drive back. But when they pulled into Jeff's driveway and parked, Skyler handed Jeff his house key. "I'm sorry about all this, Jeff. It *will* get cleared up."

"You believe me, right Skyler? That I didn't, *couldn't* do such a thing?"

He took his friend's hand. "Of course. This is just a crazy

mistake. They'll get the guy and then you can finally get some closure."

"Closure." He sat back in the seat, obviously not anxious to go into the house. "That's what people always say, isn't it. But it seems that Evan and I have been following that elusive dream for a while. All we wanted was an Army career, to serve. And then all we wanted was Evan to recover and get closure about his leg. And then we were looking for closure for my appeals. When does it end, Skyler?"

"I don't have an answer to that."

Jeff looked down at Skyler's hand in his own and sighed. "I miss him, Sky. I miss his advice and his laughter. But I've been missing that for a while. I feel so guilty because I wished that sometimes it would just end. But not like this." He shook his head. "You've been a good friend. The best. Thanks for everything."

"No problem. I'm hoping you can clear your name soon. Your VA rep came by the other day."

"VA rep?"

"Yeah, James Fischer. He stopped by—"

"That asshole? What the hell was he doing here?"

The vehemence stopped him cold. "When I was here getting your meds last night he stopped by. I thought—"

"He was the bastard that kept giving us shit about our 'lifestyle.' He wasn't helping me at all. He kept dropping over and harassing Evan about something. If I ever see that bastard here again I'll—"

"Jeff, calm down. That's just the kind of thing you don't want to be doing or saying."

Jeff deflated. "God, you're right. I'm already in enough trouble." He dug into the plastic bag and fished out his wallet. "I have a lawyer's card in here. I'll have to give him a call and get this mess cleared up."

But Skyler was staring at his friend. "Do you know what Fischer was harassing Evan about?"

"What? I don't know. Some kind of deal. He wanted Evan to do something. He'd always drop over when I was out and Evan just said it was some stupid thing. He'd never elaborate. Why? What are you thinking?"

"I don't know. Just thinking."

Jeff gave him a quizzical look before Skyler waved the thought away. "Look, I have to get to class."

"Sure. Sorry. Thanks again, Skyler. I owe you so much."

"It will be fine. Want me to walk you in?"

"No. You better get to work. See you. And thanks."

Jeff got out of the car and Skyler watched him go up the stairs and unlock his door. He paused and waved from the doorway.

"Call me!" Skyler shouted and Jeff nodded before trudging inside and closing the door.

♫ ♫ ♫

Skyler made it to the high school before lunch but too late to catch his second period class. When he arrived to the main building to check in, a pert secretary named Pauline Hingle told him to go in to see the principal.

Skyler knocked lightly on his door and went in. He'd never had to deal so much with the principal before, and never when he was a student at James Polk High. Mr. Sherman, a man nearing fifty with mousy brown hair, sat behind his desk typing something on his keyboard. He looked up briefly and said, "Have a seat, Mr. Foxe."

Skyler wondered what this was about. Was it because he was gone so much lately? Yes, he'd only just started teaching in September and he'd already taken days off and been late to work. Though some of that was to deal with Mr. Sherman's son's murder.

Mr. Sherman finished up and finally turned to Skyler. "I understand you just got into work."

"Yes. I'm sorry, Mr. Sherman. It was unavoidable. I was

helping a friend in a very bad situation."

The principal gave a wary smile. "Yes, you seem to do that a lot."

"Well, my friend's partner was murdered."

Sherman jerked in his seat and Skyler felt like slapping himself for insensitivity. "I'm sorry. That was rather abrupt of me."

"No, that's all right."

"H-how are *you* doing?"

Sherman pinched the bridge of his nose and looked down at his desk. "It's different at home. My wife…is not adjusting well. She's seeing a therapist."

"But not you?"

"I appreciate your concern, Mr. Foxe, but…"

"But stay out of it. Sorry. I guess I just can't help getting in it."

"Like with your friend?"

"Yeah."

"How is he handling it?"

Skyler sighed and flopped back in his chair. "It's pretty messed up. He's the one being accused of his murder. I just bailed him out this morning."

"Oh! Well, are you sure that's the best thing?"

"He's not guilty!" And just as he declared that, he was certain. "It's all a horrible mistake. It's a nightmare."

"One that never quite stops."

They both sat in silence for a time until Sherman adjusted his seat and took a hold of his coffee cup, gripping it so tightly that his knuckles turned white. "Well, then. Just see that it doesn't interfere with your class schedule again."

"No, it won't. I'm sorry about that." He rose, went to the door, and turned back. "And I know I should butt out, but I don't think it's a bad idea you going to that therapist with your wife. You should think about it."

Unexpectedly, Mr. Sherman smiled. "Thank you, Mr. Foxe. You're a good man."

Skyler smiled back.

§ § §

Later, Skyler got an email from Jamie. The S.F.C. wanted a mid-week trip to Trixx and "why don't you bring Hunk on a Stick along?"

Skyler sat back in his chair as his fifth period sophomores bent their heads to their schoolwork. This thing with Keith was so new. Did he really want to subject him to his friends? But then he started thinking about what Philip said about commitment. Wasn't it one of those grown-up things to introduce your friends to your…your…um. What was Keith, exactly? Date? Lover? Boyfr—

"Nope." He looked up, embarrassed that he had said that out loud. Only Amber raised her eyes to him from her book. She smiled coyly, tucked her red hair over her ear, and returned to reading with a slight blush to her cheeks.

It had been a stressful few days. He did need to unwind. It would be nice to go to Trixx but how weird would that be going with a…*date?*

He decided and typed an email to Keith.

A few of my friends have invited me tonight to our favorite bar. Want to come?

He hit send and sat back, watching, waiting. *He's not looking at his computer. He's probably doing footbally things or biology things or…shit!* The computer dinged with a new message from kfletcher.

Love to. What time?

Shit. Now he had to meet him there. *Okay. Calm down, Skyler. It's only at your favorite bar with your favorite people.* Should he also email Sidney? No, he was mad at her right now. She arrested his friend and then hung up on him. She could stew in her own juices at home. And then that thought grossed him out.

He typed:

Meet me at Trixx on Citrus and 6th at 8:30.

Send. There. It was done.

CHAPTER EIGHT

The air was thick at Trixx with the smell of sweat, beer, and layers of different colognes. Skyler went to the bar first and ordered a Grey Goose on the rocks. While he was waiting, he watched the video on the flat screen above the bar. A man, tanned, ripped and wearing a tiny white bathing suit, lay on a sandy beach with turquoise water behind him unfurling on the shore. He slathered himself with oil until his six-pack abs and pecs shined. He slipped his fingers down into his suit and showed a tantalizing bit of carefully shaved pubic hair. The whole time he smoldered into the camera with a come-fuck-me expression. He was dark-haired and blue-eyed and sort of reminded him of Keith.

The bartender had to snap his fingers in front of Skyler's face to finally get his attention. He glanced up to the monitor and gave Skyler a sly smile. The bartender was pretty cute, too. Was he new?

No! *Stop thinking of hooking-up!* Keith would be there any minute.

He gave the bartender a weak smile and grabbed his drink. When he turned he spotted Jamie on the tiny dance floor. Arms high and shimmying up against a tall, buff African American man, he looked mighty busy to Skyler. It was seething with men and loud music thumping through the speakers. Lady Gaga's "Boys, Boys, Boys" was currently keeping the dancers hopping.

He flagged down Jamie who cheered and leapt off of the dance floor, grabbing Skyler's arm and making him spill his drink.

"Hey!"

"Sorry, Sky. It seems like it's been forever since we've gotten together." He dragged him over to a table where Philip was sitting uncomfortably next to Rodolfo. Sidney was leaning against Philip.

"Oh," said Skyler stiffly to Sidney. "It's you. Cop of the walk."

"What's that supposed to mean? Oh for Chrissake. I was just doing my job."

He slammed his drink down. "Just so you know, I'm not talking to you."

"You're talking to me now."

"Only to tell you I'm not talking to you."

"Children!" said Philip, standing and motioning to them. "Both of you, settle down. You, Skyler, sit." Skyler pulled out a chair and did. "Sidney, tell us why Skyler is pissed off at you."

She folded her arms over her chest. "I...um..." She gnawed on her lip. "I may have arrested a...a friend of his. I guess. For murder."

"What?" Jamie sank to a chair, grabbing Skyler's other arm. The drink spilled a second time.

"Dammit, Jamie, I never even got to drink this and it's already half gone."

"Who, Skyler? Who got arrested for murder?" He looked around the table as if thinking it was one of them.

"My friend Jeff. Remember him? You know, the one whose partner just got murdered?"

"I thought he committed suicide?" asked Philip.

"No, it was murder," said Sidney and Skyler at the same time. Skyler glared at her, crossed his arms, and turned away.

Philip faced Sidney. "And now you think this Jeff did it?"

"All evidence suggests he did."

"He didn't!" said Skyler. "It's all a mistake."

"He had opportunity, motive, not to mention those scratches on his arms."

"That could have been from anything. From sex, maybe."

"That's what he claims, but his DNA was found under the victim's fingernails."

"Just his?"

Sidney clamped her lips shut.

Skyler pointed at her across the table. "Aha!"

"I can't talk about this."

"But you just said—"

"I *didn't* say anything."

"Sidney!"

Philip threw a wet, balled-up napkin at Skyler and he jerked back, startled. "Skyler. Down boy. It's out of your hands. Let the wheels of justice work it out."

"The wheels of justice didn't do such a bang up job last time. Something's up. I know it."

Sidney's eyes widened. "Oh no you don't. You will not investigate this murder. Didn't you learn your lesson the last time?"

"I learned that the investigation needed help."

"Skyler, I'm warning you."

"I'm still not talking to you."

"Stop it!" Philip slammed his hand on the table. It wobbled and everyone's drinks sloshed over. "We are all out tonight to relax and have fun. So fun we will have... And to hear about Skyler's date."

Skyler was bringing his drink to his lips when Jamie screeched, "Omigod!" and slapped his shoulder. The drink spilled again, this time into Skyler's lap.

"Jamie!"

"Sorry." He grabbed a napkin and dabbed Skyler's trousers until Skyler snatched the napkin out of his hand. "I just want to hear about it."

"Wait a minute," said Rodolfo, looking at everyone in turn. "Who is this man, this *date?*"

"Skyler works with him," said Sidney, sipping her margarita. "He's a teacher."

Rodolfo bristled like a rooster. "A teacher! No, I don't think so."

Skyler blinked at Rodolfo. "Um…"

"Our little Skyler has lost his heart," said Jamie, hand over his own heart.

"I haven't lost my heart. It's just…something different."

"I had a boyfriend once," said Philip. "In law school. We split because he didn't want to move to Redlands."

"I've had boyfriends," said Jamie. "Lots. This has been a very long dry spell."

"He's *not* my boyfriend. We're just going out."

Jamie hip-bumped Skyler. "So, when do we meet him?"

"Well…"

"Yes," said Rodolfo, pouting. "When do we meet this…*man?*"

Skyler cringed. "How about never?"

"Come on, Skyler," said Sidney. "These guys would love Keith. He's tall, dark, sexy, with light blue eyes, muscles to die for—"

Jamie fanned himself. "I'm feeling faint. When, when, WHEN?"

"Skyler?"

Everyone turned. Standing above his chair was the man in the flesh. The table fell silent.

Keith smiled at everyone and gave a little wave. "Hi."

"Hi, *Keith*," they chorused.

The smile fell slightly.

Skyler shot to his feet. "Keith. Hi! Uh…" He turned to everyone. "Everyone, this is Keith. Keith this is Jamie—"

Jamie stood and offered a hand. Keith took it. "*Enchanté!*" Jamie giggled and sat again.

"And that's Sidney, whom you've met."

Sidney wiggled her fingers. Keith gave her a wary nod.

"And that's Philip...whom you've also met."

Philip leaned forward and offered his hand in a business-like shake. "Good to see you again," he said quickly.

"And this is Rodolfo."

Rodolfo just sat and glared.

"These are my friends."

"It's nice to meet you all." He beamed at Skyler and looked around. "This place is great. I'm going to get a beer. Anyone need anything?"

Everyone shook their heads.

He turned and left for the bar and there was a beat before Jamie squealed. "Oh my *God*! He *is* a hunk. Skyler!" He grabbed Skyler by the shoulders and shook him affectionately. "He's gorgeous. You lucky dog."

Skyler tried not to but he couldn't help but smile. The truth of the matter was Keith *was* gorgeous. And he did feel lucky.

Keith returned shortly, drinking a Corona from the bottle. He set it down on the table

The music subdued a bit and they were able to talk. Philip, bless him, engaged Keith right away and they talked a bit so that when Sidney slipped out of the booth and tapped Skyler, he got up and went to the bar with her without anyone noticing. As soon as they reached the bar he pushed her back. "Hey, I'm not supposed to be talking to you."

"What are you, twelve? Get over yourself." She leaned on the sticky bar and motioned to the cute bartender, who was finishing with the other customers. With an eye roll Skyler turned to the bar and leaned, his shoulder pressed to her shoulder.

"Okay, but that was a lousy thing you did."

"If he's guilty, then it wasn't. But we are not talking about it," she added quickly, cutting off any protests. "The case is what it is."

"Okaaay." He toyed with a beer mat when another thought struck him. He turned to her with a predatory smile. "So…who's Mike de Guzman?"

Sidney froze. "Oh…shit. He's…a guy. My…uh…new partner. I'm sort of…dating him?"

"And you never *told* me? Sid!"

"I know, I know."

The bartender slid over with the drinks. "Margarita on the rocks for the lady and Grey Goose for the hot blond, right?"

Skyler smiled even as his cheeks reddened, but as soon as the bartender moved away he shook it off. Damn. It was hard getting into a new groove. "So you're an item already?" he said to her. "Mike seems to think so."

"Mike?"

"He told me to call him that."

"Oh. We are not an item. We just fuck." As soon as the words left her mouth she screwed up her face, grabbed the margarita, and slammed it back, wiping the wet from her upper lip. She signaled to the bartender for another. "Shit. I didn't mean to tell you that."

"Why the hell not? How long has this been going on?" It suddenly occurred to him with a pang in his heart that Sidney was growing away from him. If she was carrying on with a secret affair without his knowing what else didn't he know? "Jeez, Sid, you used to tell me everything. So what's with making me tell you all *my* juicy details?" He imitated Sidney's voice, "'I'm living my sex life vicariously through you, Skyler.' Bullshit! It's all bullshit."

"I just didn't… God. He's Filipino and I didn't want any crap from my mother."

"I'm not going to tell your mother. Not like you tell mine."

"You know, she's always '*schwartze* this' and '*schwartze* that.' Anybody with the least little skin tone is a *schwartze* to her." She pushed her curls out of her face and heaved a sigh. "But it's more than that. It's…dating someone at work. My partner, for

Chrissake."

"Wait a minute. You egged *me* on to date Keith and he's someone at work."

"That's different. It's you. We're talking about *me*. And he's my partner. That's a big no-no in the department."

The bartender returned and set down the glass for Sidney. He winked at Skyler before moving to the next customer.

"Are you going to get in trouble?"

She shrugged. "It's just complicated."

"I guess. I mean with Keith and me, it seems to be all right. The work part. The angry relationship part, not so much."

She clutched her salt-edged glass. "Do you think he might get violent with you? Because if you do I'll kick his ass."

"No, I don't think so. It's just that jealous thing he does sometimes. But I appreciate your ass-kicking offer."

"Anytime." She saluted with her glass and drank.

"You should do more than fuck the guy, Sidney. He seems nice. Go out with him."

"I work with him every day."

"Oh horrors! God forbid you should have something in common with the man you're dating."

Her face fell. "I like him. He *is* a really nice guy. But what happens if it doesn't work out? I mean we're partners. It could get dicey."

"Take your own advice, detective. You'll never know until you try."

"My mother's going to have a fit."

"What's Yiddish for Filipino?"

♫ ♫ ♫

They returned to the table and Keith grinned, a dimple forming in his cheek. "Hey, Skyler. Want to dance?"

He'd never danced with Keith. Never thought to. But he was on the dance floor without thinking twice and he and Keith were quickly gyrating to "Blow." For a big man, Keith moved gracefully. Skyler chalked it up to his football training. Keith's eyes were on him the whole time and his grin was wide.

"You're a good dancer," Keith yelled over the music.

"So are you."

"You seem surprised."

He shrugged.

And then Keith surrounded him with his arms, tugged him into his chest, and slid his body up and down. Skyler got a good whiff of his cologne and closed his eyes, just feeling the sensations of both jean-clad cocks skating against each other. Fingers pulled his chin up and warm lips covered his. God, Keith was a fantastic kisser! He loved the soft touch of tongues, the warm slide of his mouth. Before it could get too heated, Keith pulled back, giving Skyler a wicked smile that made Skyler's insides swoop.

Suddenly Jamie was dancing with them. "Hi," he said.

"Hi." Keith gave him an amused expression.

"I just have to say that you guys look great together. Tall and dark, short and light. Like salt and pepper shakers."

Keith laughed. It was a great rumbling sound in Skyler's chest.

"The Skyboy here's done nothing but talk about you," he went on.

Keith couldn't keep the grin off. "Is that right?"

Skyler reddened. He plucked at Jamie's sleeve but he didn't get the hint. "Oh, yeah. It's been 'Keith this' and 'Keith that.' Honestly, I didn't think you were real."

"Jamie…"

"But I'm so glad you finally got a chance to meet the S.F.C."

"S.F.C.? What's that?"

"*Jamie…*"

He was leaning on Keith's shoulder now, moving with the music. "The Skyler Fuck Club. S.F.C. for short, see? All of us were Skyler's hook-ups before we became friends. All except Sidney, of course."

"JAMIE!"

Keith's grin faded. "All of you?"

"Oh, yeah! Rudy came into the group only about a month ago. And there's probably *quite* a few others here, too." He looked around, squinting through the flashing lights, hand over his brow as a visor.

Keith stopped dancing. He looked at Skyler with a shuttered expression for a long moment before he turned abruptly and left the dance floor.

Skyler stopped to give Jamie a scathing look before he went after the taller man.

"Keith! Keith, wait!" Damn, he was heading for the door.

Keith stopped. There was hurt in his eyes. "Is that what I am? Just another inductee in the—what did he call it? The Skyler *Fuck* Club? What the *hell*?"

"It's not like that. Well, it *was* like that, I guess, those other times. But you're different. This is different."

"So what happens? We fuck a few more times and then just become friends? Is that what you want?"

Skyler could hear Philip's voice in his head, haranguing him about his commitment issues. Because hooking up and becoming friends was exactly how it *had* worked for the last eight years.

"Look, Skyler, far be it from me to step on your lifestyle. But that is just not me. I don't do that. I don't hook up. Not...not with that kind of frequency."

Skyler wilted. "Go ahead and say it. You think I'm a slut."

"Well, are you?"

It hurt. But he thought about the basket of condoms he kept on his nightstand. "Probably. I *was*. Not now. Keith, I like you.

I've never dated anyone before. This is weird for me—"

"Great." He turned again but Skyler grabbed his bicep and pulled him back.

"Look. I...I can't change my past but it is *in* the past. Jamie and Philip, they've become really good friends."

"Don't forget that Rodolfo guy."

"Yes, and Rodolfo, too. They're good for me. And they're good *to* me. I wouldn't trade them for anything. But they are just friends now. Just friends."

He ran his hand through his hair. "Jeez, Skyler. It's not safe sleeping with that many guys, you know."

"I get tested all the time and I'm Mr. Clean. Really."

Keith stared at the floor, his head moving from side to side like a bull in a bull ring. Finally he looked up above Skyler's head to where his friends had gathered again by the table. Jamie was looking devastated and Philip looked murderous. Sidney calmly glared with narrowed eyes but Skyler knew that was when she was most dangerous. Rodolfo looked a bit smug with his arms crossed over his bare chest, but also a little defensive.

"Skyler, I...I guess I just have to think about this. I'm the monogamous type. Always have been. If you aren't, then this is never going to work."

"Does it have to be so serious? Can't we just...you know..."

"No. We can't. *I* can't. Sorry. I'll...I'll call you later." And then he was out the door.

CHAPTER NINE

"I'm *so* sorry, Skyler," Jamie hissed in his ear. "I wasn't thinking."

"It's all right, Jamie."

Skyler kept looking at the door, thinking that maybe Keith would change his mind and return. But as the time ticked on it certainly didn't look as if that was going to happen.

"He'll calm down," said Philip. "And then you can talk to him."

"I think you should let him go," said Rodolfo. "He doesn't look worth it to me."

"Who asked your opinion?" said Philip, getting up in his face.

Rodolfo bristled. "My opinion is just as good as anyone else's."

"Not when it's a stupid opinion."

Skyler stood. "Guys! Just give it a rest, okay. I think I'm going to go."

Jamie patted the vacated seat. "Skyler, you just got here."

"I know, but I don't feel much like partying right now. I'll see you guys later."

They called out to him but he didn't stop, didn't slow, and made it to the parking lot alone.

All through the drive home he kept thinking of Keith and his own rather risky lifestyle, and he could see how Keith would be concerned. The man said he was monogamous. That was something Skyler had never been before. Hell, he'd never had a boyfriend before. Not that Keith was his boyfriend. Not at this rate, anyway. Did he even want a boyfriend? Things had been going just fine until he met Keith Fletcher. Was it worth changing his life for this guy? Although, maybe it was time to stop fooling around so much. He'd been lucky. No bare-backing, no broken condoms. Yeah, he swallowed. He loved the taste, the whole sensation of hot cum shooting in his mouth, but it never seemed like a big deal.

But looking at it from Keith's point of view, he must seem like the most casual of man-whores. But he wasn't all that casual. He had plenty of feelings. He always liked the guys he fucked or at least they all seemed nice to him. It just never occurred to him to go further. With the S.F.C., they all became friends once he had given up all interest in sleeping with them. But maybe it was like Philip said. He was afraid to commit. Was he still afraid? He was giving Keith a chance but Keith wasn't giving him the same opportunity. It was beginning to piss him off again.

He turned the corner to his street and pulled up front. Shutting the engine off, he climbed out of the car and hit the key lock. He grew angrier as he stalked up the walkway and trotted up his stairs. It just seemed that *he* had to go through all these changes and Keith didn't. What about give and take?

Inside, he switched on his Tiffany lamp and dropped onto the sofa, staring at the dark TV. In the blank screen he could see himself, alone. He had been really looking forward to tonight. Getting together with his friends and Keith, too, just to see how they all meshed. A little drinking, a little dancing. And Keith was apparently a good dancer, one of Skyler's favorite pastimes. He was also good at Skyler's other favorite pastime and he had wanted to do that, too.

Skyler thought Jamie had more tact than that but oh well.

Rather than continue to stare at himself reflected on his TV screen, Skyler got up and went to his desk situated in the bay window. He couldn't see much out the window except for a street light or two glowing in the darkness. He needed to take his mind off of Keith but when he did that it inevitably slid toward thoughts of Jeff and Evan. Okay, fine. If no Keith then he would work out Jeff and Evan's problem. He was good at that, at least. He proved that the last time he had solved a murder case.

He took out a piece of paper and grabbed a pen. On the top of the paper he wrote "Possible Suspects in the Slaying of Evan Fargo."

And then his pen wavered over the paper. He didn't really know anything yet. Except. Reluctantly, he put down Jeff's name. "In the sake of all honesty, it has to be done," he muttered.

Next he wrote "James Fischer." After he finished the "r" he looked at it. He had absolutely no reason to suspect him except by virtue of his weird encounter and because Jeff so vehemently hated the guy.

He tapped his pen on the paper. "Who else? Who else?"

There was always the possibility of a burglary gone wrong, but given the circumstances of Evan having cleaned his gun in a lighted room, why would someone break in?

He shrugged and wrote "Random Burglar."

Well, this obviously needed more investigating but there was little he could do now. *Might as well grade papers.* But when he reached down to get his satchel it wasn't there. "Oh crap! I left it at school."

He couldn't leave it till tomorrow. His first period kids needed their test scores before they could go on to the next project. He'd just have to go down to the school and go get it.

He grabbed his car keys and switched off the lamp, then he was flying down the stairs to his car.

Since the parking lot gate was locked up tight he pulled his Bug in front of the school. Climbing up the front steps he fitted his key in the lock and opened the glass doors. Once inside he quickly locked it again.

The hallway was dark except for a few recessed lights shining soft pools of illumination on the polished linoleum floor. Heading for his classroom, Skyler turned the corner and noticed a light in the office. "That's strange." He looked at his watch. It said ten-thirty-five. Did the janitor work this late?

He peered into the open office area and saw the light coming from Mr. Sherman's office. His door was solid wood but his office walls were glass. One light was on at the desk along with the light from the computer monitor. But it wasn't Mr. Sherman at his desk. It was Keith! He was earnestly typing something into Mr. Sherman's computer, and then he sat back, fingers on his chin, eyes tracking the screen.

Skyler ducked back into the corridor, heart pumping a million miles an hour. What the hell was Keith doing hacking into Mr. Sherman's computer? The old suspicions reared their hydra heads again. Skyler had thought that Keith's mysterious behavior had to do with his hiding the fact that he was gay from his homophobic football coach. But there was clearly something else afoot.

Carefully, keeping low, Skyler peered around the corner again. Keith was still there, going through more documents. He wrote down some notes in a small notebook and then he started closing it all down.

Skyler snapped back again and rested against the wall. Should he confront him? Alone, in an abandoned school? No, that didn't seem like a good idea. Wait a minute, what was he thinking? It was probably something entirely innocent. Of course it was! He was just being excitable. And what would poor Keith think if Skyler came barreling forward flinging accusations?

Except. Why was he on Mr. Sherman's computer? The principal probably kept his office locked. That meant that Keith had broken into that as well.

How could this be happening? What was going on?

He heard Keith switching off the lights and closing the office door. Skyler took off, padding quietly in the other direction. He scrambled onto the staircase, hiding behind the walled railing.

He heard Keith's steps as he walked along the corridor, thankfully going in the other direction. He listened for the sound of the front door being unlocked, opened, then closed and locked again before he came out of hiding. This was not good at all.

Slowly he went up the stairs, walking to his classroom as if in a dream. Try as he might, he couldn't imagine what Keith would have been doing in Mr. Sherman's office on his computer that would be on the up and up.

He was surprised to have reached his classroom so quickly.

Unlocking the door he found his satchel in his desk where he left it and hastily snatched it up. He locked the door behind him again and hurried down the corridor. When he got back to the top of the stairs he stopped. His car was parked right in front of the school. Keith couldn't have failed to see it. He looked down the stairs and noticed a light suddenly go out.

While he had been in his classroom, far from the front door, someone could have easily come in the front entrance without his hearing it. Or come *back* in.

Terror froze him to the spot. *Don't let it be Keith.* He didn't want to be afraid of him, couldn't really imagine it now, but he *was* afraid of the soft sounds he could hear downstairs. *Now* what should he do?

He looked behind him. There was another stairwell at the other end of the corridor. But which would be better? This one was closest to the front door, but the other way might be smarter. But he was right here. He might as well go down.

Slowly, one tread at a time, Skyler edged his way down the steps. He couldn't help but think of poor Julia, the calculus teacher, who had been pushed down the stairs. That crime had not yet been solved and Skyler knew the culprit was still at the school. He didn't want to mingle these thoughts with Keith. *It couldn't be him.* Or was it that he just didn't want to believe it?

When he got to a point where he could see something below, he crouched down behind the railing and peeked over the side. He saw a man's shadow and he was holding a long stick of some kind. Shit!

Just as he turned to go back up, there was a shout.

"Hey! Who's up there?"

Skyler froze and turned.

A man in gray coveralls with a mop in his hand stood at the foot of the stairs. Relief flooded him. He loosened his feet and came down the stairs, one hand over his heart. "Oh Mr. Bishara. I didn't expect you."

"Mr. Foxe? What are you doing here so late?"

He lifted his satchel in answer. "Forgot it. I had papers to correct."

"You shouldn't be here so late," he said in a heavy Middle Eastern accent. He looked out at the damp floor he just mopped, no doubt thinking that Skyler would have to tramp across it.

"I'm sorry, Mr. Bishara. I'll try to tread carefully."

The janitor headed for the front door with Skyler, took the wad of keys from his belt, and unlocked the door. "Goodnight."

"Goodnight, Mr. Bishara." The door locked behind him and Skyler all but sprinted to his car.

He drove too fast toward home and he almost hit a lamp post when he turned the corner a little too tightly and saw Keith's truck parked in front of his house. Skyler slowed to a stop fifty feet away and just stared ahead at the quiet street lit by vintage lamp posts.

This was ridiculous. He was not going to be afraid to go to his own apartment. He revved up the car, pulled in behind the monster truck, and got out.

Keith was sitting on the bottom step of the stairwell and when Skyler approached he rose.

"Hey, Skyler."

"Keith."

They stood awkwardly for a moment before Keith punched his hands into his jacket pockets. "Look, that was rude of me leaving like that."

"And entirely unfair," added Skyler. He clutched the handle of his satchel.

"I know. I keep getting off on the wrong foot with you. You really drive me crazy."

"*I* drive *you* crazy?"

"I never met anyone like you, Skyler. You're so carefree. I'm just not used to it."

"So you just give up at the first shot across the bow?"

"It keeps throwing me, that's all. But I've been driving around, thinking."

"Just driving around?" Skyler watched his face, searching for any kind of deception. Keith showed none. That was a little disturbing.

"Yeah, just driving around and thinking about you. And you're right. Your past is your past. It's not fair judging you by that."

"That's *right*. I'd appreciate a little give and take here. You're doing that jealous thing again and it's not endearing."

"I know. I'm sorry. But like I said. You drive me crazy."

Skyler pushed back his long bangs. "That's not *my* problem, it's yours."

"No. I mean…" Keith moved closer, almost toe to toe. A cloud of the man's cologne as well as his own underlying musky scent enveloped him. Keith was breathing hard. Skyler's eyes were level with that wide chest falling and rising. "I mean, you drive me crazy. In a good way."

"Oh." His skin tingled when Keith gently raised a hand and stroked his cheek with the tips of his fingers.

"I find it hard to stay away," he whispered.

I'm just finding it hard, Skyler thought to himself, jeans tightening uncomfortably.

"Skyler." Keith's warm body was suddenly pressed against him. His breath puffed at his ear. "Can I come up?"

Skyler pictured Keith in Mr. Sherman's office. He wanted to ask but also didn't want to know. Instead, he looked up into soft blue eyes, dark lashes, heavy black brows. It was a good face, a handsome face, wholly without guile. At least it seemed so. He stepped away from him and headed toward the stairs. When Keith made no move, he said over his shoulder, "Come on."

The heavy steps behind him turned him on like nothing else. He couldn't say why. Maybe it was because Skyler seemed to have some sway over this big man. Maybe it was because he'd never been so attracted to someone.

He conveniently stored away his misgivings and opened his door, and when it closed and he locked it again, arms encircled him and he dropped his satchel where he stood.

They kissed, and while their mouths slid together, Skyler eased his hands underneath Keith's shirt. The man gave a moan when fingers drew over his taut nipples. Skyler pushed back the jacket and lifted the shirt off, replacing his fingers with his lips. He dragged his nose across Keith's torso, inhaling the man's scent. Cologne, sunshine, grass, and maleness. It was irresistible.

He licked his skin, hands going for Keith's jeans. His nimble fingers undid the belt buckle, sliding the leather through the metal and letting it hang there. Then he flipped open the button and pulled down the zipper. He used both hands to open and peel it away, letting it slide down those muscular thighs. They fell with a clank to his feet.

Skyler's fingers dipped into the waistband of his briefs and pulled, looking down in time to watch that erection spring upward. Keith's cut cock was an awesome example of male flesh. Upright, the tip wet, with dark pubic hair framing it on either side, it was breathtaking. That plump sac below, rosy and round, begged to be touched.

Keith reached for him and nearly tore Skyler's shirt away, yanking down his trousers and briefs once the shirt fluttered to the floor. Skyler gasped when Keith grabbed his stiff cock. Only the reddened crown peeked out from those clutching fingers and a bead of precum glistened there. "Skyler," he breathed, his hand slowly stroking up and down the stiff shaft, "you have an amazing body."

Skyler groaned. "So do you. I want to suck you." Keith released him and he dropped to his knees. He nuzzled the dark pubic hair, inhaling the muskiness, and pressed the flat of his tongue at the root of the shaft in front of his face, drawing his tongue upward in a languorous sweep. Keith moaned and ran his fingers through Skyler's hair.

Skyler moaned at the taste of him, tongue licking its way up his straining cock. His lips nibbled gently at the ridge of the reddened head before he took the whole thing in his mouth and sucked it hard while one hand squeezed the shaft. Keith gasped above him, muttering "Fuck, fuck," all the while Skyler sucked and lashed that cock with his tongue, moving his head up and down. He drew back and sucked at the tip, lapping the dripping moisture bubbling up and moaning at the taste. He grasped his own dick with his other hand and slid his fingers up and down his hard flesh.

Suddenly, Keith grasped his face and pulled him off. "No. I don't want to come this way. I want to fuck you. Come inside you." He was still holding Skyler's face, looking for confirmation.

Skyler panted, nodding.

He got to his feet and pulled Keith to the bedroom. He let go of his hand and clambered up the bed to lie on his back, propped against his pillows. Opening his legs he ran his hands over his nipples enticingly. "Want this, Keith?" He opened his legs wider and bent his knees upward, exposing himself.

Keith grabbed a condom from the basket, tore the packet open with trembling fingers, and quickly sheathed his dick. He got on the bed on his knees, holding his cock in his fist. He was breathing through his mouth and staring at Skyler's hole. "Yes," he rasped. He grabbed Skyler's legs and shoved his knees up to his ears. A pump of lube from the container by the bed and the gooey stuff was swathed over his entrance. Keith kissed him once before he guided his cock to Skyler's rim, running the tip in circles over the puckered skin, and suddenly shoved it in.

No foreplay for Mr. Fletcher! And then he forgot to think. Because Keith's thick cock was gliding inward with a hot burn, filling every inch of him. He breathed, easing the path. It felt incredibly full and unspeakably sensual. Keith twisted his hips while he literally screwed forward, touching all the nooks inside Skyler, including the one that mattered the most. And then he was thrusting in and out, and Skyler, his limbs pinned helplessly up by his head, was unable to wrap them around him. He rocked his hips, stabbing them forward to take in as much of Keith as he could.

"You're so goddammed tight," Keith grunted above him. His face was screwed up as he rammed into him with all his might. "God!" He repositioned and shoved upward, catching Skyler's prostate with each hard thrust. And just as he did so, he grabbed Skyler's rock hard dick and pumped it.

Skyler wasn't going to last. He was going to unload all over Keith and he so wanted to. He felt the pressure building in his balls, felt that anguished, weightless moment and then Keith pounded into him and jerked him and Skyler had time for one gasp before the world went white and he shot long ropes of cum over Keith's chest and thighs.

Keith stiffened and grunted out his orgasm, and then the two of them were rocking with hips thrusting in the last throes.

Skyler slowly floated back down. Keith relaxed enough for Skyler to wrap his legs around the man's waist at last. He pulled him forward and Keith braced himself just above him, rubbing Skyler's cum onto their chests with his body. They embraced and kissed languidly. The air was filled with the acrid smell of spunk and Skyler inhaled, loving it. *God, I am such a man-whore.*

He raised his chin as fingers gently caressed his face. He reached up and ran his hands over Keith's stubbled cheeks and jaw. He kissed and gnawed on that chin until Keith sighed, his hands stroking down Skyler's flanks.

There was no time to remember secret trips to Mr. Sherman's office, no room for thoughts on strange goings on. There was only a hard, warm body pressed to his, sweat cooling on his skin, and moist lips mouthing his ear. He fell asleep that way, without wondering about tomorrow.

∫ ∫ ∫

But tomorrow intruded with the discordant buzzing of his alarm clock and an unusual weight of a masculine presence draped over him.

Last night—all of last night—came into sharp focus and Skyler shot up in bed, knocking Keith off of him.

"And good morning to you," grumbled Keith. He lifted a pillow-dented face and squinted at Skyler. Bright morning light streamed in from the window. Skyler hadn't had time last night to shut the blinds.

"Uh…good morning. We'd better get going if we aren't going to be late."

"Mind if I shower first? I have to swing by my place and pick up my gym bag."

"Okay, go ahead. I'll make coffee. Black, two sugars, right?"

Keith grinned and grabbed Skyler before he could get away. He planted his mouth on Skyler's, making a smacking sound when he released him. "You're sweet. I wish we had time this morning." He waggled his brows and squeezed Skyler's bare butt before moving off toward the shower, stumbling once over Skyler's jeans.

Slipping into his sweats, Skyler stood in the kitchen and watched his coffee maker brewing. Now was the time to bring up the fact that he saw Keith in the principal's office last night. As soon as he came out of the shower.

He kept glancing toward his bedroom door, expecting Keith to pop out of there at any moment. When he finally did, Skyler was still startled even though he expected it.

"Shower's free," Keith said merrily. He took the cup Skyler offered and inhaled. "You make the best coffee. I'll have to stop by your friend Phil's place and pick some up."

"If you want to stay friends with him you will never *ever* call him Phil."

"Oh? Then Philip it is." He drank a moment, eyeing Skyler over his mug. He leaned against the kitchen counter and looked up sheepishly. "Thanks for giving me another chance. I want this to go somewhere, you know? I know it's different for you, this one man kind of thing. But I promise to make it worth your while."

Skyler stared into his own coffee mug, inhaling the dark aromas and watching the kitchen lights' reflections dance on the murky surface. "That does sound promising."

Keith didn't say anything more and when Skyler looked up, the man wore an amused grin. "I like your just-rolled-out-of-bed look. You're pretty scrumptious. Especially the hair."

Skyler's hand flew to his hair to smooth it down.

"Skyler, shouldn't you be hopping into the shower? You'll be late."

Ask him, ask him. "O-okay."

"I gotta go. Thanks for the coffee. I'll see you at school."

"Keith, I have to ask…mpf." Scooped up again and smacked with a coffee and toothpaste-flavored kiss. Keith sucked on Skyler's lips and Skyler opened his mouth and gnawed back, tongues teasing each other. Keith released him and, dazed, Skyler fell back, holding on to the counter.

"Mmm mmm, Mr. Foxe." He winked and turned toward the door.

Ask him, ask him, ask him…too late.

Coward.

CHAPTER TEN

Skyler pulled into the parking lot and only then remembered that he hadn't graded his first period tests. Boy, Keith was distracting! He slammed the car door and glanced across the parking lot, looking for Keith's truck, and spotted a van parked across the street. It was a white van with a logo of a large flower and the words "Redlands Orchid Farm" scrawled across the side. Why did that name sound familiar?

He shook it off and headed in, hurrying up the stairs. He'd have to skip the teacher's lounge so he could at least get started on grading those tests.

He'd gotten a third of them done when the bell rang for class and students started trickling in.

The first part of the day went as expected. There was another email from Mr. Sherman about the Sophomore Winter Formal, reminding Skyler that he was to be a chaperone.

When the lunch bell rang Skyler headed for the cafeteria. The air was cooler today and though the outside tables beckoned it was too windy to eat and read. So he entered the cafeteria and the cacophony of disparate voices overwhelmed him for a moment as it always did, and then the aromas of chili, salty soups, and floor cleaner blended to an unappetizing bombardment. He looked over the special and opted for a tuna sandwich. He added an orange and a milk to his tray, paid, and then headed to the teacher's lunch room.

When he walked in, he immediately spotted Keith. He was sitting with Ed Fallows, Mac Simpson, and one of the other coaches Skyler didn't know, devouring a sloppy joe. His tray was piled with carbs and Skyler could only blink at the sheer volume of it. Keith's eyes flicked up and caught Skyler's gaze. He made no acknowledgement except for a chin raise. Skyler returned it with an awkward smile.

When was he going to ask Keith about the computer thing?

Not now, apparently, he told himself. When he looked up he was hailed over to a table by Kate Traeger, the girls' volleyball coach. Threading his way over he set down his tray. "Good afternoon, ladies." Besides Kate, Pauline Hingle, one of the office assistants, looked up, and beside her was the calculus substitute, Tricia Hornbeck. She had come in on temporary assignment, replacing the hospital-bound Julia Meyers.

Tall and red-haired, Tricia seemed a little shy to Skyler. She wore reading glasses that she tended to hide behind. They were currently hanging from a colorful beaded chain around her neck. She scooted closer to the table and nodded toward Skyler. "Mr. Foxe."

"Please, Ms. Hornbeck. Call me Skyler."

"Then you'll have to call me Tricia." She smiled. "Skyler. That's such a cheerful name."

"It's very retro," said Kate. Her ponytail bobbed as she giggled.

He unwrapped his sandwich, laying the cellophane open. "What can I say? My mother was a rebel. I've always liked it. I guess it *is* a cheerful sort of name. I'm generally a cheerful sort of guy."

"That's what they say," said Pauline distractedly, riffling through some papers in a manila folder.

Kate slurped a scoop of yogurt from a plastic spoon and ticked her head. "Can't you put that down for a second, Pauline?"

"I can't. These records are a mess. Something is seriously wrong with them. Do you want to know what I think?" She looked around conspiratorially and then leaned in close to the table. Everyone followed her example. "It's odd. These records are sort of haphazard. But only some of them. If I didn't know better, I would say that someone's been messing around, switching the grades," she said quietly.

"What?" shrieked Tricia.

"Shhh!" She made quieting motions and glanced quickly to

the table where Keith was knocking back a Coke like it was a beer and laughing at something Ed Fallows said. "There's been a rumor that Wes Sherman Jr. was hacking into the school computer and changing grades."

"You're kidding me," said Skyler. "Why would he do that?"

"Hired by someone. Who, I wonder?" And she glanced back at the group of assistant football coaches.

"No," said Kate. "I refuse to believe that. Grade switching so the students can keep playing? I can't see it. They're a good team."

"But do they get good grades?"

Skyler stared at the triangle of sandwich in his hands. "Have you told Mr. Sherman about this?"

"Lord, no! That man has had enough grief in his life. Why would I add to that by telling him that his dead son might have been up to something illegal and at his own school, no less?"

Skyler felt a heavy feeling in his gut and put the sandwich down uneaten. Maybe it wasn't Wes Sherman Jr. Maybe it was Keith Fletcher.

♪ ♪ ♪

Even though he had the intention of confronting Keith, Skyler chickened out at every opportunity. He even started avoiding Keith, even making sure the man was busy on the field with the players before he snuck into the parking lot to get into his car. But instead of heading for home, he diverted and drove over to The Bean.

He thought Philip's barista Cashmere Funk would come behind the counter. The tall Jamaican was a local character and philosopher, and he also had a long time crush on Philip, but he wasn't there. Instead, the man himself was busy mixing his brews. And Jamie, too. He stood at the counter sipping a frozen coffee through a mound of whipped cream.

"Hi, guys."

"Skyler!" Jamie put down his drink and hugged him, even

lifted him off the floor.

"Hey, put me down!"

"Skyler, I am so *so* sorry about last night. You know how I get when I get excited. My mouth runs away from me."

"If only it would," said Philip, wiping his hands down his green apron. "To what do we owe the pleasure, Mr. Foxe?"

He shrugged. "I just thought I'd drop by here for a change. I've missed several mornings. I didn't expect to run into you guys, though. I guess I lucked out." He smiled.

"Then what will it be?"

He looked up at the menu that he'd practically memorized. "What the hell. I need a treat. Give me a frozen caramel mochaccino."

"Coming up."

Jamie grabbed his arm and steered him to the cushy chairs. "I'm really sorry, Skyler."

"It's okay, Jamie. It turns out...well, Keith was waiting for me when I got home."

"He was? Ooo. Tell me more."

Philip came from around the counter and joined them at the chairs. He handed Skyler the frosty plastic cup. "I knew you wanted to keep your girlish figure so I left off the whipped cream."

They both looked at Jamie, who was nearly fellating the cream off his straw. "What?"

"Never mind," said Philip. "You were saying about Keith? Was he pissed off?"

"No, as a matter of fact, he was pretty contrite. He...uh. He spent the night."

"Omigod!" said Jamie. He had a whipped cream mustache. "You two. Going at it like bunnies. Mmm mmm."

"Yeah, well. We're really good at that. Maybe not so good with other things."

Philip straightened the napkin coaster on the table between them. "What do you mean?"

"Dude." He shook his head. He had to tell someone. "I got home last night and realized I'd forgotten my satchel so I went back to school to get it. And I saw Keith there. He was typing something on my principal's computer."

"So?"

"So? He's not supposed to be doing that! It was a locked office. A password protected computer. You get it?"

"Oh. Did you ask him what he was doing there?"

"No. I chickened out. He's already called me twice and I let it go to voice mail."

Jamie was alert now. He was the computer expert, after all. Web designer extraordinaire. "It's probably something innocent. I mean, what could he be doing?"

Skyler leaned in close and the others followed. "I heard today that someone's been hacking into the school computer and changing grades."

"I used to do that all the time when I was at high school," said Jamie. "Well, not the school computer. Don't actually know if they had one. But I got good at changing the grade on the report cards I brought home."

"No, this is serious. If the football team is fixing grades so the players can play, then that's all kinds of illegal. It's all about grade point averages and scholarships. We're talking fraud. It's a *very* big deal. Plus, get this. There's also a rumor that Wes Sherman Jr. had something to do with it."

"The dead kid you found?"

"Yeah."

"But that didn't have anything to do with his murder."

"No, but I just remembered something. A while back I was in the boy's gym and I overheard the coach talking to someone on the phone. He talked about the job that *Sherman* did for them but that problem was *solved*. Like dead? And then he said that they just had to *skirt Meyers* and everything would be okay. Don't you get it? Meyers! That's Julia Meyers. She's the teacher that got pushed down the stairs. She's still in a coma. And she was worried about something going on at the school, something to do with the jocks."

Philip and Jamie looked at each other. "I'm sure Sidney is investigating it," said Philip.

"But she doesn't know about this. And there were holes in Keith's records. She checked. Wes is gone now but that doesn't mean that Keith hasn't replaced him. And I know that the coach had something to do with Julia's accident."

"You don't know that Keith is responsible. And what holes? What do you mean?"

"I had her check on Keith a while ago. She said it was not exactly missing information but just holes. Like what's *not* said is important."

Philip shook his head. "God, the two of you. Conspiracy theories. Maybe he was on the grassy knoll or faked the moon landings, too. Jeez. This sounds like nothing more than suspicions and a little unusual behavior."

"Unusual behavior? He was hacking into the school computer!"

"You don't know that. You haven't asked him."

"Oh, and how will that conversation go? 'Hi Keith, I wondered if you wanted to come over. And by the way, are you hacking into the school computer and illegally changing grades?' That will be a fun evening."

"Or you can just harbor your suspicions and continue to act crazy around him. And you can break it off."

"Break it off?"

"Yes, it's what people do when they dodge each other's phone calls and refuse to date each other anymore."

"Well…I…I don't want to do…that." He sipped the drink through his straw without really tasting.

Philip hunched forward while Jamie sat back in the cushions, giving Skyler a concerned look. "Skyler, do you have…feelings for this guy?"

He looked down into his drink. "I don't know."

"Yes, you do. You do know."

There was Mother Hen Philip again. But Skyler couldn't deny it. He stirred his drink slowly. "Okay," he said quietly. "I guess I do have a sort of…*crush* on him." He sighed. "So what am I going to do? I never felt like this before. I don't want him to be guilty of anything."

"You *have* to talk to him. It's the only way."

"You're right." He looked up at Jamie who had been unusually quiet. "Is that what you think I should do?"

"You know Philip's right. He's the smart one."

"Hey, what about me?"

"You're the passionate one."

"I am? Then what does that make you?"

Jamie struck a pose. "I'm the *fabulous* one!"

♫ ♫ ♫

Skyler had to admit that it was for the best. He had to talk to Keith and the sooner that was done the better. Tomorrow. At school. With people nearby but not too close.

As he made his way home from The Bean, his mind drifted back to Jeff and that terrible night. He so wanted to help, to make a difference, and he decided to drive by and see if Jeff needed anything.

He turned the corner and glanced at the house. But all was dark. He slowed and decided to park. Getting out, he stood on the sidewalk and measured the house. A square box with boxy hedges. It was funny. The house seemed to fit their personalities. Both Jeff and Evan were square, conservative types. They probably even voted Republican, for all he knew. While Skyler lived in a house with curves, frilly design elements, and old world charm. He wondered what that said about him.

He stood on the walkway just staring at the darkened house and remembered that night he was here picking up Jeff. There were all kinds of cops wandering around, doing various things. But he also remembered something about the bushes. Something had been taped off. He wondered what it was they found.

Curious, he left the concrete path and walked across the grass, heading for the garden border. He took out his phone and switched it on, using it as a light. The bushes were manicured and the ground beneath it raked free of leaves and weeds. He didn't see anything, but that didn't mean they hadn't found something that night. He wished he knew what that had been, but Sidney would never tell him. Could it be something someone dropped? A spent shell? Or something as simple as a footprint?

He stepped over the short bushes and crept around to the back as far as he could go before encountering a fence. He looked up the stuccoed wall to a metal-framed window that was shut up tight.

A window opened behind him and a flashlight beam hit him square in the face when he turned around. Oh crap!

"What are you doing there!" cried a man in the window.

Skyler raised his empty hands. Well, one hand had his phone in it. "Hi! Hi there! I'm a friend of Jeff and Evan's."

"You just wait right there. I'm this close to calling the cops."

Skyler heard a scramble and the man left the window. He was coming around. Should Skyler bolt?

Instead, he waited like an idiot for the ax to fall.

But wait. He wasn't guilty of anything. It was perfectly innocent what he was doing. Sort of.

The neighbor came barreling out of his house baring a flashlight, which he continued to shine in Skyler's face. "Who are you?"

"My name is Skyler Foxe. I'm a friend of Jeff's."

"What are you doing skulking around his house in the middle of the night?"

"It's hardly the middle of the night—"

"Just answer the question." He was a middle-aged man with a pot belly and receding hair. He was wearing sweat pants that were more a fashion statement than used for exercise, and a zip-up jacket.

"Well, I'm friends with the police detective in charge of the case and I was just doing a little looking around."

"Oh yeah? What's the detective's name?"

"Sidney Feldman. She's mid twenties, pretty, long hair in ringlets…"

He lowered the flashlight. "Yeah, that was her. She gave me her card and told me to call if I thought of anything. What did you say your name was?"

"Skyler Foxe."

"Oh. I think I remember Jeff telling me about you. I'm sorry about the flashlight thing, but you can't be too careful. Especially about what happened. We're all kind of freaked out in the neighborhood."

"I can imagine."

"So. You're helping out the detective. Are you a policeman?"

"No. A high school English teacher."

The man frowned. Maybe he was having second thoughts about calling the cops. Skyler thought he'd better get out of there. But he wanted to ask something first.

"Did you ever see anything suspicious out here the night Evan was killed?"

"I thought they said it was a suicide?"

"Well, it might not be. Did you?"

"No. Not really. Jeff would come out here sometimes. At

night, kind of late. He'd just stand here in the garden—kind of like you are—and stare into the window. I know things were tough for those boys, what with Evan's legs and all."

"Where would he stand, exactly? Here?" Skyler stepped back into the garden border.

"Yeah. About there. Just staring inside."

That was kind of odd. It made him feel a bit sick inside. He didn't want to be suspicious of Jeff. No intention of it. But that was certainly unusual behavior.

"Did you by any chance mention that to the detective?"

"Yeah. Why not? She asked, I told."

"No reason. Anything else?"

He shrugged.

"Well, thanks. I guess I'll be going now."

Skyler headed quickly to his car and got in. He watched as the neighbor sauntered back up his own path and went inside.

Why would Jeff just stand outside and stare into his own house? Skyler couldn't ever remember doing anything of the sort himself. Not alone, and not in the dead of night. He didn't like the sound of that or the feeling it left in his gut.

He started the car and headed for home.

Chapter Eleven

He went to school the next day, thinking about Jeff but also about Keith. He was determined to have it out. He absolutely *had* to ask him what he was doing on Mr. Sherman's computer.

Walking the halls he passed an assortment of flyers and handmade posters for various school activities stapled to bulletins boards. There was a poster for the Sophomore Winter Formal. The theme: Life in a Snow Globe. He knew his fifth period student Amber Watson was one of the organizers. She was sophomore secretary and was bubbling with ideas. This sounded like something she'd come up with. The fall play was over but some posters were still up. And then he stopped dead.

Tucked between a goldenrod flyer for a food drive and cheerleader carwash fundraiser was a flyer saying: "Gay-Straight Alliance. Join our group and support diversity in our school. You don't have to be gay to be a member. You just have to be cool." And then a big happy face.

Skyler's heart gave a lurch. The meeting room was Ben Fontana's art class. That should have been him. He should have had the courage to sponsor it. Instead, it was the art teacher, the guy Skyler always took for slightly homophobic. Obviously he had woefully misjudged him. The meeting was for after school today. If Skyler had any guts at all, he'd turn up for it. But he knew in his heart of hearts he wouldn't.

Turning away from the bulletin board, he trudged to class, his satchel hanging heavy at his side.

All day he thought about it and especially when his fifth period class rolled around and Rick Flores loped into the room with his bright white smile and slouched into his chair.

Amber sat in her place in the front row directly in front of Skyler's desk. She handed him a flyer, the same one he'd seen earlier about the dance. "It's the Sophomore Winter Formal, Mr. Foxe. It's in two weeks. I'm in charge of the decorating committee."

"Yeah, I saw." He looked at the sheet. "'Snow globe,' eh? Sounds great."

"It's going to be magical, just like being in a snow globe. I hope you can come."

"Actually, I'll be chaperoning. So prepare to see me in a tux."

Her eyes lit and Skyler realized that had been the wrong thing to say. But her friend Heather reined her in.

"Down, girl," she said with her black-lipsticked mouth. "I'm sure Mr. Foxe will be busy that night, what with making sure the punch isn't spiked and other teen hijinks like that."

"Uh…yeah. Lots of standing around looking like a waiter, mostly. And a few 'none of that, boys' here and there."

Amber was still smiling when he tucked the flyer under his blotter. He picked up his paperback of *Fahrenheit 451* and lifted it up to the class. "Everyone get their books?"

"Yes, Mr. Foxe," came the chorus back.

"Did everyone memorize a page like I told you to?"

"Yes, Mr. Foxe," came the unenthusiastic response.

"Really?" He thumbed through the book, frowning. "Sounds like a lot of work."

"Then why did we have to do it?" asked a grumpy Alex from the back of the room.

"That's a good question, Alex. Class, why did I have you do that?"

Rick lazily raised his hand and Skyler nodded to him. "Because the book is about burning books and people walking around in the woods memorizing them."

"Not just burning books, Rick. But destroying thought, critical thinking in the *form* of books. Those people were *becoming* the books, memorizing them so that not only the literature but the thoughts generated because of them wouldn't disappear from the world. I only made you memorize one page. Imagine if you had to memorize a whole book and keep it in your head forever. Why would anyone want to make that sort of sacrifice? Drew?"

"Because really good books—and ideas—shouldn't be lost?"

"Yes!" He pumped the air and paced back and forth in front of the class, tucking the book under his arm and continuing his conversation. Once he was in the groove and the kids were listening and reacting, he could forget everything else. No thoughts of Keith or of poor Jeff hidden away with his lawyer, could intrude. It was just him, the students, and literature: his idea of Heaven.

A few brave souls volunteered to recite their pages and the class duly applauded after each stumbling presentation. Whether they recited or not, Skyler gave them all points toward their grade and they all cheered.

It was a good note on which to end the class and when the students all shuffled out the door, he wasn't surprised to see Alex and Rick hanging back.

Rick took Alex's hand and hid it by his thigh so that no one walking by the glass wall of the classroom would see. Skyler noticed that he seemed to do it naturally, smoothly, almost without thinking. Yes, they were getting the hang of it.

"Hey Mr. Foxe," he said. His sunglasses sat at their usual place on the back of his head. His perpetual smile was dimmed somewhat. "We're having our first GSA meeting tonight."

Skyler scuffed the floor with his shoe. He felt his face warm. "Yes, I saw the flyer. Mr. Fontana's a good guy."

"Yeah. He was nice about it. And he's a big guy so no one will give us shit…uh, I mean hassle us while he's around."

"Well, that is an important consideration."

"I wish that you would be there, though. I would never have come out if it wasn't for you."

"I appreciate that Rick. Boy, do I." If there had only been a teacher in high school for Skyler. "But…"

"Dude, he already said he can't," said Alex. "I know what it's like, Mr. Foxe. I can't go to that meeting either. Football."

Rick smiled fondly at his boyfriend before he turned back to Skyler. "So Mr. Foxe, who do you think will be there? All the school losers?"

"I don't know, Rick. The people there may surprise you."

"Or maybe no one will show and I'll be the only one."

"Maybe not. In any case, you will have had the guts to do it." *Whereas I...*

He raised a large hand and swiped down the back of his neck. "Yeah. I just hope the other jocks are too busy at football practice."

Alex nodded solemnly. "Don't worry. We will be. I'll make sure of that."

Rick took a quick glance toward the windows and not seeing anyone in the hall, he grabbed Alex around the neck and kissed him on the lips.

Alex blushed from his cheeks down to his neck. "Crazy Mexican," he said affectionately. He checked his watch. "I better go. Don't want to be late. I'll be running extra laps."

"Oh, Alex," said Skyler as the boys headed for the door, hands dropping away from each other. "Is Coach Fletcher going to be at practice with you guys?"

"Yeah. Why?"

"I just have something I have to ask him."

"He's pretty hot stuff, isn't he?" Alex smiled broadly.

Rick punched him in the arm. "No wonder you always want to go to practice. You better stop drooling over that guy. He's a freakin' teacher. And he's *old*. Although...he *is* pretty hot stuff. Have you seen him in his running shorts? Woof."

Skyler clamped his mouth closed.

"And, *mi pequeña*, you don't want to start sounding like Amber, eh Mr. Foxe?" Rick fluttered his eyelashes and held his cheeks. "*Oh, Mr. Foxe*," he said in falsetto, "*are you coming to the Winter*

Formal? I'd love it if you'd come."

Ears still pink, Skyler ushered them out the door. "Thank you, gentlemen."

Rick laughed, a rolling, joyful sound. Alex waved and took off, trotting ahead, his backpack bouncing on his shoulders. Rick gave a chin raise to Skyler and sauntered slowly after.

Skyler quickly assembled the homework papers he planned to grade at home and stuffed them into his satchel. He locked the door and hurried through the corridor.

Out onto the quad, he could finally feel the chill of November. The wind gusted a few dried leaves. Some of the trees were finally changing. Fall was always late in southern California. He pulled his jacket tighter around him and started trotting toward the field.

The sun was far from setting, but it was edging toward the horizon. How did these guys do it day after day, he wondered. Those poor kids were at practice at five-thirty in the morning and stayed after school for more punishment.

He spotted Keith right away. No shorts today, but those clingy sweats. He wore a heavier jacket over his broad shoulders and he was blowing a whistle. Oh yeah, he was hot stuff, all right.

Skyler stood on the sidelines. He wasn't sure what the etiquette was. Should he walk over the white chalk line and across the grass?

Keith turned to direct some boys onto the field. Skyler could tell the moment the man caught sight of him. He paused and stared for a heartbeat then started up again, checking his clipboard and talking to someone—a kid, an assistant coach? Skyler couldn't tell. Then he sauntered toward Skyler.

"Skyler? What's up?"

"I wanted to ask you something."

Keith smiled. "The answer is yes."

"What? Oh, no, nothing like that," he said, flushing. "I have a confession to make."

Keith looked up and sized up his surroundings. He touched Skyler's lower back and gently steered him toward the middle of the field where no one could hear them. "Okay."

"Well, last night, after you left Trixx—" Keith's shoulders stiffened but he said nothing. His eyes were fixed steadily on Skyler. "I went home pretty much right after. But then I realized I left my satchel at school so I ran over here to pick it up. And I saw you. In Mr. Sherman's office."

Keith never changed expression. His gaze remained steady.

"And…well, it looked like you were…uh…typing something on his computer."

Keith seemed to snap out of it and with jaw stiff he said, "Oh right. I was doing something for Mr. Sherman."

"In the middle of the night?"

"Well, when I left you I was a bundle of nerves. I figured I might as well do the job then."

"Sooo if we go to Mr. Sherman right now and ask him, he'll corroborate your story?"

"'Corroborate my story'? What is this, Skyler?"

"I just want to know if it's the truth."

The jaw clamped even tighter. A vein bulged at his temple. "If it's the truth? What do you mean?"

"I mean I saw you in the middle of the night doing something on someone else's computer and I would just like to know what that was."

"Maybe it's none of your fucking business."

He lifted his chin. "And maybe it is."

"You still don't trust me."

"I didn't say that—"

"You all but said it!" He seemed to realize he had yelled the last and looked around, but there was enough noise from running and grunting football players that nobody heard them.

More quietly he said, "Why can't you just trust me, Skyler? There are just some things that are really none of your business without being something sinister."

"I…I really want to…"

"I see. Okay. Nothing's going forward unless we talk to Mr. Sherman. So let's talk to him right now." He stomped across the grass and headed for the office.

Skyler ran after and caught up. "Look, Keith, there's just a lot of suspicious things going on here."

"And you still suspect me. Great." He stared straight ahead, never slowing his pace. Skyler moved double-time to catch up.

They climbed the stairs to the main building and when they reached the office Mr. Sherman was still in there, wrapping up his work for the day.

His door was ajar so Keith moved forward and pushed it open. "Mr. Sherman," he said. The principal looked up. "Mr. Foxe would like to know if I did or did not have your permission to do a little job for you on your computer in your office."

Sherman's brows were arched and he looked from one to the other. "Uh…why yes, Mr. Foxe. Mr. Fletcher does have my permission. Not that I understand why *you'd* want to know."

"Oh. Well, okay then." Skyler felt like an idiot. But more than that, he could see the hurt along with some other emotion swirling in Keith's eyes.

Sherman continued to glance from one to the other. "If that's all, gentlemen, I was just getting ready to leave. Oh, by the way, Mr. Fletcher, I'd like you to chaperone the Winter Formal as well. It will require formal dress. I hope that's not a problem."

"What do you mean 'as well'?"

"Mr. Foxe is also going to chaperone. Low men on the totem pole get this kind of duty, I'm afraid. But it will be fun. You'll see."

Effectively dismissed, they both left. Keith's pace was a little slower but no less directed. He was heading back to the field, saying nothing.

"Look, Keith, I just—"

Suddenly Keith stopped and spun on Skyler. "You just had to put your nose in it and accuse me of...of...what I don't know. Because you don't trust me. Because you think I'm up to something illegal or dangerous. Is that it?"

Skyler blinked. He didn't know what to say. "I'm really sorry. But you have to admit, it did look suspicious. And with all these rumors about...stuff..."

"You think *I* would do something crooked?"

"I didn't know what to think, okay! I'm glad we cleared that up. Now I guess...you don't want to see me anymore."

Keith chuffed a laugh. "I would think you wouldn't want to see *me* anymore."

Embarrassed, Skyler looked away. "But I do want to see you," he said quietly.

Keith paused. He was breathing hard. His fingers were restless on the clipboard hanging at his side, loosening and tightening. "And I want to see you. If you could just see your way to trusting me."

He jerked his head up. "I do! I really do."

Keith sighed and ran his hand through his hair. He looked over his shoulder toward the field. The wind had died down to a rippling breeze, still strong enough to stir up dried leaves that ran in circles around the school benches. The lights on the field were coming on and the sun hung at a lower angle near the purpling mountains. "Okay. How about dinner tonight?"

"I was meeting my friends for dinner."

"Oh."

"But why don't you come? No more surprises, I promise."

"Okay, Skyler. If you can trust me then I can trust you."

∫ ∫ ∫

The Taquito Grill's ceiling was painted with a twilight sky. Strings of paper lanterns lit the dining area with soft lighting. Sidney was absent. She said she was too busy with work, but Jamie, Philip, and Rodolfo were sitting in a booth when Skyler arrived. "Hi guys."

"Hi, Skyler," said Rodolfo flirtatiously. "I'm glad to see you're alone."

"Not for long. I've invited Keith to come."

"Oh." He wilted, scooped up a chip, and crunched it loudly.

Jamie poured some margarita from the pitcher into a glass and passed it to Skyler. "So all is forgiven? Did you ask him about the computer thing?"

"Yes, and it's all perfectly innocent, I guess."

Philip sipped his drink. "What do you mean, you guess?"

"Mr. Sherman confirmed his story. Kind of did it in front of the both of us." And Skyler explained what happened.

"Smooth," said Philip. "And the guy still wants to see you? Give him points for perseverance."

Skyler shrugged and took a gulp of his margarita. "So it's okay between us. Like I said, he'll be here any minute, so *please*, you guys, don't say anything embarrassing."

"We never say anything embarrassing, do we Jamie?"

Jamie shook his head at Philip. "Not me."

"Guys," he warned.

"Here's Hunk on a Stick now!" chirped Jamie.

That was just the sort of thing— Skyler turned around and there he was. All right, so he was Hunk on a Stick but he hoped Keith hadn't heard that.

When he got to the table he leaned down and kissed Skyler on the lips. No one had ever done that. Not in Redlands. Not at his favorite restaurant. Not out in the open like this. He quickly looked around but there was only a young waitress in the back who was looking at them and smirking. What if one of his students was here?

Keith seemed oblivious and scooted in next to him. "Hi, everyone. So what's good here? I'm starved."

Philip rested his chin on his hand. "So Keith. How are you finding life in Redlands?"

Keith lowered his menu and smiled, turning to Skyler. "I'd say that things are looking up."

Jamie "awwed" while Rodolfo rolled his eyes and loudly crunched another chip.

"Keith," said Jamie. "Skyler tells us you're from Seattle."

"Yes, I'm from there. I lived in a lot of places, though. Went to school in Boulder."

"That's in Colorado," Jamie stage-whispered to Rodolfo.

"I know where Boulder is," he snapped. "A boulder is also just a big rock."

Keith narrowed his eyes slightly at Rodolfo but said nothing.

The cute waiter showed up to the table, looking them over until his eyes fell on Skyler. He sighed. "I'm guessing you want the number three with no beans."

Keith nudged him with his elbow. "Skyler, if you order the enchiladas ala carte with rice on the side you save twenty-five cents."

He looked at Keith's sincere expression and said, "I'll do that then."

"I've only been saying that forever," said the waiter under his breath.

Everyone ordered and then filled up their glasses as the waiter left.

Philip turned to Skyler. "Any word on your friend Jeff?"

"No. In fact, I'll have to call him. I could just kill Sidney for arresting him. How could she think that?"

"Some people seem innocent when they're not," said Keith

casually, munching on a chip. Skyler glared at him. "I'm just saying."

Skyler brooded into his drink. He wished that Keith hadn't said that. He kept thinking about their quick meeting with Mr. Sherman and it all seemed so spurious, like what *wasn't* said was making Skyler uneasy. And then he remembered that Sidney said the same thing about the holes in Keith's records: What *wasn't* said was the suspicious part. What sort of "job" would he be doing on the principal's computer that he'd have to do it late at night? Because Skyler was just not buying the nerves-on-edge excuse. Why did the man have to be so mysterious? Wasn't there enough mystery surrounding them? Damn, he thought he was okay with this but the least little thing made him question it all over again.

His phone buzzed. He took it out and saw that it was Sidney. "Hi, Sid."

"So you're talking to me again?"

"You're such a beyotch! Yes!"

"Okay, then. Just clearing that up. I thought you'd like to know. Julia Meyers just woke up."

CHAPTER TWELVE

Skyler made his excuses. Keith even offered to go with him, but with a pang of something unnamed, Skyler didn't think that the first thing Julia would want to see was Keith Fletcher.

After stopping at the florist, he made it to the hospital in fifteen minutes. Sidney had told him which room and when he exited the elevator and walked toward the room number, he expected to see a police guard standing outside of it. But the hall was empty except for a frail old man in a hospital gown, holding the back closed with one hand and clutching a rolling IV stand with the other. The place smelled of antiseptic and floor cleaner. He hated the smell of hospitals.

Skyler looked through the window on the door and saw Sidney inside. Tentatively he knocked and Sidney glanced up. He pushed it open. "Can I come in?"

She motioned for him to come forward. She turned back to the bed, which was still hidden behind a curtain, and said, "A teacher from your school is here. Skyler Foxe."

"Skyler?" said a hoarse voice. When he came around the corner he was shocked by what he saw. Julia had been a hefty woman, but three weeks in a coma gave her a waxy, sunken look. Sidney had told him she woke up yesterday but since she had no family she hadn't had any visitors except for police. The poor thing had had a tube down her throat for nutrition and she told him that her voice was going to be sketchy, and *not* to ask her any questions. But of course, he was itching to do just that.

A tiny Asian nurse fussed at the beeping machines at her bedside and she turned a stern eye on him as he got closer.

Skyler clutched a bouquet of flowers. Her eyes followed him as he moved into the room. He forced a smile. "Hey, Julia."

"You're the new English teacher," she said in that harsh voice like a raspy whisper.

He flicked a glance at Sidney. She had a look that said she would tell him more in a bit.

"Yeah." He set the flowers on her nightstand. "I'm the one who was there when you had your...accident."

"I don't remember it," she said. And by her eyes, he could tell she barely remembered him. Until something in them came into sharp focus. "You have to be careful, Skyler. Something isn't right at the school. Jordan Stacey was paid to leave. I know she was."

"Jordan Stacey...the biology teacher? The one Keith Fletcher replaced?"

"Yes. Fletcher. I think he's trouble."

Skyler's gut flipped. "But he seems okay. He seems like a nice guy."

"Looks can deceive. It was Jordan who first told Mr. Sherman about the grades."

Skyler moved closer. "What about the grades, Julia?"

"Skyler," warned Sidney. "You don't want to tire her."

He ignored her. "What about the grades, Julia?"

"She knew that some of her students—those on the football team—were getting lower grades than what was showing up on the computer files. She filed an objection and she said the football coach warned her to stop."

Skyler glared at Sidney. *See?* he wanted to yell. "Julia, why didn't you tell me all this before? You just gave me a bunch of cryptic warnings."

"I didn't know you either. I guess I've grown a bit paranoid." She gave a wry laugh that sounded more like a cough.

Sidney moved in front of Skyler. "Ms. Meyers, do you know personally of any direct threats to you?"

"Yes." She licked her lips. "I went into the computer and checked the data for two years back and rechecked it to my own records. The grades had been changed. I bypassed Sherman and went directly to Carson and he laughed me out of the gym."

"Did he threaten you?"

"He…he…"

The machine began to beep louder and the nurse approached the bed. "I'm going to have to ask the two of you to leave. Ms. Meyers' blood pressure should not be elevated like this."

Sidney held up a hand to her. "Ms. Meyers, what can you tell me about your accident?"

She frowned. Her eyes showed her distress. "Nothing. I don't remember it."

"Ms. Meyers, I can't proceed without more information."

"But it had to be Carson!" cried Skyler. "Who else?"

"Okay, that's it," said the nurse. She grabbed Skyler's arm in a pretty strong grip and reached for Sidney, but she swept her coat back, showing the badge pinned to the waist of her skirt. "Uh uh," she warned.

She left under her own power and the nurse deposited Skyler outside the door. Another nurse came trotting down the hall and went into Julia's room. Skyler stared at the movement of the nurses through the window until one pulled the curtain and blocked the view.

Skyler chewed his lip. "I hope she'll be okay."

"The fact that she woke up is a good indication." Sidney paced across the shiny floors. "But that she can't remember the incident sucks big time."

"What are you going to do?"

"I have to wait and see. Maybe she'll remember more."

"What about Carson? You heard her. The man's a menace."

"Skyler, I already investigated him. He wasn't there at the time."

"Well, what about his flunkies?"

"Like Keith Fletcher? Julia Meyers doesn't seem to have a very good opinion of him."

"That's because she doesn't know him."

"Oh yeah? When were you going to tell me about the computer thing in Sherman's office?"

"How did you hear about that?"

"Jamie. He's my source for all information Skyler-related."

"I'll kill him."

"Well? So what did Keith say to convince you that he *wasn't* up to no good?"

"He said he was doing a job for Mr. Sherman. And then we went to Mr. Sherman and asked him. And he agreed."

"A job? What sort of job?"

"They didn't tell me. I assume because it's none of my business."

"Has it occurred to you that maybe Mr. Sherman might be in on it? Might be collecting some sort of kickback?"

"Mr. *Sherman*? He's as straight-laced as they come. But I did hear a rumor about Wes Sherman *Jr.*" Skyler related what he had heard, especially the phone call he'd overheard from Carson. "So what do you think of that, detective?"

"Hmm."

"Is that an interested 'hmm' or a go-away-and-shut-the-fuck-up-Skyler 'hmm'?"

"An interested 'hmm.'"

A shadow fell over her and Skyler turned around. Mike de Guzman stood there, looking like he stepped out of *Law & Order* with his short black hair and a well-fitting tan suit on his trim shoulders. "Skyler."

"Hi, *Mike*," he said with a smile. He turned that smile on Sidney.

A blush tinged the man's bronzed cheeks. "So Sid finally told you about me."

"Uh huh. I think the two of you should come over to my

place some night for dinner. Get things rolling."

"'Things'?"

"You know. This dating thing."

Mike glared at Sidney, who turned away but not before punching Skyler in the shoulder. "Ow!"

"You told him *that*? You finally tell your best friend about me and you tell him *that*?"

"He's my best friend. I tell him everything."

Skyler gave Mike a shit-eating grin. "I'm afraid that's true. So *Mike*." He put his arm around the man's shoulders and steered him away from Sidney. "Get her to come over some night. We'll double date."

"Oh. You have a boyfriend?"

"Well, he's not exactly a boyfriend…"

"Skyler," said Sidney catching up and walking on his other side. "I don't think you should see Keith anymore."

Skyler stopped. "What? Why? Is it because of what Julia said?"

"Yes. What do you really know about that guy?"

"The boy scout with the holes in the record?" asked Mike. God, he knew, too?

"Yeah. That guy. Skyler, I think it would be safer if you just cooled it."

"He didn't do anything. And it sounds like all this stuff with the computer happened way before Keith got to the school. Maybe you should follow up on this Jordan Stacey. Ask her what the deal is."

"We are. But she moved out of state and she's been hard to locate." She seemed to cut herself off in mid-thought. "Still," she resumed, "it's better to be safe than sorry."

"But…I like him."

She sighed and exchanged glances with Mike. "Skyler, I can't tell you how many times a guy that looked perfectly innocent turned out to be very guilty."

He looked at Mike for confirmation and he nodded apologetically.

"Really?"

They both nodded together.

"Shit." It did seem like a lame story—doing a "job" for Sherman, but the principal said it was true. Except maybe he was up to something, too? This was getting insane. At this rate, he wouldn't be able to trust anyone!

He didn't say anything, but secretly, he decided he wasn't going to stay away from Keith. The only way to be sure of him was to get to know the guy, right?

"But what about Jeff Dwyer? Are you guys still investigating that? Sidney said that there was someone else's DNA under Evan's fingernails." But Skyler couldn't help picturing Jeff standing outside his own house in the dead of night, watching Evan, thinking, planning.

Mike gave an accusatory look at Sidney. "You really do tell him everything. Ever consider that a civilian shouldn't have that info?"

"Shove it, Mike. I never told him that. *You* just did."

Skyler repressed a smile of triumph. But as soon as he thought about what they were discussing the smile faded fast. "I'll see what more I can find out from Jeff," said Skyler, moving down the hall again.

Sidney nabbed him by the collar and dragged him back. He sputtered. "You're choking me!"

"I'll do more than that if I catch you doing any investigating. Stay out of it, Skyler. I mean it."

"That's what you said last time and *I* cracked the case."

"You did not crack the case. What the hell do you think this is, *Murder She Wrote*? This isn't a game, Skyler. People get hurt. Look at Julia back there—" and she waved a hand vaguely back down the hall toward Julia's hospital room. "Someone wanted to silence her. Maybe you should think about that."

"These guys were my friends. My ex-lovers. And no one gives a damn about them. I do."

"We do give a damn," said Mike kindly. "It's really great that you want to stand up for your friends, but you have to let Sid and me do our jobs. It only makes it harder when you get in the way. Because then we have to protect you, too."

Oh my God, he thought. They were doing good cop, bad cop. He wondered if they even realized it.

"I can protect myself," he said in a small voice.

"Like when that guy took a pot shot at you?" Sidney asked.

Skyler still remembered the sound of the bullet smacking the wood on his front stoop while he and Jamie had been outside talking in the dark. Wes Sherman's killer had tried to stop Skyler that night and it *had* scared the shit out of him. But it also gave him a renewed sense of justice. This did, too. Evan and Jeff had served their country. Something terrible had happened to Evan in the course of that service, leaving him disfigured and disheartened. And then homophobic COs drummed them out of the only life they had ever wanted, effectively ruining their careers and any chance of a decent job. And *then* someone killed him, and his partner was perhaps set up to take the fall. That was all just bullshit, plain and simple.

Sidney and Mike talked quietly together and Skyler, feeling like a third wheel, moved away from them. Now more than ever he was determined to do what he could for Jeff and Evan. Screw Sidney and screw Mike. He didn't want to even contemplate the possibility of Jeff being guilty. He had to talk to someone who knew them, someone with an Army connection.

He suddenly thought of that VA guy that came to Jeff's house—what was his name? He reached into his pocket for his wallet and opened it up. Pulling out the VA card he looked at the name again. James Fischer. He needed to talk to him himself.

CHAPTER THIRTEEN

When he got home, Keith was sitting on the bottom steps to his stairwell again. He held up two Styrofoam containers. "I brought your dinner. And mine, too. I thought we could still have dinner together."

Jeez, that was really sweet. Would a bad guy be really sweet?

He nodded and led the way up the stairs, unlocking his door.

Inside, he checked the fridge to see if there was any beer. "I've got Corona. Want some?"

"Perfect."

The Styrofoam containers were set on the table and Skyler brought out two glasses and two forks. They began eating quietly, only glancing up at one another from time to time.

Finally Keith spoke. "Do you think we'll ever manage to spend an entire evening with your friends?"

Skyler chuckled. "Eventually. There's just a lot of stuff going on right now."

"How's Julia Meyers?"

He chewed and looked up at the man. God, he was gorgeous. *Could anyone with those gentle eyes really be a...a...well, go ahead and say it, Skyler. A killer?* He'd had some amazing sex with this man and he wanted more amazing sex with him. And maybe something else too, he had to admit. He really did want to get to know Keith and not just to see if he was hiding something.

"She's okay. I mean, for someone who'd been in a coma for a few weeks."

"Did she say who attacked her?"

"No. She said she couldn't remember the attack at all. I understand that isn't unusual. To not remember the thing that put you in a coma."

"Wow. That's too bad. How will they ever catch the person who did it then?"

"Oh they'll catch them. My Sidney's a great cop."

Keith stuffed more rice into his mouth without commenting. It was funny—or was he just being paranoid—but every time he mentioned Sidney, Keith always clammed up.

He decided on a different tack, trying to gather as much information on Keith as he could. "Hey, do you remember when we met up at Beat, that defunct dance club in San Bernardino?"

"You mean when I stopped that bartender from pummeling you?"

"Ha…yeah. You said you were there with some friends."

"Oh." He took a swig of his beer. He hadn't used his glass. "Yeah, they're my best friends. Went to school in Boulder with me. They're girlfriends."

"Y-you're old girlfriends?" There was an unpleasant jealous feeling welling up inside that Skyler tried hard to tamp down.

He chuckled. "No, you idiot. Girlfriends with each other. Ever heard of 'lesbians' in your male-centric world?"

"Hey, I'm not male-centric. Sidney is my best friend. She's not male or a lesbian. She's porking her male partner, as a matter of fact."

The beer was halfway to Keith's lips before it stopped. "Her detective partner?"

Skyler cringed. "Oops. Wasn't supposed to tell. Pretend you never heard that."

"Agreed. Well, anyway, they're my best friends, Keisha and Sheryl. But they live in San Diego and I don't see them often."

"That's quite a drive from here."

"Yes. But I'm dying for you to meet them." He grinned. It was a very affectionate expression and Skyler couldn't help himself but be entranced by it.

Keith gazed at him a few moments more before sighing and

getting to his feet. "It's a school night and I'd better get going."

"What? Aren't you going to stay?" That sounded a bit too whiney to his ear but Keith didn't point it out. He merely walked to the door and Skyler trailed after.

"I'd love to. Believe me." He adjusted his jeans. "But I think it might be a good idea for us to slow things down. Get to know each other. That way we can work through our trust issues." He looked at Skyler pointedly.

"Oh. Well, I guess you're right. If you really feel like you have to go."

"I really do." He leaned over, took Skyler's chin in his hand, and bestowed a gentle kiss to his lips. "But don't expect such a grandiose gesture next time," he said quietly, lips still feathering on Skyler's.

Skyler inhaled his scent one last time before the man escaped out the door. He leaned out of the doorway and watched him thump down the stairs, turn once at the bottom to wave up at Skyler, and disappear into the night.

Skyler rested against the shut door. "Well, shit." Did bad guys act like *that*?

♫ ♫ ♫

The next day at lunchtime, Skyler GPSed the Veteran's Affairs Center and drove there. It was across town from the school and he hoped he wouldn't be late getting back. He pulled into a parking space in front of a meter with some time left on it and got out. He held the business card in his hand, read it, and then looked up at the building on the busy street. It was probably built around the late forties, with curved walls and small windows that looked like they belonged on a Packard. Pocketing the card he walked up the steps and went inside. A wide counter of laminated wood stretched before him with a young man wearing a polo shirt and a name tag that said "Brian" sitting behind it. "Hello."

"Hello," said Brian, raising his head.

"I wonder if you can help me. I'd like to talk to James Fischer."

"I'll see if he's in. A lot of our personnel are currently out for lunch. May I ask who you are, sir?"

"Skyler Foxe. I'm a friend of...of Evan Fargo."

The man made no expression of recognition at the name so Skyler waited as he hit a button on the phone and then talked into it.

"You can go in, sir. Right through those doors and to the right."

"Thank you."

Skyler pushed through the double doors and saw the name "Fischer" on the first door he came to. He knocked and heard the answering, "Come."

Fischer was wearing a suit. He got up from behind his desk and stretched out his hand to Skyler. They shook and he sat back down. "I remember you from the house," he said in greeting.

"Yes," said Skyler, trying to get comfortable on the old metal and vinyl chair. "I just wanted to ask you some things. Uh...you sort of left abruptly the other day."

"Yes. I apologize for that. There just didn't seem to be anything more to say and it was rather upsetting business."

"I agree. You know, I was just talking to Jeff Dwyer, Evan's partner—"

"His gay lover, you mean?"

There was no change to his expression or even any emphasis or inflexion in the words, but there was something in the tone that made Skyler immediately bristle. "Uh...yes. His *partner*," Skyler emphasized, just so Fischer knew exactly where he stood. "And he was telling me quite a different story about your interaction with them."

Fischer sat back, toying with a pen. "Yes, I rather imagine he would. You see, Skyler—may I call you Skyler? You see, Skyler, Lt. Dwyer and Lt. Fargo were fully aware of the government's policy regarding Don't Ask Don't Tell. I explained to them that there was little to be done from here. Lt. Dwyer was insistent on changing his dishonorable discharge. We could advise but there was little else we could do. I told them to contact their local GLBT center for lawyers and, of course, gave them information on their congressman. Naturally they were upset over the quandary they found themselves."

"Pardon me, Mr. Fischer, but 'quandary' doesn't really quite cover it. But be that as it may. Jeff Dwyer—Lt. Dwyer—indicated that your presence particularly upset Evan—Lt. Fargo. And that you had wanted him to do something he was reluctant to do. Lt. Dwyer didn't know the nature of what it might have been to upset Lt. Fargo, so what I'd like to know is—"

"Excuse me." He leaned forward. "Are you a lawyer, Mr. Foxe?" So it was "Mr. Foxe" again.

"No."

"Are you legally authorized in any other way to represent Lt. Dwyer?"

"Well, no. I'm just his friend."

"Then I really don't think we have anything else to discuss, do you?"

"As a matter of fact I do think there is more to discuss."

"Mr. Foxe, while it was true that Lt. Fargo was honorably discharged, he was an injured veteran and entitled to those benefits, which he received. That was certainly not in question. But Lt. Dwyer was *dis*honorably discharged. He had three appeals in Iraq and none of them stood. I wasn't his counselor but I am the team leader here, and I told him over and over that there was nothing left for me to do. He had the option to contact his Congressman."

"And I know all that. But there were some awfully suspicious circumstances surrounding Lt. Fargo's murder and you were there at the house where you didn't belong and weren't exactly welcome…"

"Just wait a minute. What are you saying?"

"I'm saying that it's awfully suspicious you're hanging around there. And what I'd like to know is—"

Fischer shot to his feet. "Who the fuck are you to accuse me of shit like that?"

Skyler got out of his chair and edged behind it. It did no good because Fischer came barreling around his desk. "What do we have here?" he said, looking Skyler up and down. "'Friend' of Dwyer's you say?" He made air quotes around "friend." "Aren't you just another *faggot* friend of these guys? God, I've had it up to here with whiney homosexuals. They knew the consequences. It's too late to cry about it now."

Skyler aimed an index finger at the man's chest but it was trembling with anger tinged with fear. "You know, they fought for this country. The man lost a goddamned leg in the service of this country. What the hell difference does it make who he slept with?"

"What the hell difference? It matters to God, that's who. 'Thou shall not lie with mankind, as with womankind: it is abomination!'"

"You are a fucking disgrace to the Army and to this country."

He got right up into Skyler's face. "What did you say to me?"

"You heard me. You're not fit to counsel people here or anywhere else. You're not fit to even represent this country—"

Pain! Stars. When Skyler was cognizant again for the half second it all took to happen, he realized that the bastard had hit him and he was on the floor.

"Get the hell out of my office!"

Scrambling to his feet, Skyler was too incensed, too shocked to say anything further. He stomped out of the office and through the lobby. He got into his car and sat, clutching the steering wheel with whitening fists, adrenaline-dazed. His face hurt like a sonofabitch.

He hit me! He actually hit me! The fucking bastard. People just don't *hit* people. It was only then that Skyler glanced in his rearview mirror and saw the shiner forming at his eye. "Holy shit!"

He didn't know what else to do. He drove hell for leather to The Bean.

♪ ♪ ♪

Cashmere Funk, with dreads hanging from under his cap, danced behind the counter to a beat playing in his ear buds. At least, Skyler hoped he was wearing ear buds.

"Cashmere!"

The tall man turned to him and his eyes widened to saucers. His accent was thick when he cried, "Oh man! What happened to you, Skyler!"

"Cashmere, is Philip here? Can you get him?"

"Someone popped you but good."

"I *know*, can you just get Philip, please?"

"Mos def!" He spun and ducked through the open kitchen doors. It only took a few seconds for him to return with Philip.

"Holy shit, Skyler! What the hell happened to you?"

"I can't go back to school like this." Skyler was looking at his distorted reflection in the shiny brass espresso machine behind the counter. "Fuck, it's like sophomore year all over again."

"Cashmere, go get some ice and put it in a towel." The barista disappeared again. Philip grabbed Skyler by the arm and maneuvered him to the cushy chairs. "What happened?"

"I did something really stupid."

"It's Keith, isn't it?"

The *non sequitur* threw him off for a second. "No. *No!* That's not what happened."

"I'll kill the guy. No, *Sidney* will kill the guy 'cause she has a gun."

"It wasn't Keith—"

He grabbed both his shoulders and looked him in the eye. "I blame myself. I told you to go for it. But you tried to tell me how violent he is."

"Philip, listen to me—"

"I'm calling Jamie." He reached in his pocket and pulled out his phone.

"Philip, just listen for a second—"

"Jamie, get your ass to The Bean right now. That dickhead Keith went and hit Skyler. *Yes, way!* Get the hell over here now!" He threw it on the table, stared at Skyler, and tears formed at his eyes. He clutched Skyler into a hug. "We'll get that guy, and then we'll make sure he stays far away from you."

Skyler pushed back with all his might. "Will you shut up for a second and listen to me! *It wasn't Keith!* I went over to this Army guy's office at the VA Center and pretty much accused him of killing Evan, just like Sidney told me not to do, and he punched me."

"And you expect me to believe a lame story like that? Why are you protecting that guy?"

"I'm not protecting anyone. It was the Army guy, James Fischer, the one I ran into at Jeff's house. Remember me telling you about him?"

"Skyler, he's not worth it. Trust me."

"Philip!"

Cashmere returned with the ice and by then some of the customers had come over to see what the ruckus was.

"His boyfriend. Domestic violence," Philip explained tearfully.

Everyone began offering advice, including calling the police, calling a TV station, and calling the paramedics.

"No, everyone, thank you all for your concern but that's not what happened."

"Same thing happened to a friend of mine," said a young woman to her companion. "She defended the bastard all the way to court."

"Stop, stop! Everyone just stop!" The buzz of concerned voices came to a halt. "I'm only going to say this once. It. Was.

Not. Keith! I started investigating my friend Evan's murder and the guy I suspected did this to me."

Everyone exchanged glances and the soft buzz of conversation started up again.

Philip narrowed his eyes at him. "Skyler, is this the absolute truth? You're not just saying this to protect that guy, are you?"

"No! But we cannot call the cops because Sidney can't find out about this. I swear, Philip. It really was the Army guy." He prodded his sore cheek with his fingertips. "Does anyone have any make-up?"

"Make-up won't hide the swelling. You'll just have to keep away from Sidney. But I swear to God, Skyler, if you're lying about this—"

"I'm not. Really." He looked around and the customers slowly retreated back to their tables or lidded their cups and left.

"*Oh my God!*" screeched Jamie from the doorway. Rodolfo skidded through the door a second later.

"*Amante!* That beast! I told you he was no good for you."

Skyler sat back, pressing the ice to his face.

After explaining it for the fiftieth time, it seemed, Jamie and Rodolfo appeared to believe him, at least a little. Skyler then thought of calling the school to make a lame excuse as to why he couldn't return. "They're so going to fire me."

"Mr. Sherman is on your side," said Philip. "You said so yourself."

"I can't do it. I have to go back. How does it look?" He pulled the towel away and scanned their faces.

Jamie's eyes were wide and his mouth seemed set in a permanent "o." Rodolfo winced. Philip patted his hand. "I'll get some make-up."

ʃ ʃ ʃ

Skyler kept checking his face in his rearview mirror as he drove back to school. His cheek and eye were hopelessly swollen and beginning to turn dark. His eyeball was red from broken blood vessels. Definitely a shiner. He already had a story prepared and he hoped he could just get through the rest of the day.

But as luck would have it, he literally ran into Keith first thing upon entering the school.

Keith pushed him back, a joke ready on his smiling lips until his gaze focused on Skyler's face. His eyes grew wide and something dark shadowed his expression. He said nothing as he dragged Skyler into the first available empty classroom and shut the door. "Who hit you?"

"What makes you think anyone hit me?"

"For God's sake, Skyler. I can tell someone hit you. Who was it?"

"It was an elbow. It was a simple mistake."

"Was it that Rodolfo guy? Because I'll kill him."

"No, no! I swear!" Almost the same words Philip used but an entirely different feeling slithered up his spine. Keith wanted to protect him. He could read it in the concern in his eyes, in the way he pawed at Skyler's shirt.

"Skyler, don't lie to me to protect him."

He laughed, he couldn't help it. And Keith drew back, perplexed. "That's the same thing Philip said to me…about *you*!"

And now he was sorry he said it because Keith suddenly looked devastated. "He thinks that I would hurt you? Do *you* think that?"

"No, of course not!" His arms had somehow gone up around the taller man's neck. He brought him forward for a soft kiss, risking it at school to calm the expression he caused on his face. "Keith, I know you'd never hurt me." And this time he believed it. Keith might get angry or jealous but he would never raise a hand to Skyler. He didn't care what Sidney or the others thought. This man was different, sweet, loving. He just wouldn't do it.

He rested his head on his chest a moment, just relishing the contact before he pushed away. They couldn't take the chance of someone walking in.

"So someone really elbowed you? Really?"

"Yeah, it was Jamie." He felt an acute pang of guilt as he lied, but he also knew, just like if he told Sidney, that they would both be all over James Fischer with some big time whoop ass, and Skyler would just as soon put the whole thing behind him. For now. Fischer definitely bore watching, though. Obviously, violence was in his repertoire. Looked like he had a hot button for gays. "I was helping him move some stuff. He has a really good left hook, elbow-wise." *Don't overdo it, Skyler. He's already looking at you suspiciously.* He decided to take out the big guns. With a pout he said, "It hurts, you know."

"Oh." Keith took him carefully in his arms and cradled him gently. "That okay?"

"Uh huh...well. Maybe we shouldn't do that here."

But Keith leaned in and dropped another gentle kiss on Skyler's lips and then a feather soft one near his bruised eye. "That should make it all better," he whispered.

Be damned if it didn't! Skyler gazed up at the man he had just lied to, who had tried to sooth him, and who had threatened to defend him to the death...and sighed.

Keith released him, straightened, cleared his throat. "You're going to be explaining that all day."

"I know." He shrugged.

"I wish I were going to be free tonight," he went on, "but I have a previous obligation. Otherwise I'd be there to pamper you."

"Damn. Pampering sounded good."

"There's always tomorrow night."

"It's a date. I mean..."

He mussed Skyler's hair playfully. "You *can* call it a date, you know, and the sky won't fall in."

He felt his cheeks heat up. "I-I know."

Keith shook his head. "God, you're cute. Even with a black eye. I'd better go. See you, Skyler."

"Bye, Keith." He let the bigger man go first and then waited a beat before he stuck his head out the door and walked down the empty corridor.

As predicted, he spent every class explaining the shiner, but when he got to the last period and Rick and Alex stayed behind at the end of the day, Rick whistled and got a finger close to it. "Damn, Mr. Foxe. Who punched you?"

"Nobody punched me," he said, stuffing papers in his satchel. "I told the class at the beginning of the period—"

"But that was such a lame story. Who really hit you? It wasn't that guy that brought you flowers, was it?"

"Yeah," said Alex, a determined look on his face. "'Cause I'll kick his ass for you."

Alex too? "No, boys. Really. It's no big deal. It went down like I said it did." He grabbed his satchel and walked out the door, locking it behind him. The boys hovered in the corridor. "How'd the GSA meeting go, Rick?"

Rick gave a crooked smile. "There were two lesbians that showed up—didn't know them. Another guy who said he was gay—he was a junior, I think. I'd seen him around."

"Not too close, I hope," said Alex, pinching his arm.

He ignored Alex. "And then there were two chicks who said they were gay friendly."

"Wow. That sounds like a pretty good turnout. What did you talk about, if you don't mind my asking?"

"I guess some people knew me and they said they were surprised to see me there," he said sheepishly.

"Dude, you didn't say anything about me, though, right?"

He touched Alex's chin and tilted it up. "Of course not, *mi pequeña*," he said softly.

Alex's eyes scanned the corridor fiercely and he stepped away from Rick's fingers. Skyler could tell the Hispanic boy's feelings were hurt but his eyes soon shut down the emotion.

"But it was a good meeting?" asked Skyler.

"Yeah. Yeah, it was. I still wish you were there, Mr. Foxe."

"I know."

"Gotta go. Coming, *mi rosa*?"

"In a minute," said Alex, shuffling his feet.

Rick waved a large paw and loped down the empty corridor until he disappeared down the staircase. Skyler clutched his satchel and gazed at Alex expectantly.

The boy ran his hand over his spiky hair and licked his lips. "Here's the thing. It's okay to make excuses. Just don't start believing them."

"Excuses? About what?"

Alex sighed and stared down at the floor until he seemed to square his shoulders. "About who hit you. And you don't need to deny it. I know what it looks like…to get hit."

Skyler's jaw fell open. "Oh, Alex. Are you telling me—?"

"There's been a lot of rough-housing in my life, okay. A lot of stuff at school."

And there was a pause and Skyler wondered if he had meant to fill that gap with "and at home, too." But Alex didn't. He just let it hang there. Letting Skyler know in so many words and a lot more unspoken, that Skyler didn't have to take it, didn't have to be a punching bag. Maybe he'd wanted to tell *himself* that in the mirror, but it was always a lot easier dispensing advice to someone other than oneself.

Skyler's eyes prickled.

Alex never looked up. He just kept scuffing his dirty running shoes on the shiny floor. "Just don't fall for it, okay, Mr. Foxe. Don't let the guy do it anymore. I think you're better than that. I *know* you're better than that."

All he could do was nod. Alex touched his shoulder

comfortingly and then he was gone, dragging his backpack behind him, starting off in a quick walk and becoming a trot as he turned the corner at the stairs.

♪ ♪ ♪

Skyler walked slowly down the stairs, thinking of Alex's gentle and undeserved reassurance. Sometimes you taught the kids and sometimes the kids taught you. Silently, he went through the main office. He gave a half-hearted wave to the student assistants, checked the bulletin board and the schedule for anything he needed to know, and sluggishly left the building toward the parking lot.

Wow. So much to think about. It was bad enough he had to lie to everyone, but now even his students were coming to his aid. And if Alex Ryan was confessing to abuse at home, Skyler was obligated by law to report it. But *had* he? Such a mess.

When he raised his head, his gaze spotted that white van again parked across the street. The last few minutes were abruptly forgotten. He stopped and stared at it. "Redlands Orchid Farm. Why is that so familiar?" And then it suddenly hit him. He had seen a business card with that name and logo on it in Evan Fargo's wallet. He had to call Jeff.

CHAPTER FOURTEEN

He phoned Jeff from the car as he navigated the late afternoon traffic. "Jeff, how are you doing?"

"Okay, I guess, for a wanted criminal."

"You're not a wanted criminal and I have it on good authority that you probably won't be the prime suspect long."

"Are you shitting me, Skyler? 'Cause that would be the only good news I had in a long time."

"I, uh, can't tell you details." *I shouldn't even have told you that, but screw Sidney.* "But I think it will be all right."

"Damn. That's...that's great." He sounded teary.

"But Jeff. I wonder if you could tell me a few things. One, your neighbor reported some, well, odd behavior. Like you standing outside your house in the middle of the night."

"Yeah, so?"

"Well...what were you doing?"

He snorted a laugh. "Getting away. Only as far away as I dared. I didn't like to leave Evan alone. It was bad enough I worked two jobs and was gone a lot. I knew he was depressed. But sometimes I just needed alone time. I could see him inside, just sitting there. And yeah, it made me angry and it also made me a little bit sad. I sure wish he was still there to stare at."

It made Skyler choke up a little. "I can see that." And he could. Suspicion could be a dangerous thing. He could see himself doing something like that.

"And two?" said Jeff. "You said there were two things you needed to know?"

"Oh yeah. Why did Evan have a card for the Redlands Orchid Farm?"

"Orchid farm? No idea. Neither of us liked orchids. Hated

them, in fact."

"Oh. Well, do you still have that card? I wonder if there was a name on it."

"Sorry, Sky. I emptied that wallet of anything that wasn't relevant. Tossed it."

"Damn."

"What's this about?"

"I don't know. Just thinking outside the box. By the way, do you want to come over this week?"

"No, my sister is coming to town. Wouldn't you know it took a crisis like this to make amends with her?"

He hadn't known Jeff had a sister, let alone that they were on the outs. "That's great, Jeff."

"Yeah. She's going to stay with me. The house will be less lonely that way. And we can reconnect."

"I'm glad."

"Also...the funeral is Saturday."

"What time?"

There was a pause and Skyler could hear him swallowing. "Thanks, Sky," he said quietly. "One o'clock at Mt. View in San Bernardino."

"I'll be there."

"Thank you, Skyler. I love you, dude."

"I love you, too."

God. A funeral. Well, it meant some sort of closure for Jeff and being reunited with his estranged family. Maybe some good could come from this, though Skyler wasn't one to attribute these events to Fate or God. God couldn't be *that* mean.

He automatically headed for home, feeling a little down, but as he drove and thought about it all, he hit the button for his GPS. "Redlands Orchid Farm," he told it, and the calm female voice told him to, when possible, make a legal u-turn.

He followed the instructions until he was driving down Alessandro and then across the railroad tracks to San Timoteo Canyon. Groves of orange trees offered vistas of green to his left, while the canyon flattened to a wide pasture on his right. It wasn't long until he saw a worn plywood sign with the orchid farm's logo on it, along with an arrow pointing down a long dirt road.

Giving only a brief thought to his white Bug's paint job, he turned onto the road and bumped along, kicking up a cloud of dust behind him.

The late afternoon sun tinged the outlying pasture's brown grass and mustard plants with a golden fringe of light. Turning with a bend in the road, he pulled up to a wide greenhouse and turned off the engine. A rusty tractor was parked off to the side under a large out-spreading oak tree. A flatbed trailer with a couple of empty plastic garden pots lying on it was hitched to the tractor, but there was no one and nothing else to be seen.

Skyler got out and stood by his car. He looked down at it and winced. Covered in dust. He sighed and walked toward the greenhouse. He tried to wipe the window to look inside but the glass was soaped from the inside so you couldn't see in. He tried the door but it was locked with a substantial padlock. There were no posted hours of business. The only thing indicating what the place was at all was the logo above the door.

"You there!"

Skyler jumped ten feet, he was sure of it. With a hand over his heart he turned around. A man wearing dusty coveralls and a few days' growth of gray whiskers was eyeing him. He clutched a rusty rake.

"We're closed," he said. His gaze rose to Skyler's shiner.

He ducked his head, trying to hide it. "Oh. Well, I was wondering if there was someone around to talk to—"

"No, no one's here."

"What time tomorrow should I—?"

"Better call first."

"I don't have the number—"

"Ever hear of the internet?" He turned away and walked back seemingly into the underbrush, but Skyler noted a gray shack just behind the foliage. A dusty ATV was parked beside it and the man was headed for it. He glanced at Skyler once more before straddling the thing and starting it up with a roar and a belch of smoke.

Skyler returned to his car and got in. Why all the secrecy? And what was with the creepy Scooby-Doo caretaker?

But more importantly, what did Evan have to do with this orchid farm?

$\int \int \int$

He scarfed down a hasty dinner of instant macaroni and cheese and called Jamie.

"Want to do some investigating with me tonight?"

Jamie laughed. "Not another Nancy Boy Mystery!"

"Ha, ha, very funny."

"Skyler, seriously, what are you getting into? I thought Sidney told you to lay off that stuff."

"I know, but she's the one who arrested the wrong guy. She has only herself to blame."

"Oh, so this is about your friend Jeff? Okay, I'm in. Can I call Rudy?"

"Why not? Let's get the whole Baker Street Irregulars together."

$\int \int \int$

Jamie insisted they *not* call Philip because he was a spoilsport and would talk them out of it.

Which didn't seem like such a bad option after all when Skyler turned down the dirt road in the dark with Jamie chatting nonstop beside him and Rodolfo clinging to his seat back.

He turned off his headlights, hoping to be a little stealthier about it. And then he decided to park well up the road and walk the rest of the way in.

Jamie zipped his weathered Fossil leather jacket and looked down at his Converse All Star Duck boots. "These will get ruined," he said.

"They're just shoes," muttered Skyler, using his flashlight discreetly.

"You say that, but you know it isn't true."

Rodolfo put his arm around Skyler. "Uh, Rodolfo, honey. What are you doing?"

"It's scary out here. I thought I'd protect you."

Skyler could see Jamie's smile even in the dark. "Rudy is so sweet, isn't he?"

"He's adorable, but he needs to keep his hands to himself." Skyler grabbed the hand on his shoulder and pushed it gently but firmly away. "I'll be fine."

"You used to be more fun, Skyler."

"Yeah, I know. That was before...never mind."

Jamie looked smug. "You were going to say 'before Keith' weren't you."

"I don't know what's so great about this *Keith*," said Rodolfo, saying his name with particular vitriol.

Jamie snickered. "Are you *blind*? He's fucking gorgeous, that's what. And if he's half as good in bed as he looks like he is—" He glanced at Skyler for confirmation. Skyler nodded enthusiastically.

"See? I think you should give Skyler some credit. He's never had a boyfriend before and he's just feeling out the new territory."

Skyler sniffed. "He's not my boyfriend."

"Then he's a Fuck Club member," said Rodolfo.

"No, he isn't that either. He's not likely to ever be that."

"Oh my God!" said Jamie, lurching to a halt.

"What? What is it?" Skyler waved his flashlight around, peering into the darkness ahead.

"Do you realize that this might be the end of the S.F.C. as we know it?"

"Jesus Christ," breathed Skyler.

"No, I mean it. An era is ending. Rudy, you might just be the last inductee."

"Goody for me."

Skyler grabbed Jamie's arm and urged him along. "Isn't that supposed to be a good thing?"

"Well, I suppose. God, it seems like we're all growing up."

"We're twenty-five. Don't you think we should?"

"Ahem," said Rodolfo.

"Oh yeah," said Skyler. "You're older than twenty-five. By the way, dude, just how old are you?"

Rodolfo's shirt shimmered in the darkness. "I never kiss and tell."

Skyler smiled. The man was probably pushing forty, though he wasn't pushing it very hard. He always looked damned good.

Skyler turned his attention to the path ahead, aiming his flashlight down along the rutted dirt road. The air in the canyon cooled and the swaying of the eucalyptus trees on either side of them cast eerie shadows along their starlit path. A rustling in the underbrush to the left stopped them all cold.

Two sets of hands grabbed him and he gave a startled squeak before he realized it was Jamie and Rodolfo. "Would you guys stop doing that!" he whispered. No one moved. The rustling in the foliage continued and Skyler whipped his flashlight in that direction. He couldn't see anything past the deepened shadows. "Probably just a raccoon or possum."

Everyone seemed to relax...until the screech.

They all screamed and ducked as the white apparition swooped over them and then arced up into the distant trees behind them.

Skyler waited for his heart to slow before he could trust his voice. "A screech owl."

"Damn," whispered Jamie. "I guess there's a good reason they call them that. What a horrible sound."

Skyler huffed an uneasy laugh. "I had a trick once who pretty much sounded like that."

Jamie gasped. "Doug, right? Dark-haired guy with a star tattoo at each shoulder? I did him, too."

"Maybe he should start his own fuck club," said Rodolfo.

Jamie giggled. "He could call them the Screech Owls."

"Yeah," said Skyler, feeling more at ease, "cause 'Hooters' is already taken."

They collected themselves and started out again. Skyler looked around, eyes adjusting to the dark, and saw lights in the distance up on the hills above the railroad tracks that snaked through the canyon. There were a lot more houses in the canyon than there used to be but this stretch of it was still fairly lonely. Nothing but fields, a few horse ranches, and one orchid farm. If someone jumped them here it would take a long time for a rescue, if one ever came.

He swallowed. Once again, he had led his friends into danger. But even with the fear tickling the edge of his senses, there was also an adrenaline rush, the kind he felt while prowling at Trixx. Could he be an adrenaline junky?

The road made a long curving sweep to the right and the shadows seemed to deepen. Crickets softly chirped in the background and the breeze kicked up just enough dust to obscure their path, making the use of the flashlight a necessity.

"I've never been out here at night," said Jamie quietly. "It's really lonely here."

"This reminds me a lot of my town in Ecuador," said Rodolfo.

Skyler turned to him and tried to discern his expression in the dark. "You never talk much about life back in Ecuador."

He shrugged. "There was a lot of discontent. And a coup. That's why I'm here."

Jamie smoothed his hand over Rodolfo's shoulder comfortingly. "I'm sorry you had to leave your homeland, but whatever the reason, we're glad you're here."

He took Jamie's hand, kissed it, and smiled. "Me, too."

Skyler sighed. If only Rodolfo and Philip could get along as well.

They continued on in silence, and after a careful walk that seemed to go on forever, Skyler's flashlight beam finally swept over the greenhouse ahead. He switched the light off and everything seemed to fall quiet in the darkened night.

Skyler crept forward toward the shack. It was slow going without his flashlight on, but he managed to get near enough to see that no one was there. He returned to his friends and motioned for them to follow. He got to the front of the greenhouse and tested the padlock. It was secure. Then he tried looking through the windows and even shone his flashlight through, but there was no way to see through the dried soap. "Let's go around the other side," he said quietly.

Jamie took Rodolfo's hand and followed. "I still don't know what you expect to find, Skyler."

"I don't know either. But Evan obviously had some reason to keep that card."

"Maybe he just wanted some flowers," said Rodolfo.

"No. Jeff said they both hated orchids."

"So the reason to have a business card," said Jamie, thinking, "is that you intended to do some kind of business?"

Skyler nodded. "Makes sense."

Rodolfo took the lead and pulled Jamie along, right up next to Skyler. "But what kind of business?"

"Don't know. That's what we're here to find out."

Jamie's eyes were bright in the darkness as he looked anxiously around. "Why are we doing this at the dead of night again?"

"Because..." Skyler stopped. "Um...because I wanted to just look around without anyone stopping me. And I wanted to take my mind off this stupid black eye."

They all picked their way carefully over the rutted dirt path as brambles and other dark foliage stretched out branches to snag on their clothes.

"What *about* that, *amante*?" said Rodolfo at his ear. Skyler felt the man's hand resting on his shoulder. "Are you going to report that guy for hitting you?"

"Yeah, Skyler. That was physical assault. It could even be classed as a hate crime because he only hit you because you're gay."

"I don't know. I figure Sidney would hear about it and then I'd be doubly in trouble."

"She's gonna hear about it anyway. You know she will. She's got Spidey sense or something."

"I know. But the longer I can put it off the better— Hey! Another door."

He turned the flashlight on it and examined the door with its peeling paint and soaped window. He turned the rusty doorknob but it seemed to be corroded in its position. Yet when he pulled on it the door moved. He pulled harder and it slowly scraped along the ground, dusting Skyler with dried bird droppings and flaking paint. "Whoa." He yanked and pulled it opened just enough for him to slip through. He was about to go in when Jamie stopped him.

"Skyler, this is breaking and entering."

"But the door is open."

"It's still breaking and entering. I thought we were just going to look around."

"We are. Inside. A little."

"Skyler," said Rodolfo in a harsh whisper. "This can get you into lots of trouble."

"I'm just going to look." They both stared at him. "A really quick look and then we're out of here."

"I don't know what you expect to find," said Rodolfo, leaning against the doorway as Skyler took a few steps over the threshold. He clicked his flashlight on and moved it around. Lots of plants. Expected. Wait a minute.

"Dude. Do these look like orchids to you?"

They both stuck their heads in, careful not to cross the threshold. Skyler shined his light on the nearest row of plants in boxes. They were bunched together on long wooden planks with tubes of drip lines strung along them. The potted plants seemed to go on for a long way, row after row of them.

"Skyler," whispered Jamie. "These look like—"

"Marijuana," said Skyler. Lots and lots of marijuana plants.

♫ ♫ ♫

Back by the car, the three got in and faced each other in the dark. "We should call the police," said Rodolfo, the surprising voice of reason.

Skyler shook his head. "But I've got my fingerprints on the doors and locks. That's the last thing I need."

Jamie was biting his fingernail. "Maybe we should tell Sidney."

"That's the same as calling the cops, you do realize."

"Oh, yeah."

Rodolfo suddenly smacked Skyler upside the head.

"Hey! What's that for?"

"Why did you take us along on this? We could all get into trouble."

"I didn't know we'd find that!" But now he had to think. Why did Evan have that card? Was it to get illegal weed from these guys? Did he need it for the pain? Was he going to sell the stuff to subsidize their dwindling income?

"Shit. I think Evan was going to sell the stuff."

"You can't be sure of that," said Jamie.

"Oh!" Rodolfo clutched Skyler's shoulder painfully. "That's why they killed him! To shut him up."

Skyler pried the man's fingers from him. "But if he was going to sell the stuff, why would they want to shut him up?"

"Oh. You're right. You are good at this, Skyler."

"No, I'm not. I think I've only scratched the surface. Let's go home. I've got to think."

∫ ∫ ∫

While Jamie and Rodolfo chatted on the way home, Skyler put his mind to the problem. It seemed likely that Evan was going to go into business. Was it these guys that killed him? Maybe it had nothing to do with his murder. He had to talk more with Jeff.

When his friends left, he turned on his phone and then looked at the clock. It was getting late and maybe he didn't need to disturb Jeff just now. He put down the phone and sat back on his sofa. He wondered what Keith was doing right now, and with a weirdly pleasant glow in his chest, he thought that the man might be thinking about him, too. Keith was a really special guy. Smart, funny, sooo good-looking. Such a jock.

He found himself thinking of Rick and his jock boyfriend. They were opposites. One tall and thin, the other stocky. One smart, the other a jock. But they seemed to go together. It was really sweet the way Rick interacted with Alex. He hoped it lasted between them. And thinking of Keith, Skyler hoped it lasted between them, too. He realized he hardly knew the guy but he wanted to get to know him. He couldn't wait to meet Keith's best friends. Two lesbians, huh? He wondered how Sidney would react to that. Of course, she might have a boyfriend, too, by then. Everything was changing, but now it didn't seem to be as scary as he once thought it might be.

Before Skyler knew it, all of these disparate people were all soon to come together as a makeshift family. And, strange to think of it, it was all because of Skyler.

"Weird," he said to the empty room.

♪ ♪ ♪

Weirder still, late afternoon the next day, Skyler saw that orchid farm van parked across the street again and he decided to stake it out.

He tried to be casual as he hung out in front of the school after the last bell, even had the chance to talk to a couple of kids from his junior class and keep half an eye on the van, when he saw the assistant coach Ed Fallows talking at the curb with fellow coach Mac Simpson. They bid their farewells before Ed looked both ways and then crossed the street. He got into the van and drove away.

Huh?

"What's so interesting over there?" came Keith's voice at his ear.

He jumped. "Jesus! Why does everyone like to sneak up on me?"

"Sorry," he said with a chuckle. "But you were so concentrated on something."

"Oh, I just noticed one of your coaches, Ed Fallows I think the guy's name is, get into a van from some orchid farm and drive away."

"That's because he only works here part time. Most of the assistant coaches have other jobs. Ed works at that farm. They're offering a discount to the school for the Winter Formal."

"He works there, huh?"

"Yeah. Why so interested? Gonna bring me flowers?"

Skyler reddened. "No! I mean…d-do you w-want—"

"Relax, Skyler."

"Oh. Okay." He tried not to look too relieved. "I guess I didn't realize. I mean I thought all the football staff were full time."

"If I didn't teach biology I'd be working somewhere else, too."

"God, that's terrible. You work darned hard on the field with those kids."

He smiled, cheeks glowing. "Thanks. I love those kids. It's a great job, even at part time status."

"You're really into football. If we hang around long enough, you're going to make me watch a game on TV, aren't you?"

"Yup. Steelers are playing next Monday. Shall I bring over beer and sandwiches?"

Skyler grinned. It seemed like such a jock thing to do. Why not? "Yeah, okay."

"Great… Whoa. Who's this guy?"

Skyler turned and saw James Fischer stride up the front path to the main building. He spotted Skyler and headed straight toward him.

Shit! Should he run?

His fear made up his mind for him and he stood rooted to the spot.

CHAPTER FIFTEEN

Fischer wasn't swinging fists. In fact, he looked contrite. "Mr. Foxe, can we talk?"

"Just talk?" he asked cautiously.

"Yes, just talk."

Skyler looked at Keith, who got the hint and wandered away, calling to some boys to stop roughhousing.

"Look, Mr. Foxe, I really apologize for the other day. I don't know what came over me. It was completely unprofessional and uncharacteristic."

Skyler couldn't help it. The bitch just couldn't wait to crawl out of his mouth. "I think some homophobic bullshit came over you." And then he crossed his arms.

"Okay, I deserve that. I'm a kind of religious guy, been surrounded all my life with the military, and I just see gays as a detriment to discipline." He seemed contrite in his words, but Skyler missed the sincerity in his bearing. He got the feeling it was staged, as if he were following a script.

"I guess you're entitled to your opinion, no matter how stupid and small-minded it is."

"Look, I'm trying to apologize here. I've seen the damage of gays in the military. I've seen the damage in a young life when they make that choice."

"It's not a choice. And there are probably thousands of gays in the military and they serve with honors and no one ever knows that the guy or girl beside them is gay. Because it doesn't effing matter!"

"Don't get excited."

"You *hit* me," he said as firmly but as quietly as he could.

"I know. And that was way out of line. So I am apologizing and I would like you to reconsider pressing charges."

Not that he was pressing charges. "Oh really?"

"Yes. I don't want this going on my record."

"Oh that's a shame. Because your boss really should know what an asshole he has working under him."

"Mr. Foxe." He looked to be struggling to remain polite. "Please. I'm asking as a personal favor—"

He pointed to his black eye. "May I remind you that you fucking *hit* me?"

"He did *what?*"

Shit. Keith, suddenly right behind him.

"I *knew* you were lying to me," he growled and pushed Skyler out of the way and went nose to nose with Fischer. "Want to try hitting *me*, asshole? Huh?"

"Look, mister, I don't want any trouble with you. This is between Mr. Foxe and me."

"Oh no. I am very much afraid it's now between you and *me*."

"Keith! Don't. People are beginning to look." And gather. The students, like hungry sharks, sensed blood in the water and they began cautiously approaching, making a wide circle around them.

Keith hands closed into fists and he clamped his mouth shut.

But Fischer was looking from Keith to Skyler, all pretense of contrition falling away. "Oh for the love of Jesus. You, too? Is this whole town full of fairies now? I remember when this was a god-fearing neighborhood."

Skyler pushed Keith back, and it wasn't easy. "Leave, Fischer. Or I'll call a cop! Now!"

Fischer snorted as he turned. He didn't seem one iota afraid of Keith or his fists. "Jesus H. Christ! Fucking fairies. You know what? Okay. I don't give a shit what you do. Call the cops. Press charges. And I'll tell you something else. Fargo had it coming. Yeah, that's right. Too bad they didn't get the other one, too. That would have solved everyone's problems."

Skyler didn't know what came over him. The one minute he was standing there, trying to keep Keith from hitting the guy, and the next minute he was swinging his own fist.

Except he missed.

He spun 360 degrees and slipped on the grass. Fischer howled with laughter. "Fucking sad."

The security guard trotted forward at last, standing between a furious Keith and Fischer. "Sir? I'm here to escort you off the property." His hand was on his Taser.

"No, need officer. I'm on my way."

They both watched Fischer leave followed by the security guard, and when he was in his car, Keith turned on Skyler with a black expression. "Care to explain that? How about not lying this time?"

 Kids were whistling and catcalling. Some were deriding Skyler but still others were saying, "Go, Mr. Foxe!" Skyler was still flushed from having his blood up…and missing the chance to do anything about it. And then a wave of embarrassment at his actions in front of the students made him redder still.

"Shouldn't you all be going home?" yelled Keith to the crowd. "Or would you all rather be running laps?"

The crowd quickly dispersed, but some hung around on the sidewalk, outside the sphere of the school's influence.

Skyler turned and stomped toward the gym. He shook out his arms and blew out a breath. He was shaking all over. Must have been the adrenaline. Damn. He'd never gotten physical before, not like that. He almost actually punched the guy! Except that he never even got close to him. But he *almost* did.

No one was in the boys' locker room when they got inside. Keith suddenly grabbed Skyler's arm and spun him. "So he hit you. There was no accident with Jamie."

"Yes. I'm sorry I lied to you but I wanted to prevent that very scene from taking place."

"Skyler, why the hell did this guy hit you? Under what

circumstances—"

"I was following up on some information about my friend's murder. I thought that this guy might be responsible."

"Wait. Wait. You thought this guy might be a murderer so you went to see him and got him so mad *he hit you!*"

Keith dragged his fingers through his hair in obvious frustration and walked in a circle, running shoes squelching on the damp cement floor. Facing Skyler again, he still looked murderous. "Skyler…Skyler…" He blinked in disbelief. "What the fuck! No investigating!"

"You're not Sidney. You can't tell me what to do."

"Oh yeah? If you won't listen to me I'll call her."

"No! Don't do that!"

"Goddammit, Skyler." He glared at him for a moment before engulfing him abruptly in his arms. All the air was whooshed out of him in that hug. "I don't want anything to happen to you, do you understand?" he rasped in his ear. "I…dammit, I *care* about you."

"I know," came his muffled reply.

"There's no reason to do this. Let the police do their job."

"Okay."

"Skyler, I mean it."

"Keith…I can't…breathe."

He released him and Skyler fell back, breathing in great gulps of air. He held up his hand to the man who looked ready to grab him again.

"Look. These guys were important to me. And they got a very raw deal. I'd like to help them."

"That's very sweet of you but there must be some other way."

He stared steadily at Keith. "I can promise…that I will try."

"Skyler!"

"What if it was your friends, Keisha and Sheryl? Wouldn't *you* do something?"

That brought him up short. He could see Keith trying to find excuses and coming up empty. Finally, Keith heaved a big breath and lowered himself to a bench. "I wish you wouldn't do this."

"I kind of have no choice."

"Don't ever go alone. Not ever."

"Okay. Good advice."

He shook his head, obviously still angry and probably angrier that he was impotent to stop Skyler. Skyler kicked at the floor, scuffing the cement. "I gotta go. So…I'll see you later? Weren't you going to come over…or would you rather not?"

"No. I'll come over."

"Good. I'll see you in a little bit, then."

Keith said nothing. He fumed quietly to himself on his bench while Skyler hurried out of the gym.

∫ ∫ ∫

Skyler worried what they were going to talk about. He didn't want a long night of Keith trying to talk him out of doing what he knew he had to do. It was bad enough Sidney pushing him around; he didn't need it from Keith, too.

He ordered Thai food and when it was delivered, it sat in its cartons on the kitchen table. Skyler was flopped on his sofa, trying to read a book but not getting past the first sentence over and over again. He gave up and tossed it aside, just as the doorbell rang.

He opened it and there was Keith, looking gorgeous and concerned, wearing a tight T-shirt and worn relaxed jeans.

As soon as Skyler closed the door he was engulfed in a hug. "What am I going to do with you?" Keith said into Skyler's hair. He kissed the top of his head, drew back, lifted his chin, and planted a kiss on his mouth. It started out as a few gentle pecks but soon blossomed into something deeper. His lips sucked on Skyler's and then he dipped his tongue between them, tasting and teasing. Skyler sank against him, floating on the intense sensation of Keith's mouth on his and those hands caressing his back and dipping down to his backside, cupping. Slowly, he pulled back and gazed into Skyler's eyes once Skyler pried them open from the wonderful haze he had dropped into. "You so drive me crazy."

"Same here," he said languidly.

"Skyler, I'm not leaving tonight."

"Oh? Good. I have dinner."

"I don't want dinner. I want you."

"Okay." He allowed himself to be tugged to his bedroom and while still in a haze, Keith slowly undressed him.

He peeled Skyler's shirt away then reached for the hem of his own shirt and pulled it up, tossing it aside. There was no sight greater than Keith's naked torso, muscular and defined. His nipples were dusky ovals and the cold air hardened them to tight nubs. Skyler wanted to bite them but he was pushed onto the bed on his back and suddenly hands were at his jeans, flipping open the button and yanking down the zipper. Fingers curled into the waistband and pulled them down his legs, stopped by his Nikes. With a growl, Keith yanked the shoes off along with the socks and tugged the jeans all the way off, pitching them to the floor.

He stared at Skyler's small briefs while he toed out of his own shoes, one at a time, and undid his belt and jeans. He pushed down the pants along with his underwear, revealing that amazing erection. Skyler's eyes were glued to it. He licked his lips, remembering the taste, the feel of its velvety steel on his tongue.

Keith swallowed hard and peeled Skyler's underwear off, tossing it over his shoulder, and stared a long time at Skyler's dick, leaking its string of precum over his stomach. His hands slowly teased up Skyler's torso, spreading upward until his fingers encountered his nipples, two hard pebbles. Keith's big fingers closed over both of them and pinched before giving each a little twist. Skyler writhed and gasped. A tongue suddenly replaced one set of fingers and lapped at the tiny pink button until warm lips closed over it and sucked.

Skyler dug his fingers into Keith's hair and held his head in place. "Oh, man," he moaned.

The mouth and tongue left his nipples and feathered up to his neck, closing over the soft skin there, alternating between sucking and nipping. He drew back and just gazed at Skyler, at the love bites he'd surely left behind, at Skyler's face set in a languid smile with heavy-lidded eyes, at his cock, so red and so hard it ached.

"You are so beautiful," he said huskily. A hand dragged down his skin again, knuckles making circles in his blond pubes, and stroked down his dick. It twitched and bobbed at his touch. Catching some of the moisture from the tip on his fingers, Keith brought them to his mouth and sucked them between his plump lips, closing his eyes in ecstasy. "Mmm. You taste fantastic."

Skyler stared up at him, at that hungry gaze, and he couldn't help bucking his hips toward him, trying to get his dick closer to those hands or that mouth. With a trembling breath, he said, "Come on, Keith. I'm dying here."

"Turn over," said Keith, voice hoarse, and he reached for a condom from the basket.

Skyler turned. He decided to give Keith his money's worth and got up on his knees while laying his head on his folded arms. With his butt up in the air and his legs spread wide, Keith had the full view of wide-open ass and enticing, dangling balls.

Keith grabbed the lube and squelched it over his sheathed dick. Skyler jumped a little as the cold of the lube touched his hole, but he moaned as the finger slowed and made tiny circles on his puckered flesh. Keith moved his finger away too soon, but commenced touching Skyler's butt instead, smoothing his hands over both plump cheeks at once, sometimes squeezing them and bunching them together. He dropped a kiss on each pale cheek in turn, and Skyler wriggled his backside appreciatively.

"Oh, fuck," Keith murmured. Yes, Keith seemed to like the view.

A hand cupped his sac and toyed with his testicles for a bit. Keith kissed them, licked them, and then kissed them again. He ran his tongue along the bottom of the sac before sucking gently on one orb within. Skyler moaned into his hands and arched his back, offering them to Keith.

Keith fondled them a moment more before the bed moved and Skyler knew that the man was positioning himself. Yes! He felt that cock at his moistened hole, pushing. Skyler tried to push back to make it easier, but try as he might, he couldn't take Keith's girth the first few inches without some sort of pain. But it didn't matter. A little pain for so much pleasure!

Keith's fingers dug into Skyler's ass as he pushed in, determined to be seated deeply as soon as possible. He usually waited for Skyler to get comfortable, but there was none of that today. "Want you so much," rasped Keith behind him.

He began to fuck him immediately. The thrusts were smooth and rhythmic. Skyler rode with it, rocking back and forth as the strokes delved deeper with each plunge. He was hitting his prostate almost every time and Skyler gasped and keened. His head was floating in a wooly cloud of bliss. He grabbed his dick and pumped it, sliding his fingers down the large vein and over the damp crown.

Keith was getting close. Skyler could tell because he was stabbing more wildly into him and his breathing sped up. His body slammed the back of Skyler's thighs and his balls slapped over and over against his wide open ass before they rose. Keith was going to pop at any moment.

But then, in a surprising move, Keith suddenly yanked out of him. Skyler looked over his shoulder. Keith stripped off the condom and clutched his dick, aiming it at Skyler's backside, and came in long spurts of white. Skyler felt the hot spunk fleck against his bottom and he moaned again at the hotness of that, of the thought of Keith coming *on* him instead of *in* him. He squeezed his cock tighter as he stroked it.

Keith seemed to have covered his entire bottom in cum and when he finally finished, his large hands began to slowly rub it into his skin.

"I so wanted to come on your ass, baby," he said breathlessly, fingers sliding over Skyler's wet butt. "I wanted to spread it all over you."

"Oh shit." And with one more stroke he came hard onto the sheets.

Keith held Skyler's ass as Skyler came, squeezing the wet cheeks, almost pushing the jizz out of him.

Skyler held his moist dick until it was completely milked and then let it go, panting with his head hanging low between his sloped shoulders. "Damn, dude. You are too good."

Keith grabbed his waist and tugged, gently turning him over. He laid Skyler down beside him. The sheets stuck to his wet bottom, but it didn't matter. He was floating and Keith was nuzzling his neck, licking the salty sweat. "You're pretty marvelous yourself." He pulled Skyler in until he was nested against his chest, an arm cradled around him. He ran a finger down Skyler's sharp nose, over his lips, and down his chin. "How about we forget about the world and just spend the next week right here?"

"Sounds like a plan," he slurred.

"At least I'd know you'd be safe."

His lassitude suddenly jolted away. "Don't start with that again."

"Skyler, I just think that you're living a little too dangerously."

"*You* could get hurt on the football field, you know."

"Oh really? How's that?"

"Well, someone can come barreling into the sidelines or something and take you out. Seen it a hundred times on TV."

"Where on TV?"

"Well...the movies."

"You're funny." And he gave him a squeeze. "Mind if I bring in some of that food that smells so good in your kitchen? I'm suddenly starving."

"Yeah, sure. Chopsticks are on the counter."

"Chopsticks?" Keith snorted as he rose, wiped his dick on the sheets, and threw them aside. Skyler watched that perfectly round backside retreat and heard him messing around in the kitchen, opening drawers, and then the tinkle of flatware. Keith returned with the cartons in the crook of his arm and a fork and chopsticks in his hand.

He set the cartons on the nightstand on his side of the bed and offered Skyler a pair of chopsticks still in their paper wrapping. They began opening cartons and then dove in. Skyler scooted back against the headboard and Keith joined him, stretching his long legs out and crossing them at the ankles.

They ate ravenously for a full minute, offering each other's cartons for sampling before Skyler looked over at Keith who had noodles dangling from his lips. His heart seemed to flutter. "This is...nice," he said, and then felt his cheeks heat with embarrassment.

"Never ate in bed with someone? It's one of life's little pleasures."

But Keith's comment got him to thinking and it was an unpleasant sensation in his gut in counterpoint to the good feeling of just a moment ago. "So." He stirred his *pad see ew* with his chopsticks. "Have you had many...significant others?"

Keith looked at him, sucking a noodle up through his lips. It smacked against his mouth before disappearing.

"*You* know." Skyler looked down into his carton, continuing to stir. "Shared a lot of meals...like this?"

"Well, not a *lot*. A few."

"So how come they didn't work out?"

Keith lowered the carton to his thighs and wiped his lips with a paper napkin. "I traveled a lot, looking for my niche. And that's not a euphemism," he said with a smile. "I'm just a rolling stone, like I told you. Not conducive for long-term relationships."

"I thought you were into those."

"I'm into monogamy. But I'm certainly not averse to long-term relationships."

"But if I was a psychiatrist, I'd say that you were avoiding them by all this stone-rolling." Skyler felt the man's pointed stare at the top of his head and finally looked up to meet it. "Seems like," he added quietly.

Keith raised his brows and frowned. "Maybe. I don't know. Maybe Mr. Right hadn't come along yet. Maybe I was still looking for him."

"Or maybe you're avoiding commitment."

"Are we talking about me or you?"

Skyler hastily stuffed the *pad see ew* in his mouth and chewed, giving him time to answer. Keith leaned over and Skyler thought he was going to kiss him, but he kept leaning until his face was almost in his naked lap. A warm tongue lapped a stripe across the pale skin below his navel. Keith gave him a weighted gaze. "You dribbled some sauce there."

"Thanks." He gulped. His cock stirred.

Keith seemed satisfied with himself. He sat up again and resumed eating his noodles.

CHAPTER SIXTEEN

When Skyler got to school, he couldn't help but notice the GSA flyers…with swastikas scrawled on them. Others had charming epithets like "Die Fags!" He grabbed one of those and tore it down, crumpling it in his fist.

He felt a presence beside him, which stopped him from saying what he wanted to say out loud. He glanced over and saw that it was Heather Munson, the Goth from his fifth period class. "Sometimes I hate this school," she said. "I am so tired of living in the Inland Evil Empire."

"It's not all bad," he said automatically.

"Yeah, I just love these high-minded Christian types with their 'die fags' slogan. So loving. So inviting."

"It's a small group of misguided kids."

"Yeah? Well how come they aren't committing suicide because *they* can't cope? Give me that flyer." She snatched it out of his hand and smoothed it out on her thigh below her short plaid skirt. "I'm going to this meeting and I'm joining because this school just pisses me off so much. And I'm bringing Amber with me whether she wants to go or not." She turned on her heel and stalked away, the multiple buckles on her heavy boots jangling.

A small smile grew on his face. She reminded him a lot of Sidney.

He hadn't gotten very far down the corridor lined with lockers, when he encountered Rick Flores looking pretty upset and talking with a group of Hispanic girls. They saw Skyler coming and made hasty farewells. Rick looked up, spotted Skyler, and turned away toward his locker.

"Rick? Is something wrong?"

"It's all right, Mr. Foxe."

"Rick, I'm here to help, all right?"

Rick spun. His face wore an uncustomary grimace. "Some kids found out I was at the GSA meeting last week and I've been getting shit ever since. I suppose I expected that, but it's really getting around, you know. Those girls said my brother heard about it. If *he* knows then my parents will know."

"How do you think your brother would feel about that?" Skyler tried to picture Rick's brother and came up with an equally tall senior, another Flores who owned his year of students.

"He's always joking, calling something 'gay' to mean stupid. He tells those jokes. You know the ones."

"But…if he's your brother—"

"Does *your* family know?"

Point.

Rick leaned back against his locker. "You tried to warn me. No wonder you didn't want to get involved."

Skyler shook his head. "You made a good decision, Rick. Much braver than…than me."

"Yeah? It doesn't feel brave right now. My father will kill me."

His voice broke on the last and Skyler's heart ached for him. "I'll go with you to your father. I'll talk to him."

"You don't get it. He won't want to talk to you. He won't want to listen to anyone about this, least of all me."

His eyes were glossy and he looked around the corridor uncertainly. Finally, he pushed away from the lockers and headed down the hallway.

"Rick!"

But the boy ignored him. Dammit. It had all been so promising and Rick had been excited about joining. Today there was another meeting. Rick should definitely go and get the support he needed. Skyler wondered where Alex was. He glanced at his watch and knew he had to get to class. When he looked up again Rick had disappeared.

The day dragged. When he finally got to his fifth period class, all the students filed in. All except Rick.

He glanced at Alex but he seemed just as perplexed as anyone.

Skyler checked the roll and had to ask. "Does anyone know where Rick is? I saw him earlier today."

Everyone rustled but no one said anything.

Finally, Heather spoke up. "I saw him sitting on the bleachers. He didn't look like he was going to be moving anytime soon."

Skyler looked at all the faces staring back at him and made a decision. "Everyone, just read your books and I'll be back."

As soon as he left the classroom he broke into a run. He flew down the stairs and out the building, heading fast for the football field. He finally stopped when he reached the edge of the bleachers. He was a bit out of breath. He hadn't jogged in the mornings for weeks…which was Keith's fault. He tended to get up too late when the man stayed over.

He scanned the bleachers and saw the lone figure sitting in the middle.

He jogged up the stairs and walked toward him. Rick was staring off into the middle distance before he looked up in shock. "Mr. Foxe? Didn't class start already?"

"You didn't come to class so class came to you."

He looked around, maybe expecting the rest of the students.

Skyler sat beside him and stared ahead. "You gotta come to class, Rick."

"Why? My dad will take me out of school once he finds out about me. Shove me in a Catholic school. Like a Catholic school has no homos."

"I'm the world's biggest hypocrite, but you've got to go to the GSA meeting after school today."

"What good will that do?"

"They'll have some suggestions for you. And support. That's what it's about, remember? Besides, Heather's joining today."

"Munson of the black leather?"

"Yeah. She'll kick ass, too."

"Mr. *Foxe!*"

"You know she will," he said, ignoring Rick's shock. "And she'll come up with some good ideas, too. Don't give up now, Rick."

Rick glanced at Skyler's profile until Skyler turned to face him. "I don't want to. It's just…"

"I know. Trust me, I know." He gave a regretful smile. "I'm sorry I'm such a lousy role model."

"No you're not. I've never known a teacher who would leave his own class to come after a student."

Skyler shrugged and leaned forward on his knees.

"What do you suppose the class is doing while you're gone?"

"Oh, I don't know. Setting fire to the trash cans. Hacking into my computer. General partying. It's what I'd be doing."

He laughed and shook his head. They both turned at a step. It was Alex.

Rick rose. "Dude, what are you doing here?"

Alex looked distraught. "I wanted to see what happened to you."

"I'm okay. Mr. Foxe is the patron saint of lost boys."

Alex didn't seem to know what that meant or anything else. He only had eyes for Rick.

"I'll give you boys a few minutes," said Skyler, standing and threading his way through the benches. "But then you'd better both get back to class. I'll sic Heather on you if you don't."

Rick held up his hands. "No need for drastic measures!" He almost sounded like his old self again.

As soon as Skyler had gotten down the bleachers a few feet, Alex enclosed the taller boy in a hug. Skyler smiled. Looks like support had arrived.

But when he reached the bottom, he noticed Ed Fallows dragging the blocking dummies out to the field. And he was looking up at the stands.

Skyler hesitated. It was insane leaving his class alone this long, but he didn't like the look of Fallows' body language.

The boys were finally headed down when Fallows called out to Alex. Alex motioned for Rick to go on, which he did, going down the opposite stairs from Skyler and didn't notice him. Skyler was too far away, but he got the gist of what Fallows was saying to Alex. The boy was turning red and barely composing himself. Skyler moved forward, close enough to catch the tail end of, "...don't need any pansy-asses on this field, you understand me? Carson will hear about this and you'll be off the team faster than I can spit your name, Ryan."

"Is there a problem here?"

Fallows glared at Skyler. "It's none of your damn business, Foxe."

"It's my business if you're throwing your homophobic diatribes at a student." He turned to Alex. "Go on back to class, Alex."

"I'm not through with you, Ryan."

"Oh yes you are. Go, Alex."

Alex didn't hesitate. He sprinted away, head down, and continued in a hard run.

"Foxe, you are in for a world of hurt if you get mixed up in this."

"Oh yeah? I already know what that's like."

Fallows' eyes flicked to Skyler's shiner. "Someone popped you one already, huh? Looks like someone knows how to make you shut up."

"You're a fucking disgrace, you know that. I'm going to make sure you can get nowhere near kids again."

Skyler spun on his heel, expecting any second to feel the guy pounce on him. But when he was a good hundred yards away, he looked back, and Fallows was still standing by the blocking dummies, fuming.

The hell with it. Skyler was feeling vindictive. He pulled out his phone, punched in Sidney's number, and waited till she picked up.

"What is it, Skyler? I'm in the middle of something."

"Want to make a drug bust?"

"At the *school?*"

"No. There's this orchid farm on San Timoteo Canyon, but it's only a front for a pot farm."

"*What?* Start at the beginning."

He cleared his throat and told her the whole story. He pulled the phone away from his ear while she yelled and when it sounded like she was done, he put it back.

"Are you absolutely sure about this?"

"Yes. I…uh…went inside."

He pulled the phone away again and waited.

"Skyler, are you fucking insane?"

"Just be aware that I might have left a few fingerprints."

"Oh that's just great. Great! Brilliant. And you, a college graduate."

"I didn't think I was going to find pot. That much of it."

"A lot? Seriously?"

"Row on row. Go get 'em, Sidney."

"So why the sudden change of heart?"

She was so on to him. He sighed. "An assistant coach here works there part time. And he pissed me off royally today. I only hope he's involved. At the very least, that will be one job he can't go back to."

"Jesus, remind me not to piss you off."

"He laid into a student about being gay. You know that is one of my buttons."

"Well, you go, girl. All right. I'll get a warrant and go out there. You didn't say anything to him about it, did you?"

"No. Mums the word."

"Okay. I'm on it."

He clicked off his phone and punched the air. "Ha! Take that you homophobic bastard!"

♪ ♪ ♪

He returned to class much less agitated, but he did cast an eye toward Alex, who was quiet and sullen at the back of the room.

He was glad to see the class hadn't devolved into chaos while he was gone—no explosions or burnt corpses—and in fact, Amber and Heather had tried to lead a discussion on the reading.

When the class was over, Alex tried to escape quickly but Rick cut him off. Amber and Heather had remained, too, and when Alex realized it, he clammed up.

"So," said Heather. "Are you two going to the GSA meeting?"

Alex glared at Rick. "What the fuck, dude? Did you tell them?"

"We aren't stupid, Alex," she said. "You make cow eyes at him all the time."

"Shit!" He ran his hand over his spiky hair and dropped into a chair.

"Chillax." She plopped her backpack on the desk in front of him. "We're here to be your escorts."

"I'm not going," said Alex.

"Are *you*?" she asked, turning to Rick.

He worried his lip and stared at Alex melting down in his seat. He raised his chin and gave a quick nod. "Yeah, I'm going."

"Awesome. You?" She leaned on the desk toward Alex.

"I can't!" he rasped. "Football. Although I'll probably be kicked off the team."

Rick sat at the desk next to him. "What? Why?"

"Coach Fallows saw us. He screamed at me about no fags on the team."

"He can't legally kick you off the team, Alex," said Skyler. "Don't you worry. I'll take care of Coach Fallows."

He looked Skyler up and down as if to say "Are you kidding?"

Skyler straightened his shoulders. "I'm serious. I won't let it happen. I have a feeling he's not long for this school."

He blinked at Skyler, his mouth hanging open.

Rick laid his hand gently on Alex's. "Come to the meeting, *mi pequeña*. Come *with* me."

Alex chewed on the inside of his mouth and wouldn't raise his eyes. "I don't know."

"It's a safe zone," said Amber primly. She had her sophomore secretary hat on now. "I've read up on it online. If we all go together then no one will know whether you're gay or just gay-friendly."

He took in her pink sweater and fuzzy head band and then sized up Heather's plaid mini skirt, purposely torn fishnet stockings, and heavy black boots. His Adam's apple bobbed as he swallowed. In a small voice, he finally said, "Okay."

Skyler's eyes bugged. He never expected that!

They all left together with backwards calls of "See you later, Mr. Foxe. Have a nice weekend."

He was frozen to the spot as they disappeared en masse around the corner. He was so damned proud of them.

And then he felt like shit for staying behind.

∫ ∫ ∫

It was a long time later that night that he let go of the guilt and felt instead the buzz of excitement about the drug raid. The phone rang. Keith had told him earlier that he couldn't come over and he thought the call was from him. But when he looked down he saw that it was from Sidney. "All *right*! Let's hear the dirt." He clicked it on. "Sid! What's the 411?"

"You asshole!"

He sat up. "What?"

"Mike and I go down there with guns drawn, and guess what? Nada. Bumpkis. Nothing there. I look like an idiot."

"*What?*"

"There was nothing there, Skyler. You have a lot of explaining to do."

CHAPTER SEVENTEEN

Sidney came over about an hour later, pushed through the door, and laid into him right away. She was in the middle of her tirade before she noticed his eye. "What the hell happened to you?"

His hand came up automatically and tried to cover it. The purple was beginning to turn a sickly yellow. "Oh. It's nothing. Jamie elbowed me."

She tore his hand away and stared at it. "Keith did it. I'll kill him."

"Keith didn't do it! Jeez, why is that the first thing everyone thinks?"

"Because you're an idiot and you keep dating that guy when I told you not to."

"You can't tell me who to date!"

"Goddammit, Skyler!" She kicked the coffee table and flopped down on the sofa. "This was one fucked up day. Not only did this whole thing blow up in my face—and my captain thinks I'm a lunatic, thank you very much—but now Mike isn't speaking to me and that's really tough because he's supposed to be my partner."

He sank down next to her. "What happened?"

"Don't change the subject. What the hell happened with this supposed pot farm?"

"I don't know. It was there a few days ago."

"Someone must have tipped them off."

"You didn't find *anything*?"

"Nope. Traces, but not enough to arrest anyone. The owner was one pissed off dude. Threatened to sue."

"So now what happens?"

"Not much. We keep an eye peeled. But chances are they won't show up there again. They probably have lots of farms all over the place."

"You mean in the canyon?"

"Yes, that, too. But sometimes these operations move into suburbia. Regular houses fronting for farms. Rooms or the whole house devoted to just growing weed. It's becoming quite the enterprise."

"Wow. I'm sorry. But isn't it better to know about it and keep an eye on the guy than not to have known?"

"I suppose. I told everyone over and over that you were a reliable source."

"I hope so." That was crazy! They must have worked all night moving that much weed. How did they find out? Maybe that shack wasn't empty after all and they saw him and his friends that night. How messed up was this?

He looked over at Sidney, fuming and angry. Of course, *he* was still a little mad at *her* for arresting Jeff. But this was kind of a big deal. This kind of thing could become a career-ender. He hoped it wouldn't come to that.

But then she had said something about a problem with Mike. Sidney was just as much a virgin with relationships as Skyler was. Maybe even worse. "So Sid, what's this other problem you were talking about? What was this disagreement you had with Mike?"

"It was about procedure. Dating procedure. I gave him shit, he gave me shit, and then it escalated from there. I *told* you dating someone at work was a stupid idea. We should have just stuck to fucking."

"But you guys were already sleeping together."

"That was *different!*"

"I don't get it. What was this shit you were giving him?"

"Why is this *my* fault?"

Skyler snorted. "No idea. Maybe it's that demure façade you're projecting that threw me off."

She squinted at him and crossed her arms over her chest. And then she wrestled angrily with her jacket and tore off her holster with the gun in it and tossed it on the coffee table. Skyler jumped back.

"Shit! Is that going to go off?"

"The safety's on, you pussy."

"It's just…you know. I don't like guns."

"Can we get back to *my* problem? I just told Mike that I didn't want to do the friend thing."

Skyler pushed the gun away gingerly with his foot until he was satisfied it was far enough away from him. "What 'friend thing'?"

"You know? I don't want to meet his friends, he doesn't have to meet mine."

"Wait a minute. You don't want him to meet us?"

"How well did that work out for you when Keith showed up?"

"We cleared that up. These are things that have to be done. Friends are important. And besides, we don't really have anything on you that we can squeal to Mike about." She was silently chewing on a manicured nail when it hit him.

"You're *ashamed* of us?"

"*No!* Don't be an idiot."

"But it's because we're gay, right? You don't want him to be uncomfortable. Well, isn't *that* nice!"

"That is not it at all. You are way out of line."

"Then what is it?"

She shook her head and leaned back. "It's not just friends, it's family. He's got a really big family."

He scooted closer. "You're afraid to meet his family and friends?"

Still gnawing on a nail she nodded.

"Ah, Sidney." He put his arms around her and laid her head on his shoulder.

"There're all these aunts he keeps telling me about and they're all like these dainty women with flowers in their hair. Skyler, I have never been a dainty woman let alone one with a flower in my hair!"

That's for sure. Aloud, he said, "But that's not what seems to appeal to Mike, right? I mean, he wouldn't want to go out with you if that's the case."

"But don't you see? He'll get to compare us. I'll be standing there all Jewish and his family will be there, all Filipino, and that will be that."

"So *that's* what this is? You think the culture clash will be too much for him?"

"Can't it just be us for a while? So he gets used to me? Likes me more than, you know, those other women?"

"Filipino women?"

"Yeah."

He rubbed her arm. "I think you're making a big deal out of this. But if it really does bother you, why don't you just tell him you just want it to be the two of you for a while? Tell him you're not used to dating."

She looked up at him. "Is that what you told Keith?"

"He knew I never dated before. So he was cool with that. And he's cool with a lot of things. He's not a criminal, Sidney. He's sweet and loving and he would never lift a hand to me. Why can't you trust me on this?"

"Because I love you too much and don't want to see you hurt."

"I won't be. Keith is very protective of me. When the guy who hit me came to the school— Oh shit!"

Sidney snapped upright. "Skyler! You fucking lied to me! Who is this guy?"

"Okay, okay!" He related the whole James Fischer incident

without mentioning names, while she seethed at him. He was glad the gun was across the table.

"You are such an idiot! What am I supposed to do with you?"

"That's what Keith said."

"Well for the first time I agree with the guy. I must be wrong about him because he's got to be a saint to put up with you."

"He ain't no saint," he said, waggling his brows.

She punched his arm.

"Ow! What was that for?"

"Being a jerk." She touched his cheek below his eye with a surprisingly gentle finger. "Does it still hurt?"

"No. It just looks horrible. I tried make-up but it doesn't work. Maybe I need a pair of Jackie-O's."

"Aviator goggles." She grabbed his chin and turned his head this way and that. "Want to press charges?"

"I don't know. I tried to hit him, too."

"Tried?"

"I missed."

"The thumb goes on the outside—"

"Shut up!"

They both sat quietly until Sidney finally said, "Where is the goddamned alcohol?"

♫ ♫ ♫

Drinking margaritas, they watched old movies on TCM till around one in the morning. Sidney yawned as she rose from the sofa.

"I'd better get home," she said, heading for the doorway. "Fishbreath misses me and I'm sure I haven't cleaned the litter box in days."

"Pet your kitty for me. He's the only pussy I like."

"Oh ha, ha." She kissed him on the cheek. "Whatcha doing

tomorrow?"

"I'm going to Evan's funeral."

"Oh. Well, goodnight, Skyler. Love you."

"Love you, too."

He locked the door, suddenly dreading the weekend.

∫ ∫ ∫

He could think of better ways to spend a Saturday. But that's what friends did. And it was such awful circumstances. After the funeral at the chapel they all made their way to the graveside. Hills of green were speckled with white crosses and plaques gleaming in the sun almost as far as the eye could see. Jeff wore his uniform with its medals on his chest and Skyler still couldn't believe that this multi-honored man had been dishonorably discharged. How did these generals sleep at night with that on their conscience?

Jeff's sister, Cindy, was a prettier, slimmer, version of him. She wore a dark dress and pumps and had her arm through his the whole time. Jeff had other friends there. Some were in their dress uniforms—other grunts—with a sprinkling of both gay and straight friends. A pastor read a few words Skyler was sure Jeff had written and then two old retired vets removed the flag from the coffin and ceremonially folded it. Once it was a tight triangle, the uniformed veteran tried to hand it to Jeff's sister and in a strained moment, she whispered something and ended up handing it herself to Jeff.

Clutching it to his chest, his mouth quivered. His eyes were hidden behind sunglasses while he looked straight ahead. His sister, to her credit, clutched his arm tighter.

Seven retired vets with "Memorial Rifle Squad" patches on their sleeves fired off their rifles in the air three times while a recording played taps. Skyler wiped his eyes. He tried to swallow past a hot lump in his throat.

Afterward, everyone mingled a bit, leaving Jeff alone by the graveside.

Cindy came up to him. "You must be Skyler. He said you were

really, really blond."

He gave her an awkward smile. "It was good that you came."

She looked back at Jeff and shook her head. "I should have done it years ago. It was so stupid. I sided with my parents. It was a dumb thing to do."

Skyler shrugged. There wasn't much to say to that.

"He has a lot of friends," she went on. "I'm glad."

"Yeah. Jeff and Evan were a nice couple."

"Are the police still accusing Jeff? Court date's in two weeks. Jeff said that maybe they were looking at someone else."

"I don't know. But I feel something will break soon." If *he* had anything to say about it. Skyler wasn't done with James Fischer. Not by a long shot. He knew that man had something to do with the murder.

Skyler went over to Jeff's house with everyone else for cold cuts and salads. He chatted with some of Jeff's friends and after an hour or so, he took Jeff aside to wish him well.

He was about to leave when he turned back to Jeff. "By the way, that orchid farm?"

"Yeah?"

"Did Evan ever mention anyone named Ed Fallows?"

"No. I don't think so. Unless that was his friend Ed from college. He never mentioned a last name."

"At University of Redlands?"

"Yeah. He talked about this guy Ed that was a really good friend of his. Until he found out he was gay. Then he lit into Evan with some religious bullshit and never spoke to him again."

Was it possible it was the same guy? He gave Jeff a last hug and kissed his cheek. "Call me, okay? We'll get together."

"I liked your friends," said Jeff. "What little I saw of them."

"They'd love to meet you properly. Call me."

"I will."

Skyler walked down the front steps and along the concrete path. He wanted to get home to his computer and look up the University of Redlands alumni association.

§ § §

It didn't take him long at all. He logged in and did a search, and there he was. Ed Fallows. Class of 2006. It didn't mean it was the same guy but—who was he kidding? It *had* to be! And Jeff had said that Fallows dropped Evan's friendship once he discovered he was gay. How cold was that? And he certainly hadn't changed his tune when it came to football. How did they hire people for the job anyway? Gave them a "Spot the Homo" test? Except it hadn't worked very well when hiring Keith. How did he stand it over there with all the jokes and invectives? It had to really wear him down.

But what did this all have to do with Evan? Surely Fallows wouldn't have contacted Evan, would he? So maybe Evan had contacted Fallows. But why? How did he even know Fallows was working at the orchid farm? The thought that Evan would resort to growing pot to earn a living made Skyler queasy. He just couldn't see it in a million years. But desperation was a mighty stern mistress.

He didn't get it. He was missing something; that was for sure. He knew Sidney didn't want him to mess with it but there was so much going on out of his control it made him angry. Like all this stuff at the school that no one seemed to be doing anything about. Julia and the skinhead football team. It was probably them defacing the GSA flyers. Keith could only do so much to stem the tide. It was just so thick over there with hate and prejudice. He didn't know how he could have imagined Keith going out of his way to change grades for troglodytes like that. But someone had. And it *was* probably Wes Sherman Jr. He had been a computer wiz and had the know-how to do it. He must have been paid a lot. Imagine doing that at his father's own school. He probably stole the codes right out of his dad's files. What a dick.

He wished he could find out who did it and blow it wide open. Something was going to give soon. He knew it. And it didn't look good for the school.

But wait a minute. *He* knew a computer wiz.

He grabbed his phone and punched in Jamie's number.

CHAPTER EIGHTEEN

"Skyler, I don't like this," said Jamie, walking close beside him as they entered the darkened school. "You could get into a lot of trouble."

The empty hallway echoed with their timid footsteps. "I have to know."

"This is a felony, you know. Hacking into a school computer."

Skyler stopped and looked at his friend. He was just a willowy shadow with spiky hair. "Then why are you doing this?"

The shadow drew closer, put his hand on Skyler's neck, and pulled him in for a quick kiss on the lips. "Because what are friends for? Maybe we'll share a jail cell."

"Don't even joke about that." He looked around cautiously. Skyler moved ahead again, making sure Jamie was close behind him. "Can you really tell if someone hacked in and changed grades or not?"

"There are ways to look around and see. But it's not going to tell me who."

"But if it tells you how might it also tell you who? I mean, an expert as opposed to an amateur?"

"It might."

"I thought computers were all precise and everything."

"They are. But... Never mind, it's too hard to explain. Let's just get in there and get it over with."

Skyler had a key that would get him into the office but not into Mr. Sherman's. "That doesn't matter," Jamie reassured. Actually, it didn't reassure Skyler at all.

"You mean you can hack into his computer from any of these?"

"I didn't even have to come, but it's easier getting the pass codes from here." They didn't turn on the lights, didn't want to alert anyone of their presence, but Skyler had his Maglite. Jamie sat at the first computer for one of the office assistants and opened the metal desk drawer. "It's usually right here...yup. There it is." The pass code was written on a piece of paper taped to the inside of the drawer.

"You're kidding me."

"People put them in all kinds of obvious places. Behind their family pictures, under their coffee mugs, written on the sides of computer monitors. Safety schmafety."

He woke the computer and began typing. He was in the system immediately. Skyler leaned over his shoulder. "That is so scary when you do that."

"It's a good thing Mrs. Ewing raised an honest boy. Now, let's have a look at the grades."

"Will the firewalls and securities be able to tell you've gotten into the system?"

"Not with this." He plugged a flash drive into a port. "This will confuse the system to make it think that no one is here."

"Scary."

"You have no idea." Jamie tapped away on the keyboard and Skyler leaned on his shoulder, watching the screens flash by. Jamie was going deep into the system, finding holes, tunnels, all sorts of ways Skyler had no idea about. Jamie read rows of code and more foreign things than Skyler had seen since *Tron*. It seemed to take a long while and Skyler was getting nervous. He kept going to the office doorway and checking down the hall to see if anyone was coming. He looked at his watch under the dim glow of a security light. Getting late. He hoped Jamie would wrap up soon.

He came back into the office and Jamie was shutting things down, fingers still whizzing over the keyboard. At last he put the computer to sleep, pulled out his thumb drive, and snapped it shut. "Well, that's that."

"That's what? What is that?"

"Can we go and I'll tell you?"

"The Shakespearean?"

"Let's."

♫ ♫ ♫

Skyler drove him over to the pub on State Street. It was late but it was still warm and noisy inside. Portraits of kings and queens of England hung on the high walls of dark wainscoting. Flags of the various British football clubs hung around the old-fashioned bar.

They managed to find a booth and slid in. Jamie studied the picture of Shakespeare right over their table. "There is just no era when that haircut looked good," he said.

A waitress dressed in a peasant blouse, flouncy skirt, and laced bodice came up and said, "Gents? What will it be?"

Jamie smiled at her. "I love your dress."

She smiled back and traced her finger over the laces of the bodice. "Thanks."

He took a cursory look at the menu and then pushed it aside. "You order, Skyler. I never remember what sort of beer I like here."

Skyler smiled at the waitress. "Two Boddies and an order of chips."

"Coming up."

Jamie watched her walk away before leaning toward Skyler. "What did we just order?"

"Boddington's beer and a plate of fries."

"Oh good." He spread his hands on the table and then grimaced, picking them up again and wiping them on his trousers.

"So? What did you find?"

Jamie looked around for a napkin to wipe his hands. "Oh it's been hacked into, all right."

"By whom?"

"I can't tell that."

"I thought you said you could."

"Well it's not like they hack in and leave a note. 'Thanks for letting me hack. Love, Wes.' It was hacked into about two months ago. That's what I can tell just with a quick look."

Two months. That let Keith off the hook and puts Wes in the spotlight once more. It cheered Skyler. "Wow. So what was changed? Can you tell?"

"Looks like you were right. Most of the hacking is definitely in the section with the grades."

"Is it something to do with football?"

"I don't know what you mean. It's not laid out like that. It's alphabetical."

"Oh. Well, this is proof, though. Did it look like a pro?"

"Oh, definitely. But I knew what to look for."

He knew it! He knew there was something fishy going on. He was just glad they could find it out without anyone knowing they did. He didn't think there was any way to trace them to it... except by their *fingerprints*! Damn! He had to start remembering about that.

The beers arrived and they both drank through the sweet, creamy foam. "Mmm. I remember I like this," said Jamie.

"I know. That's why I order it for you every time we come here."

Jamie leaned back against the maroon vinyl seat and took in the atmosphere. "I like this place. Why don't we come here more often?"

"I guess because we either go to The Bean or to Trixx."

"Maybe now that you're all domestic with a boyfriend you won't be going to Trixx so much."

"He's not my boyfriend," he said automatically.

"He's as good as. Why are you fighting it, Sky?"

He wriggled a little in his seat. "I'm…not fighting it. It's just… Jamie, I don't know what I'm feeling. I like him. A lot. But…"

"But what?"

"It's just weird. Seeing the same guy. Sleeping with him. Only him."

"But you like that part, right?"

"Yeah! He's fantastic."

The waitress returned and set the plate of fries with a bundle of bottles under her arm: mustard, vinegar, and ketchup. Jamie grabbed the ketchup and poured a good dollop on the side of the plate. He took a fat fry and dipped it in, swirling it around until he covered the whole tip in red before popping it in his mouth and taking a bite.

"Then what's the problem?" he said between chewing.

"Everyone keeps asking me that. And I don't know what to tell them. Maybe I'm just not the boyfriend type."

"So you spend time with him, go out, stay in," he grinned and winked, "and you don't think you're boyfriends? Sweetie, you aren't paying attention. 'Cause you never did any of that with me."

Skyler tried to remember. "I guess I'd call you, you'd come over or I'd go over there, we'd fuck, and then I'd leave."

"I asked you to spend the night plenty of times."

"I know. I just…didn't want to get that involved."

"Ha, ha. Joke's on you. Now you're more involved with me than ever without even the benefit of fucking."

He shook his head, grinning. "I know. You are so needy."

Jamie threw a fry and Skyler ducked it. He sighed, hesitated, and finally said, "Monday night Keith's coming over with sandwiches and we're going to watch football on TV."

Jamie threw down his fry. "That settles it. You're boyfriends.

I mean you and *football?* De-*ni*-al!" he sang.

Skyler chewed slowly on a fry. So what *was* the big deal? So what if Keith was his…his boyfriend. He hadn't even felt like seeing anyone else since that first date. Even when they were at Trixx Skyler had looked but hadn't really wanted to touch. He had fallen into monogamy without even thinking twice about it.

Suddenly he looked up wide-eyed at Jamie. "Oh my God. I have a boyfriend!"

♪ ♪ ♪

Keith had been disappointingly busy all weekend, which meant no Sunday night with the man and, consequently, no Monday morning lying around in bed with him, either.

With no Keith to distract him, Skyler rose early to do his running before getting ready for school. The air was crisp and cold. His breath clouded around his face as he sang softly to his iPod playing Sam and Dave's "Soul Man." He got in a good few miles before getting back home for a shower, and even had enough time to slip over to The Bean. He liked getting back to his routine, but he was also finding the apartment quiet without Keith tromping around.

He stood in line. Both Cashmere and Philip were behind the counter, working at a frenzied pace. But Philip spotted him and waved.

When it was finally his turn, Philip came over. "Ethiopian?"

"With a shot."

Philip wiped his hands down his green apron, got down the jar of Ethiopian beans from a shelf and poured some in the grinder. The noisy grinder whirred for a few seconds before he moved on to the next task.

Skyler, a bundle of energy, was bouncing on the balls of his feet, hands pressed to the glass case with its carefully laid out croissants, apple pastries, and cinnamon buns. "And guess what, Philip?"

Philip had his back to him, busy taking out the spent grounds from the espresso machine and dumping them in the compost bin. He scooped the perfectly ground beans into the espresso basket. "What?"

"I have a boyfriend."

He whipped around so fast the new grounds flew out of the little silver basket. He didn't even notice. "You what?"

Skyler felt his face heat up and he shrugged, trying to act casual. "You know. A boyfriend. Like most people have."

"Who?"

He squinted at him. "Who do you think?"

"I thought you weren't dating him anymore."

"Why would you think that?"

"Oh. Right. Because you never do anything sensible that someone tells you to do. Especially someone with a detective's badge."

"She doesn't know him like I do."

"Thank goodness for that." He stooped to clean up his mess and then started again, filling the basket, tamping it down, and clicking it in place on the machine. He flipped the switch and turned back to Skyler. "We *are* talking about Keith, right?"

Skyler looked around surreptitiously. "Yes!"

Philip leaned his forearms on the tall counter and rested his chin on them. "For real? When did you come upon this revelation?"

"Last night when I was talking to Jamie. I was trying to deny it for the umpteen millionth time and I suddenly thought, why? Why should I deny it? I really like the guy. He's good to me. He's romantic."

A middle-aged woman waiting for her coffee at the counter turned toward Skyler with a dreamy smile on her face. When she noticed him looking at her, she grinned. "I think it's sweet."

"See? Even she thinks it's sweet," he said to Philip.

"All right. It's you who risks the wrath of Sidney."

"She's got her own boy troubles. Or is that *gay* troubles? I'm hoping it distracts her."

"So she's really dating her partner, huh?"

"She's giving it a shot."

Philip turned back to his business and quickly got Skyler's coffee ready. He popped a lid on and handed it over the counter. "See you tonight?"

"Keith's coming over and we're watching the Steelers play."

"Oh my God! You *do* have a boyfriend!"

♫ ♫ ♫

The day moved on quickly from there. Before he knew it, his last class of the day was over. As usual, Rick and Alex stuck around. Not usually, Amber and Heather did, too.

Skyler looked from one to the other. "So what's this?"

Amber smiled her all-collegiate smile. "Alex is my date for the Winter Formal and Heather is Rick's. See? That way we can all go."

"Oh?"

Rick was smiling his million dollar smile but Alex didn't look as pleased. "We talked about it at the GSA last Friday," said Rick, his tone seeming to add his thanks toward Skyler for the encouragement. "And we decided to maybe take the heat off me with the presence of Ms. Munson."

He looked toward Heather. She shrugged. "I'm just going along for the ride." She punched Alex playfully on the shoulder. "And this stud will hang with Amber. Don't they make a cute couple?"

"A cute couple of what?" Skyler said, unable to resist.

"Dude!" said Alex to Heather, rubbing his shoulder.

"So we'll all see you this Friday night, right Mr. Foxe?" asked Amber, batting her lashes. Was she still that clueless?

"Bye, you guys."

He watched them go with a smile. Things were looking up.

And that evening, they were even better. Keith showed up wearing a football jersey with his own name on the back. Skyler assumed it was his college jersey. He also arrived with beer and a huge submarine sandwich.

"Just how many of us will be at this party?" asked Skyler, helping him put it on the kitchen table.

"Just us. But I get a good appetite going when I'm watching a game."

O-kay, thought Skyler salaciously.

Keith sliced the sandwich and even poured Skyler's beer in a glass. Keith preferred to drink out of the bottle. They settled in the living room with the flat screen and in between bites, Keith explained the strategies.

Skyler looked at it like a medieval battle, which in a sense it was. They talked about Keith's own strategies for football and how he saw the strengths of the players and how that all went into his formulations. It was all far more complicated than just picking the biggest guys in the line and making them run toward a goal post.

Skyler found himself getting into the game and later, he made popcorn, spilling a lot of it on his floor when he jumped up and cheered when the Steelers scored.

The game wrapped up with the post game and the talking heads going over what went wrong and what went right. Skyler watched Keith watching it, noting his concentration and how his jaw clenched when he seemed to be working something out. The man loved football, no question.

Skyler scooted closer while Keith watched the TV. Experimentally, he slid his hand over his muscular thigh encased in its running pants. Absently, Keith's hand covered his, thumb rubbing back and forth over Skyler's knuckles.

All at once, Keith looked over and smiled. He leaned in and

gave Skyler a wet kiss. "I hope you weren't too bored."

"No. It was kind of fun, actually."

"More fun with a room full of guys."

Skyler traced up his thigh higher. "Maybe not."

Keith followed the trail of the hand with his eyes. His features softened and he turned toward Skyler. One hand came up to Skyler's cheek and he leaned in. Keith's mouth was warm and soft, tongue teasing Skyler's lips until he opened them and welcomed it in. Their lips caressed while Keith's other hand skimmed up his thigh to palm Skyler's balls and growing erection, and squeezed. Skyler raised his hips and ground his dick into that kneading hand.

Keith tore his lips away from the kiss to latch onto Skyler's neck at the sensitive spot below his ear. With a moan, Skyler laid his head back against the sofa, allowing Keith's lips to lash at his skin. Arousal rippled up and down his body, and his dick felt especially hard. Keith's hand rubbed his groin through the material of his jeans and Skyler thought he'd pop his zipper at any moment.

The doorbell.

Keith gave one more lick to Skyler's pale neck and sat back. His face was flushed and he was panting. "You gotta be kidding me."

"Maybe they'll go away," said Skyler, just as the doorbell rang again. "I swear to God," he said, whipping up from the couch. "If it's Jehovah's Witnesses, I'm flashing them."

He threw the deadbolt and pulled open the door, ready to give whomever what for—

"Mom!"

CHAPTER NINETEEN

Cynthia Foxe stepped into the room, wearing a lavender sweater under her black Pendleton blazer. Skyler quickly grabbed Keith's jacket from where the man left it draped over a dining room chair, and held it casually over his arm to hide his erection.

Keith sat up quickly and grabbed a sofa pillow to do the same thing.

"It's so dark in here," she said before spotting Keith. "Oh!"

Skyler flipped on the light in the kitchen and stood awkwardly by his dining room table. "Mom, what are you doing here? So late?"

She looked at her watch and ticked her head. "I know, honey, but I just got done with my book group and I thought I'd swing over before going home. Your light was on so I figured you were correcting papers or something. I have that grapeseed oil you said you wanted. I was at Trader Joe's earlier today so I picked up an extra one for you."

She handed over a paper bag and Skyler took it. Cynthia turned to Keith. "I don't believe we've met. I'm Skyler's mother, Cynthia Foxe." She held out a manicured hand with gold bangles on the wrist. Keith stepped forward, the pillow still in his hand over his groin.

"Keith Fletcher. A pleasure to meet you, Mrs. Foxe."

She glanced at Skyler and he supplied the answer to the question in her eyes. "Keith is a teacher at James Polk. We were just...uh..."

"We were just watching a football game. I'm new at the school, an assistant football coach, and Skyler was nice enough to invite me over."

Cynthia folded her hands in front of her. "Skyler, when did you get interested in football?"

When I met him. But aloud he said, "Oh, recently. One of my students was having a bit of disciplinary problems until I got him on the team."

She smiled and turned to Keith. "I knew he would be a wonderful teacher. He's so great with people. He understands kids. Probably because he's still one himself," and she ruffled his hair.

"Mom!" Vainly, he tried to smooth the mussed locks.

"Yeah," agreed Keith with a soft smile. "I hear great things from the other kids about Mr. Foxe."

Skyler felt himself blush. This was too weird. He definitely needed to get rid of his mother. He took the few steps to the breakfast counter and left the grapeseed oil there before anxiously turning to her again. "Are you staying, Mom?"

"Oh, no. I just stopped by to see my favorite son and to drop that off. I know how you like to do your gourmet cooking. Besides, it's a school night and we all have to get up early for work."

"She still thinks I'm a teenager," he lamented.

"She's right," said Keith, slowly pulling his jacket from Skyler's grasp and tossing the pillow back to the couch. "Not that you're a teenager, but that I should be going." Cynthia Foxe's arrival had successfully dissolved Skyler's hard-on, and also, so it seemed, Keith's.

"Do you have to?" said Skyler, looking between Keith and his mother.

Keith smiled. "Yeah. It's late."

"Well I won't keep you," said Cynthia. She turned toward the door first. Keith started to follow, but Skyler stepped forward on his toes and said, "Oh, Keith, you can't go until I show you the… thing…with the thing." He gestured wildly, making Keith's smile broader. His eyes glittered with amusement.

"Oh the *thing*. But shouldn't I walk your mother out?"

"Don't be silly," she said. "I'll be fine."

"It's no trouble, Mrs. Foxe. I was just leaving anyway. I'll see you at school, Skyler."

Skyler tried to mask his disappointment. "Okay. I'll show you the...the thing some other time."

"Looking forward to it," he said, stifling a laugh.

Skyler embraced his mother and kissed her cheek. She kissed his and wiped the lipstick away with a thumb. "Teach well," she said. "Goodnight, sweetie."

"Goodnight, Mom, and thanks for the oil."

"Cook me something nice with it sometime," she said from the landing.

Keith poked his head back in as Cynthia made her way down the stairs. "Maybe *we* can do something with that oil sometime," he said huskily. "Goodnight, Skyler."

Skyler leaned his forehead against the closed door and moaned.

♬ ♬ ♬

At school, all the new GSA flyers were now laminated or put behind glass bulletin boards. Skyler was pleased that nothing would happen to them, except that all week, the ones that weren't behind glass were summarily taken down. Skyler noticed, too, that Heather and Amber began sitting at lunch with some of the kids that had showed up to the GSA meetings. He was glad to see the closing of the ranks.

Rick and Alex, of course, steered clear of them when they were with the GSA members, but Skyler did notice that the two boys started to hang out with Heather and Amber when they were alone. New friendships were forming. New adventures to conquer. Ah, adolescence.

At least there were no more swastikas or hateful diatribes written on flyers, and Skyler did a lot of extra patrolling in the corridors when he had a chance, just to make certain.

Friday, the night of the dance, finally rolled around, and Skyler was ready to rock. After he got home that night and had his dinner of grilled tilapia and mustard greens, he popped into the shower.

All week, even through the drama of the GSA, Skyler had also thought about Jeff. The man had a court date next Tuesday and Sidney had seemed no closer to arresting anyone else.

Under the spray of water, Skyler rubbed his chest and arms with the foamy bar of oatmeal soap. It seemed to him that the murder might have something to do with James Fischer. The man was violent, that much was certain. Maybe he should have pressed charges, after all. Maybe he should have just told Sidney about the whole thing. He was already in trouble with her. He might as well.

He shampooed, running the foam through his fingers and using his soapy hands to wash his torso. Ed Fallows kept giving him the stink eye all week, too. Skyler had wanted to fuck up his life by getting the orchid farm shut down but instead he'd made Sidney and himself look like fools. What the hell had happened? Who tipped him off?

He rinsed himself off and applied conditioner, letting the hot water pound against his shoulder blades. It was still a puzzle, though, as to how Evan had found his friend Ed again. Jamie said that a person kept a business card because they wanted to do business. Illegal pot business? But how would he have known about that? Who told *him*? Not Jeff. They both hated drugs. Maybe it was simpler than that. Maybe Evan just wanted a job. Shit! Maybe there was an ad or something.

He quickly finished and toweled dry, and with his hair still wet and the towel still wrapped around his waist, he sat at his desk and opened his laptop. He got on the internet and looked on Craig's List for jobs. He did a search and there it was, dated three weeks ago. "Redlands Orchid Farm seeks reliable clerk. Disabled and Vets welcome." Evan had applied! He must have. He must have gone down there somehow without Jeff knowing and met up again with Ed Fallows. Did Ed tell him to go fuck himself or had he felt sorry for him and offered him a job?

Skyler Googled Redlands Orchid Farm and found the website.

He clicked it and looked around again. Nothing new, nothing different. He scanned to the bottom of the page where it said "owner." Sidney said the guy had been royally pissed at the raid and threatened to sue. Bastard. Skyler looked and read the name for the first time.

"Oh *shit*! Shit! Shitty shit *shit*!"

The owner was J. Fischer.

CHAPTER TWENTY

No, this was not happening! Fischer owned the freaking orchid farm? Maybe *that* was the connection. Maybe Fischer suggested Evan go to the farm to get a job... "But maybe *that* wasn't the job they offered him!"

Skyler paced back and forth in his underwear, stocking feet slapping against the wood floor. Shit! Sidney said that sometimes these pot ringleaders recruited people to grow it in their houses. It could be that *that* is what Fischer was harassing Evan about. And Evan hadn't wanted to. He wouldn't have done anything illegal, especially if it brought any more shame down on Jeff's head.

It seemed to fit. And then Fischer got tired of hearing him say no. He came over when Evan was cleaning his gun, got all violent, and shoved it in his mouth...

He felt queasy and sat down at the kitchen table. "I have to call Sidney." He grabbed his phone from the charging cradle and punched in her number.

Voice mail.

"Dammit. Isn't she ever around when I need her?" The beep. "Sid, it's me. Now don't get mad. But I think I've cracked the Jeff Dwyer case. Remember that guy who hit me? Well, what I didn't tell you—and I know I should have—is that he's some sort of counselor at the VA Center. I sort of accused him of killing Evan and he got all homophobic and medieval on me. I also met him sneaking around Jeff's place that night I went over to get his meds. I know I should have told you that, too. But get this: his name is *James Fischer*. Ring any bells? Yeah, it's the guy who owns our friendly neighborhood orchid and pot farm. There was an ad on Craig's List for a clerk at the farm and it said that *disabled* and *vets* were welcomed. The ad ran around the time that Evan could have seen it. Evan also went to college with one of the guys who works there, Ed Fallows who also happens to be a part time coach at James Polk High. Do you see a pattern forming? God, I wish you were there." He blew out a breath. "I have to get dressed. I'm chaperoning the school dance tonight. But call me when you get this."

Skyler clicked off, stared at the floor and then looked up at the clock. Shit. He was going to be late.

♪ ♪ ♪

Skyler arrived on the dot, when the volunteers were supposed to get there, but many were already milling around hanging last minute decorations, probably had been for hours. He straightened his bow tie as he passed through the cafeteria's double doors. Amber and her crew had done an amazing job with their theme "Life in a Snow Globe," and it looked pretty good. In the front by the stage was a miniature scene with a snow-covered cottage, pine trees, and a snowman. Twinkly lights were arranged along the walls and stage, where the DJ was doing a sound check. Giant snowflakes hung from the ceiling with spotlights on them, and there was even a projector shooting images of snow falling across the walls and dance floor.

He spotted Amber directing some kids on a ladder and he headed toward her. "Amber! This is fantastic!"

She blushed down her neck and bare shoulders. "Thank you, Mr. Foxe. Everyone really worked hard."

"I can see that. I hope you're getting lots of pictures."

"We are." She blinked at him shyly. "You look very nice, Mr. Foxe."

He smoothed down his lapels. "Oh, thanks. You look very nice, too." He perused her lilac off the shoulder dress with its tulle skirt and her medium height pumps. Very tasteful.

Then he turned around and spotted Heather.

She was wearing shiny black combat boots under her long, slim red dress with a black leather bustier over the bodice. *I guess those must be her formal combat boots.* The whole had a sort of vampire vibe. Her eye make-up was still dark and heavy around each eye, but she had opted for normal color on her lips, perhaps in deference to her date, not that they'd be kissing or anything.

And just where *was* her "date"? Ah!

Rick loped in and Skyler's jaw dropped. He was wearing a Pronto Uomo white Nehru tux, its long jacket swishing around his hips. "Wow," was all he could say.

Rick struck a pose. "'Wow' is right, Mr. Foxe. Am I stylin' or am I stylin'?"

"You be stylin', Rick, no question." He high fived and Rick smacked his hand. He looked around. Kids were still setting up chairs along the walls. Tables with snowflake centerpieces sported bowls of chips and M&Ms. There was another table by the kitchen with a couple of punchbowls with a stack of clear plastic cups beside it along with a battalion of bottled water laid out in regimented rows.

Skyler smiled and felt a little thrill of excitement in his chest. This was his first school dance as a teacher. He'd thought about this kind of thing for a long time and had been really looking forward to it. But it also gave him a pang of something else, of regret and of lost opportunities. He wished he could have gone with a boy to *his* school dances. Bringing your gay date to the prom seemed like the norm these days, but not at James Polk High. Skyler hadn't had the nerve when he was in school. He had still been in the closet then. When he'd gone to dances, he always brought Sidney.

Amber, Rick, and Heather were here. Where was Alex? If the boy hadn't been such a jock, Alex might have taken Rick to the dance, no problem, at least no problem to Alex. He guessed Rick still had issues at home. He empathized with that. He couldn't imagine sitting down to tell his own mother. What the hell would he say? What would *she* say?

He spotted the Vice Principal, Alice Goodwin, earnestly talking to Amber, with Amber nodding her head vigorously and checking a clipboard sitting in the crook of her arm. Amber had only told him last month how she had had ambitions to run for student government, and when the position of sophomore secretary opened up, a hasty election got her in. She was in her element, all right.

Skyler walked over just as Amber scampered away to do whatever it was she was doing. "Hi, Alice," he said. "You look lovely tonight."

Her eyes traveled down at her long beige skirt and sparkly cropped jacket. It was the wrong color on her and in a style too old for her age. She looked like the mother of the bride. "Thank you, Skyler. And don't you look elegant."

He brushed his hand down his black jacket. "Thanks. We certainly clean up well."

"I'm not expecting any trouble tonight, but that is why you are here. Just keep an eye on the corridors and check the boys' bathroom periodically. Encourage the boys and girls to dance together. Go ahead and chat with the wallflowers. However, we certainly *don't* encourage teachers to dance with students." That was a relief, he thought, looking across the room at Amber. "You can take a break or two. Just switch off with Coach Fletcher and Coach Fallows."

What? Ed Fallows was going to be here tonight? That sucked.

"Also, I have asked the DJ to keep the music to an acceptable intensity, but I've been to enough of these to know that the DJs prefer a decibel level that inspires leaves to fall off of trees." He laughed. Sounded like the guy at Trixx. "So keep an eye—or I suppose rather an ear on that."

Her attention was caught by something across the room. "Oh. Please excuse me, Skyler. I think you've got the gist of it."

He saluted. "No problem, Alice. Well in hand." When he turned around to survey the room he saw Ed Fallows enter. He was wearing a regular dark suit and tugging at his tie. His eyes locked on Skyler's for a moment before he sneered and turned away.

"Dickhead," muttered Skyler and wandered near the crepe-swagged tables, checking out the decorations.

It was getting close to the witching hour and still no sign of Alex or Keith. Skyler joined the kids outside the cafeteria at the check-in table and students from his classes whistled and catcalled upon seeing him.

"Mr. Foxe! Check him out!" cried Drew O'Connor from his fifth period class. He was one of the nicer football players and had taken Alex under his wing.

"And check you out, Drew. Slick."

Drew pulled at his labels with his thumbs. "This old thing? I make it look good."

His date clutched his arm and chortled. She was a slim girl in a frilly layered number. She had braces but didn't seem to mind and smiled a big toothy grin. Skyler didn't know her name.

It was fun to see his students all dressed up, like little ladies and gentlemen. This was all part of the ritual, part of the long path to adulthood. Soon enough they would have to start thinking of careers and which colleges to go to in order to make that happen. Lots of grown-up decisions ahead, not the least of which involved sex. Skyler was well aware that many of the students had already had sex before they even got to high school. But this mating dance was all a part of the socialization of their tribe. Even if that tribe had zits on their faces and braces on their teeth.

Alex finally showed up. He looked stiff in his tux with his collar tight around his barrel-shaped neck. "Hey, Alex," said Skyler, checking him off the list. "Your date's already in there."

"Huh?" His panicked face broke out in a sweat.

Chill, dude. "Amber. *Your date.* She's inside."

"Oh! Yeah. She's in there." He threaded his way through the crowd at the door and squeezed in.

Skyler rolled his eyes. This was going to be a long night.

CHAPTER TWENTY-ONE

The music had begun, thumping so loudly through the base of the speakers that everyone lining up at the check-in table in the corridor felt it in their guts.

Skyler checked his phone, hiding it in the palm of his hand, when one of the girls at the table beside him tapped his arm. "Uh…Mr. Foxe, we aren't supposed to have cell phones on."

"Oh, sorry, Jessica. You are absolutely right." He set it on vibrate and stuck it in his pants pocket. Sidney still hadn't gotten back to him and it was pissing him off.

And where the hell was Keith? He didn't want to be stuck with just Ed Fallows all night. And just as he thought of sneaking away and giving Keith a call, he saw the man coming around the corner down the corridor.

Damn. Did he look good.

Some men with broad shoulders looked too buff in a suit, as if their seams would rip if they moved. Either his tailor was superb or he was just the right size—or both—because Keith looked elegant and graceful in his black tux. He wore a white band-collar shirt with no tie and a high-cut vest in black. His dark hair was shiny with product and his beard stubble on that square jaw was neatly trimmed to form a precise curve under his cheeks. He came right up to Skyler and smiled. It was all Skyler could do not to drool.

"Hey, Mr. Foxe."

He wanted to effuse on how good he looked, but he knew that would not be a good idea in front of the students. It was bad enough that his voice cracked when he said, "Hi, Mr. Fletcher."

"Sorry I'm late. What are we supposed to be doing?"

"I was just helping out with check-in. I guess we can patrol the corridors and such." He stepped away from behind the table and walked with Keith down the corridor away from the students.

"You look absolutely edible," muttered Keith.

"God, so do you. And only two hours to go till it's over."

Keith groaned. "Want to jump you *now*."

"Stop it. Don't even think that. My dick is not behaving as it is."

Keith was breathing hard. "Did you have to say 'dick'?"

They paused and looked back down the corridor. There were fewer kids in line. Most had gone inside. Skyler looked up at Keith. "We're supposed to check the boys' bathroom."

"Skyler!"

"No! I mean *really* check the boys' bathroom. No way would I do anything here."

Keith nodded, running his finger nervously around his collar.

The bathroom was just ahead and they pushed the door open and took a look inside. It smelled like urine, urinal cakes, and the lingering stale smell of cigarette smoke.

Nothing there.

They slowly made their way back toward the cafeteria.

"I don't know about you," said Skyler, reaching for a safe topic, "but I've been looking forward to this."

"You have?"

"Yeah. I like all this teacher stuff. And it's my first year, you know?"

Keith smiled. "Yeah, I remember. I was pretty psyched about all that, too, when I first started out."

"And when was that exactly?" asked Skyler with a brow waggle.

"Back in the Jurassic period, of course. Somewhere around 1998."

"Did they have paper back then?"

"No. We chiseled our essays on rocks and played football with a T-Rex egg. Made for messy tackles."

Skyler chuckled. They made their way back into the noisy cafeteria. Students were dancing in couples and sometimes in groups of three or more. "Shall we do the obligatory check of the punch?"

"Sure," Keith shouted over the music. "I'm a little thirsty."

They headed to the drink table and a student volunteer behind the table ladled them each a cup. Skyler sipped and nearly choked. Too sweet by far. He discretely poured it in the potted plant by the door.

Keith followed his lead. "Not spiked, but jeez!"

Skyler spotted Ed Fallows chatting up some of the female chaperones across the dance floor. "Ugh. Fallows." He shivered.

Keith looked in the direction Skyler was scowling and leaned in. "What's your beef with him?"

"He's a bastard, that's what. He was yelling at one of my kids, calling him all kinds of unacceptable names."

"Coaches do that all the time."

"*Gay* names?"

"Well, yeah."

He stared at Keith aghast. "Surely *you* don't find that acceptable."

"No, and believe me, I try to curb it when I hear it but it's part of the culture."

"Well it needs to stop being part of the culture. I'm surprised at you. And a little dismayed."

"Look, Skyler. You don't understand—"

"You're damned right I don't understand. It's hurtful. I had to listen to that crap enough when I was a student here and I damned well don't want any more kids to have to suffer it."

"I think you're overreacting."

"Overreacting? He caught Alex Ryan, your newest player, in a clinch with his *boyfriend*. He laid into him, threatened to throw him off the team just because he was gay."

"Ryan is gay?" He looked around for the boy.

"Yes."

"He can't kick him off the team for that."

"I know, but he'll find another way. Like maybe adjust his grades the *other* way for a change?"

Keith's gaze jolted toward Skyler's and their eyes locked. "What do you know about that?"

"Enough to know that football's in a lot of trouble."

Keith's whole demeanor changed to something slightly menacing. Skyler took a step back as Keith loomed over him. "Look, Skyler. I want you to keep out of it, okay? I have it covered."

"I will not keep out of it! One of my students needs me!"

"I'm warning you—"

"Gentlemen," said Ms. Goodwin, coming up behind them. They parted for her and she situated herself between them, giving them each a stern expression. "Could you save your heated debates for another time? I suggest you break it up and patrol the dance floor. I need a male presence out there."

Skyler turned a sheepish expression on her. "Yeah, sorry, Alice."

She nodded and moved along, touching shoulders to make her way through the crowd.

"What do you mean you're 'warning me'?" he said, leaning in close to Keith. "What kind of attitude is that?"

Keith passed a hand over his eyes. "I'm sorry. I didn't mean to say it like that. I just... Skyler, I know it's a stretch, but could you just trust me on this?"

"How can you stand it trying to stay in the closet over there? It's so ingrained with those coaches to be anti-gay."

"I know, I know." Keith took a deep breath. His gaze drifted and he seemed to be lost in his thoughts.

"And anyway," said Skyler quietly. "I think the man's a criminal. A real one."

Keith snapped out of his reverie. "What do you mean by that?"

Skyler wanted to spill the whole thing about the pot farm, Evan, murder—but he felt Alice Goodwin's demanding gaze on him. "Look, I'll tell you later." He moved onto the dance floor, looking back once at a perplexed Keith before turning away.

Maybe that was too heavy a conversation for tonight. Keith was doing that hot and cold thing again. What was with the guy? And anyway he didn't want to spoil the mood of being at his first school dance. He mentally shook his head and tried to get into the spirit, checking out some of the dance moves he saw and storing them away in his head for the next time he was at Trixx.

He caught up to Alex, Amber, Rick, and Heather. They were all standing by the folding chairs, moving to the music but not actually dancing. Skyler waved and they all perked up.

"Hey, why aren't you guys dancing?"

Rick rolled his eyes and jabbed his thumb at Heather. "Leather Munson doesn't dance. Should have thought of that when you invited me to a...wait for it...*dance, tonto*!"

"I'm just your beard, *Enrique*. I'm not your dance partner."

Skyler blew out a breath. These guys. "What about you, Alex?" The boy had already loosened his tie and unbuttoned his jacket. His shirt was untucked on one side.

"I don't dance," he sneered.

Amber crossed her arms and blew a lock of her hair off her forehead. She looked more annoyed than disappointed.

Skyler stated the obvious. "I have a solution. Rick, why don't *you* ask *Amber* to dance?"

The Hispanic boy turned to Amber. "But I came with Leather Girl."

"And I applaud your chivalry. But you *can* dance with other people. It seems a shame to waste that tux."

"Totally." He shrugged. "You want to dance, Watson?"

Amber smiled her most beguiling toothy grin. "Yes, please."

The complete gentleman, Rick took her hand, kissed it, and escorted her to the dance floor.

Alex thrust his hands in his pants pockets and fumed.

"Alex," said Skyler out of the corner of his mouth. "Cool it. You look like you're ready to kill her."

Heather moved toward Alex and threaded her arm through his. Alex looked at her like she was crazy. "So now I'm *your* beard, sweetheart. Try to look a little less constipated and let's get some water."

Alex must have succumbed to the wisdom of it and relaxed his face. He walked with her to the table with the drinks and Skyler watched them go with amusement.

He loved his job.

"Love the little game you're playing, but it's not going to work."

Skyler whipped around to the voice at his ear. Ed Fallows.

The man gestured toward Alex, looking uncomfortable with Heather hanging on his arm. "Maybe you can fool these guys, but not me."

"I'm not interested in getting into it with you here, Fallows, so take a hike."

"We're not done, Foxe. Not by a long shot."

Skyler turned to him and with his best sneer said, "Please *do* take this the wrong way: *fuck off.*"

Fallows frowned. "I know about you, too, Foxe. It could get mighty uncomfortable here for you once everyone finds out you're a homo. Just what is it you do with your male students that makes them so attached to you? Sherman would like to know that."

"You bastard. Get away from me, or so help me—"

"What? Just what will you do? I heard about that punch you missed."

"You mean on your boss? James Homophobe Fischer?"

Fallows eyes widened almost comically.

"Didn't know I knew that, did you? I know more than you think. About all kinds of off campus…*stuff*."

Fallows paled, tightened his lips, and whirled away. Okay, maybe that wasn't the smartest of moves but that guy really pissed him off!

He snatched his phone from his pocket and looked at it again. No messages. Where the hell was Sidney? What kind of public servant was that?

♫ ♫ ♫

Hour three. Hardly any of the students showed signs of leaving. Heather and Amber obligingly stuck around Rick and Alex so the two boys could hang out. That was nice of them.

Skyler caught a kid smoking outside and confiscated his cigarettes. The punch ran out and the committee made a quick run to buy sodas, which promptly ran out, too. Skyler broke up no less than three heavy make-out sessions with teens hiding in doorways, niches, and even behind some holly bushes out in front of the school. Ouch.

All in all, it was a pretty good night. He managed to skirt Ed Fallows, whom, every time Skyler looked, seemed to be making furtive and frantic phone calls.

Whenever he found Keith in the crowded room—and it wasn't hard because he was quite tall—he had a concentrated look on his face, as if he were puzzling through a knotty problem. He wished Keith would talk to him a little. Ever since they separated on Alice Goodwin's stern suggestion, he hadn't returned.

God, Keith looked good! Really handsome. It was as if he didn't know it, either. Maybe he didn't. Keith might have his flaws of character but it wasn't vanity. He seemed comfortable with who he was and it was all there, laid out on a platter. Despite Sidney's worries, he truly felt that Keith was a straight shooter. No surprises. He found he liked that.

Suddenly Keith looked up and his eyes locked with Skyler's. He gazed at him for a long time, so long that Skyler felt his whole body grow warm. The man pushed away from the table he was leaning against and started walking through the gyrating dancers toward Skyler in a purposeful stride.

Rooted to the spot, Skyler breathlessly watched him approach.

The dark-haired man finally made it across and walked up to him. "I haven't talked with you much tonight," he said.

Skyler played it cool and turned slightly away to survey the crowd. He shrugged. "You seemed kind of pissed off with me."

"I'm sorry about that. It had nothing to do with you." He sighed. "Well, it had everything to do with you, actually."

He kept staring in that strange concentrated way until Skyler couldn't take it. "Keith—?"

"Skyler... Man." He took a deep breath and shook his head. He seemed to be silently berating himself. Taking another breath he said softly, "Skyler, the night's almost over. Will you dance with me?"

Everything shut down. The sound of the music softening to a slower beat, the projected snowfall, the twinkly lights—all seemed to disappear into a mute bubble. There was only Keith's earnest face looking at him expectantly, and then the man's hand came up, silently asking for Skyler to take it.

Lucidity finally prevailed and his senses came crashing back in. "Are you nuts? No!"

"Skyler. Aren't you tired of this? Of us standing apart? Just dance with me."

"No, Keith! No!"

The hand was still out. It was a nice hand, he noted somewhere in the back of his head, the part that was still working. The palm was smooth and dry, though there were calluses at the pads.

The man was serious. He wanted to dance with him in front of everyone. Everyone who mattered at the school. What would they say? What about his students? His heart pounded madly in his chest.

People near them started to stare. Keith's hand out like that? It was becoming obvious to other people what he was asking for. The students began whispering and turning their full attention to it. Just what Skyler didn't want.

Then he thought of Ed Fallows and all the bastards like him. And he thought of Rick and Alex and the rest of the GSA kids. He thought of his friends and how out they were. With Jamie it was unavoidable, but even Philip flew a rainbow banner outside his coffeehouse. And Rodolfo made no secret of it either. Even Mike de Guzman seemed okay with it.

And then there was Keith. He was willing to out himself in front of his coaches who seemed to hate gays with a passion. It was a far bigger deal for him and he didn't seem to care. His steady gaze never wavered and he even smiled a little, that irresistible gleam of square, white teeth and dented cheeks.

"Dance with me, babe," he said again. "Forget about everyone else."

And suddenly, without realizing he had done it, Skyler's hand was in Keith's and he was being led out to the dance floor. People around them gasped and when the dancers saw what was happening, they parted and stopped dancing. It was a slow number and the dance floor was dim, and the light-generated snowflakes were whirling all around them, and warm hands slid around his back and an even warmer body pulled him close, and before Skyler knew it, he was dancing, slow and gentle and soft.

He didn't take his eyes off of Keith's. But his heart was ready to burst from his chest, it was pelting his ribcage so hard. "What are we doing?" he whispered to his dance partner. "This is insane."

Keith wore a million dollar smile. "I know. But I like this kind of insanity."

Skyler gasped as Keith drew him even closer. There wasn't an inch to spare between them. Skyler couldn't keep his eyes off Keith's face. Independent of his brain, his mouth was saying, "You look *so* handsome."

He smiled down at Skyler. "So do you. You always do. All night I longed to take you in my arms like this."

"This is really crazy." Skyler felt his face flush hotly and he buried it in Keith's chest to hide.

"Hey," came the gentle rumble from that chest. Reluctantly, Skyler raised his face. "We'll get through it together."

It was then that Skyler got the courage to finally look around. No one else was dancing. Though people still stood around them, they were effectively alone on the dance floor. Glancing at the outer edges, he caught sight of Rick, who looked shocked and then pleased, smiling from ear to ear. Heather looked smug and Amber…the poor girl. She looked positively crushed.

Rick was motioning toward them and put out his hand to Alex, who vigorously shook his head. Rick took his hand anyway and argued with him. They were too far away for Skyler to hear but he got the gist of it through Alex's vehement body language. He tried to pull away, and when Ed Fallows came up to him, he managed to yank his hand from Rick's. He gave Rick one last look and tore out of the room, slamming the double doors open. Rick scowled at Fallows and tossed his hand up in a gesture that seemed to say "fuck off" before following Alex out the door.

Uh oh.

A flash. Skyler looked up at a boy with a camera who gave them the thumbs up. "That just got into the year book," he groaned. Then others seemed to wake up and suddenly there were a lot of mini flashes from cell phones. "And that just made it to the internet."

"Does it matter?" said Keith. "I mean, in the great scheme of things, does it really matter? I don't want to hide my feelings for you anymore, Skyler."

"Gentlemen."

They stopped and turned to Alice Goodwin. She wore an unyielding expression that brooked no argument. "Would you two mind coming with me?"

Chapter Twenty-Two

She led them out to the corridor. It was only when they stood out in the blaring lights of the hallway that Skyler realized he had been holding Keith's hand the whole time. He let it go.

Alice folded her arms over her chest and glared at each one in turn. "Would someone please explain to me what happened in there?"

Keith stepped forward. There wasn't an ounce of fear on his face. "We were dancing. Couples dance. And we're a couple."

She looked at Skyler. He knew he must have looked like a deer caught in the headlights but he couldn't quite pull off as relaxed an expression as Keith was wearing. "Well, yeah. I mean…he's… he's my…boyfriend."

This was the first Keith heard of that, and his head whipped toward Skyler, grinning madly.

She closed her eyes and pinched the bridge of her nose. "I see. Well, what you do on your own time is your business. But when you are on school property fulfilling your obligations of your contract on school business, I expect you to conduct yourselves with a little more aplomb. That was a spectacle I don't want repeated."

"Excuse me, Ms. Goodwin," said Keith. And Skyler just knew he was going to cause more trouble. "With all due respect, if we had been a heterosexual couple—"

"Stop right there, Mr. Fletcher. If you had been a heterosexual couple of *teachers* working at the same school at a school function as this is, I would have done the same thing. Consider this a warning on both your records." She gave them both a nod of finality and hurried away.

Skyler turned to Keith. "It's on my record."

"At least you don't have to serve detention."

"You think this is funny? I don't think this is funny. I have a warning on my record. I always had a perfect record. No matter what school I went to or what job I had, I've always had a perfect record. And now look!"

"Are you blaming *me*? Because you didn't *have* to dance with me."

"'*Dance with me, babe,*'" he said in imitation of Keith's baritone. "I was going to say no to *that*?"

Keith smiled and looked down at his shoes before cocking his head. "Boyfriend, huh?"

Skyler stopped short. "W-well, I just thought…I mean."

He chucked Skyler's chin. "You're adorable when you stammer."

He slapped Keith's hand away. "Stop that! We can't do this here." He stared down the long hallway without really seeing it. What had he done? He'd outed himself. All his careful cultivation. And it was all over the internet now. It was on every one of his students' Facebook pages, on Twitter, being exchanged in emails complete with digital pictures. Proof positive, ladies and gentlemen, that yes, Skyler Foxe was a homo, and now everyone knew it. The school newspaper would know it, the yearbook would have a lovely picture probably with the both of them in a heart-shaped border, and his mother—

Oh God! His mother!

"Oh shit! What have I done?"

"Skyler, hon, it's not the end of the world."

"Not the end of *your* world, you mean."

"Skyler—"

"We…we have to get back in there. Patrol. Separately." Dazed, Skyler walked back into the cafeteria and as soon as he entered, he was inundated with catcalls and whistles. His face was hot and red. He made his way as smoothly as he could to the drink table. Grabbing a bottled water, he unscrewed the cap and drank down almost all of its contents.

"Way to go, Mr. Foxe!" said Heather, suddenly beside him. She had her hand up for high five but he didn't return it. "Uh oh. What's wrong? Was this some unplanned moment of teacher hijinks?"

"I'm afraid you haven't caught me at my best, Ms. Munson." He unscrewed another water and drank up, wishing for all the world it was a bottle of Grey Goose.

She put a hand on his shoulder. "Don't meltdown. It's okay. No one here cares. We all sort of suspected anyway, didn't we Amber?"

Amber still looked rather stunned and she had nothing to offer.

Skyler withered. "You *all* suspected?"

Heather shrugged.

"Great. Just great."

"On the up side, it will make a great picture for the yearbook."

"I live in the hope," he said shakily.

"On the other up side, you can now co-sponsor the GSA."

Her words were finally permeating his numbed senses. She had a point. And yes, now he could man up and do what he should have done in the first place. He managed to dredge up a smile. "I guess you're right. No more excuses."

They were silent for a moment before Heather chuckled. "Soooo. Mr. Fletcher, eh? Dude! Your coolness quotient just skyrocketed. Not that it wasn't good before, but, I mean, he is hot!"

He reddened again. Jeez! He had to get away before he was forced to swap Facebook urls. "Excuse me, Ms. Munson, but I have to go do…uh…teacher things now."

"Sure. Go for it. I think Amber and I need to hunt down our 'dates,' though I suspect our career as beards just came to a screeching halt." She smiled and waved as she dragged poor dazed Amber away.

He moved around the room. Most of the kids were giving him high signs and he could swear his face never got a chance to cool down. But there were also some kids, religious ones along with the jocks, who were giving him a cool reception. Not that *that* wasn't expected.

He got to a cluster of female teachers, one of whom was Tricia Hornbeck. She disentangled herself from the pack that didn't look like it had plans to break up anytime soon, and came over to him. She was wearing a tasteful black dress with a pearl choker. "Well, that was certainly...something."

"Not you, too."

"You have to admit, Skyler, that wasn't the most discreet of moves."

He ran his hand through his hair. "I know, I know. But it all happened so fast, like in a dream, and Keith was talking to me with his hand out, and all of a sudden I was out there...I mean really *out* there. Damn." He looked back at the cluster of other female chaperones. "So, what are they saying?"

"Some said you made a really cute couple—"

"Ah *man*!"

"And some had some...not very nice things to say." He groaned again. "What did you expect?"

"I really wasn't thinking, truth be told."

"I can see that." She patted his arm. "It will be fine. It will be a bit of office gossip for a few weeks and then it will blow over."

"Thanks. Let's hope so." He pulled his collar away from his sweaty neck. "Excuse me, I need to get some air."

He made a few steps toward the doors when Tricia stopped him with, "Skyler?"

"Yeah?"

"Just for the record, I think you make a very nice couple, too." She smiled and then returned to her klatch.

He sighed and made his way to the doors. The corridors were

empty. He decided to check the boys' bathroom before heading outside. No one there. The dark glass doors to the front of the school beckoned and he walked silently down the hall toward the entrance. He pushed the panic bar and it clacked open, and the chilly air of a November evening cooled his face at last.

He could only see a few stars because of the pervasive city lights just over the treetops beyond the quiet suburban neighborhood surrounding the school. But it was a clear night and the air was fresh as he filled his lungs with it.

But even though it was a quiet, pleasant night, his roiling gut told him that he was full of regrets at what Heather so aptly called "teacher hijinks." Was Keith *that* irresistible that he would throw caution to the wind? Maybe he had been hasty about the boyfriend thing. That was kind of uncool of Keith to have put him in that position without asking him first. And he would have said no.

But would he always say no?

Keith had asked if he was tired of always standing apart. He knew the man had meant their physical relationship in a public setting, but being outed meant that he *would* stand apart. Now all the evangelical teachers and kids would make a wide berth around him. Of course, he had done the same thing to them, too. He supposed turnabout was fair play. Maybe everyone had something that isolated them from everyone else. It was perhaps a bit boorish of him to assume that just because he was gay he was the one who was different. "'Society is no comfort to one not sociable,'" he told himself, quoting from Shakespeare's *Cymbeline*.

His phone rang. Finally! Sidney.

But it wasn't Sidney. It was Philip.

"Just calling to find out what's going on tonight. Jamie and I were heading over to Trixx and wondered if you and Keith want to come. With us, that is. Or are you guys already out?"

"Funny you should mention that. I think 'out' is the operative word."

"Skyler, what are you talking about? You sound funny."

Skyler walked down the front steps and leaned against a tree. "I'm at school right now chaperoning the Winter Formal. And a few minutes ago, Keith asked me to dance with him in front of everyone."

"You didn't do it, did you?"

"Didn't I?"

"Holy shit! Skyler! What the hell?"

"This is such a fuck up, Philip. I don't know how I let him talk me into it."

"Let me guess. He batted those baby blues at you and you turned to mush."

"Yeah, pretty much. I thought I could sort of keep this under control but now it will be all over the place. Parents are going to start calling the school."

"Yeah, I guess you'd better brace for it."

"But they can't fire me, right?"

Philip, in his best lawyer voice, quoted from the California law code: "'It is an unlawful employment practice for an employer, because of the race, religious creed, color, national origin, ancestry, physical disability, mental disability, medical condition, marital status, sex, age, or *sexual orientation* of any person, to bar or to discharge the person from employment.' That good enough for you?"

"Yeah, okay. I wish you'd finished law school."

"But then I'd miss out on making you coffee every day. Seriously, Skyler. Try not to worry about it."

"The Vice Principal is putting a warning in my record. A *warning*, Philip! I've never had a warning in my life."

"Oh dear. Your spotless record now has a minor stain."

"Everyone is treating this lightly but it's no joke when it comes to tenure and budgets and layoffs. The guy without the warning gets to stay." He knew he was working himself up again and breathing hard into the phone but he was powerless to stop it. Philip must have heard it.

"Skyler, I want you to calm down. It's going to be okay. It will blow over in a little while and then it will settle down to normalcy. And Keith will be there right beside you, right?"

"I don't know. Maybe I jumped in on this boyfriend thing a little too soon. Maybe we should take a break."

"Walls, walls, walls."

"Seriously? I'm hurting here."

"You're panicking and it's normal. Just take some deep breaths and when you get home pour yourself a tall cool one."

"You'd better believe it."

"I'll talk to you later, Skyler."

"Bye. Thanks."

He closed his phone and stuffed it back in his pocket.

"Talking to yourself, Foxe? They kick you out of the school yet?"

He didn't even bother turning around. "Really, Fallows? Haven't you got anything better to do than bother me?"

"Not at the moment, no. You and Fletcher, huh? I knew something was off with that guy. Well we won't have to worry too much about him when Coach Carson gets a load of this. No one wants a homo coach watching their boys take a shower."

"And it's okay for their *hetero* coach to watch them take a shower? You know what, just go away."

"I didn't connect what Mr. Fischer was talking about when he spoke of a troublesome fag. Now I know he meant you."

Skyler stayed leaning against the tree and folded his arms. "Do you *not* understand what 'go away' means?"

"Are you going to press charges?"

"Well I don't see the point, being that he'll be in jail for murdering my friend Evan Fargo."

"*What?*" He nearly screamed it. Skyler snapped around to

stare at him. "You know Evan Fargo?" he cried.

"Yeah. He was a really good friend of mine. And I know you knew him, too, in college and dumped him just because he's gay. So just go fuck yourself."

"You know way too much."

"Yeah. I know that you won't have a job at the orchid *pot* farm soon. Was it you or Fischer who suggested Evan open up the farming business in his own living room?"

By the look on the man's face, Skyler saw that he'd hit the nail on the head. He had offered Evan a job, all right. A nice stay-at-home production sort of job.

"How much money does it cull these days? I mean, a modest little house like theirs?"

Fallows recovered but his hand was shaking as he wiped it over his face. "He had quite the smart mouth, too. Not so smart with the muzzle of a gun in it."

Skyler stopped. "How do you know that? That wasn't released to the press."

There was a pause, as if the world was holding its breath. Neither of them moved. And then suddenly Ed's hands zipped out like a rattlesnake's head, clamping around Skyler's neck. The man shoved him hard against the tree and all the wind was knocked out of him. And there was none left to inhale because his throat was being systematically squeezed shut.

He scrabbled at the hands around his throat, trying to pry him off, but it was no use. He tired to yell—no breath. His vision was closing up, a black tunnel, getting smaller…

Chapter Twenty-Three

All at once, Fallows fell away from him, hands mercifully disengaging from Skyler's throat. Skyler bent over and breathed great gulps of air.

When he looked up, Keith was beating the daylights out of Fallows. Skyler tried to yell at him, but his voice wasn't working. He stumbled forward and smacked Keith's back until he stopped. Good thing, too, because a sedan screeched to a halt in front of the school and Sidney leaped out, gun drawn. Mike flung himself out of the passenger side, gun drawn as well.

"Stay where you are, Fallows," snarled Sidney. She got right up to him and put her wedge heel on his cheek. She flicked a glance at Skyler. "You all right?"

He nodded, not trusting his voice just yet.

Keith suddenly scooped him up and held him in his arms. "Can you breathe? Do you need oxygen?"

Skyler shook his head, held up a finger for a pause, cleared his throat, and then spoke slowly. "I'm fine," he said, voice hoarse. "I will be fine." He pushed Keith's arms off of him.

He turned to Mike de Guzman as Sidney was engaged in hand-cuffing Fallows. "How did you guys get here so soon?"

"Got a tip about five minutes ago that something was going down. Sidney heard it was the high school and took the call."

A black and white pulled up with lights and siren. The siren was cut but the lights were raking a jagged streak of red and yellow across the front of the school.

"Sidney," said Skyler, pointing to Ed Fallows on the ground. "He killed Evan Fargo. He and his boss, James Fischer, were trying to get Evan to do their pot farming at his house and he refused. I guess Ed here didn't want to take no for an answer. Plus he's a big time homophobe so I'd add hate crime to the charges."

"You just let me decide that, okay, Skyboy?" She dragged the bleeding Fallows up to his feet by his cuffs and looked him over. "Who did this? Not you."

Skyler gestured toward Keith.

Keith stood defiantly, as if he expected to be arrested, too. She tossed Fallows to Mike who grabbed him and pushed him toward the car. "Nice job, Fletcher," she said.

"Thanks. What is Skyler talking about?"

"He's investigating crime again without a license." She turned back to Skyler. "I got your message, by the way."

"He basically admitted it, Sidney. He attacked me when I—"

"I'll take your statement at the station. It corroborates our own forensic evidence, just so you know. One of his boots is a match for a footprint we found outside Evan's house that night. We'll do a DNA test on him for the skin under Evan's nails. And with your statement I'm sure he'll stay jailed for a very long time."

"So Jeff is free?"

"I've already sent the paperwork to the county and all charges will be dropped."

"That's the best news I had all night."

She put her arm around him. "Are you really okay? Maybe we should drive you to a doctor." She examined the bruises on his neck. "These will match your shiner at least."

"And just when that was disappearing for good." He rubbed his neck. "I'm okay. I don't suppose you've heard yet."

She smirked and thumbed over her shoulder toward Keith. "You mean dancing with this lug? I got a call from Philip."

He dropped his face in his hands.

A warm hand skimmed over his back. "Come on, Skyler," said Keith. "We're done here. Let me take you home."

Sidney snapped the safety on her gun and holstered it, pulling her jacket over it again. "He needs to come in for a statement."

"He can do that after he's had a chance to change and take a shower, detective."

Sidney narrowed her eyes, never a good sign. She glanced once at Skyler before turning on her heel and heading for her car.

His hand lingered on Skyler's back. "Come on. I have to swing by my place first and then I'll take you home."

"What about the dance?" But when he turned around he noticed most everyone from the dance was standing on the lawn in front of the school talking about the commotion.

"I was coming out here after I told Alice we were done for the night. She heartily agreed. And then I saw that asswipe choking you."

"You saved me." They started walking toward the parking lot.

"I don't mind. Wait. I do mind."

"Huh?"

"If you wouldn't get into these messes you wouldn't need saving. I hope this is a lesson to you to stay out of it and let the police do their job. Sidney would have handled it without you getting your neck in the way."

"I had it wrong, though. I thought it was Fischer."

"He may well be just as involved. Anyway, he'll certainly be up on drug charges."

"And assault. I haven't ruled that out."

He opened the door of his truck and helped Skyler up into it. He walked around the other side and easily climbed in.

As Skyler sat back against the leather seats, he expelled an exhausted breath. "This has been quite a night, huh?"

"I guess so." He pulled the truck into traffic and started driving down the oak-lined street of old Victorians and bungalows. "Look, Skyler, I owe you a huge apology. I thought it would be a terribly romantic gesture to offer to dance with you. I just felt all kinds of frustrated hiding it all the time. And I was watching all those couples and just wishing I could hold you, too. I did it on impulse and didn't think the consequences through. I'm really sorry if it screws up things for you. I don't know how to take the blame but I will."

Skyler looked out the window as they passed quiet houses, light spilling though homey lace curtains or the blue glow of television sets flickering behind drawn shades. He realized he had never been to Keith's place before. Always they had gone to Skyler's.

"You did kind of spring it on me. It's the sort of thing we should have discussed first."

"I know. It was wrong of me. I just really care about you, Skyler. No matter what stupid thing I do, I just want you to know that."

That had a strange sound to it. He glanced at Keith for clarification but the man's jaw was set and he was staring straight ahead out the windshield.

He was too tired to even ask, to argue. He glanced at the truck clock and it read ten-twenty. He just wanted to crawl into bed and pull the covers over his head. But when he thought about that scenario, Keith was always crawling in there with him. Maybe he would stay over at Keith's...no, *no*! He was angry with the guy. He wanted to put the brakes on this boyfriend thing, give it a pause before either of them got too deep.

Say something, Skyler. "Um, Keith. About what I said to Alice. You know. About the b-boyfriend thing—"

"You're getting cold feet again, aren't you? This whole thing freaked you out. I get it. I do. But don't make any hasty decisions tonight, Skyler. Sleep on it and see how it looks tomorrow. Tomorrow may surprise you."

"Okay," he muttered.

They pulled into the driveway of an apartment complex built sometime in the late sixties. Keith pulled his truck into the carport, where it barely fit between another SUV and a Prius. They both climbed out at the same time, but Keith was suddenly right beside him. "I'm okay," he muttered as Keith offered to help him.

He followed the man up a flight of concrete stairs and walked along a gallery to a door that had a large "12" on it. In the courtyard below was a pool surrounded by potted palms and metal lounges. It was an old place, sort of retro, but in good shape. Keith unlocked his door, switched on a light, and held it open for Skyler.

There wasn't much inside but what looked like a brand new leather La-Z-Boy recliner, a lamp, a flat screen TV, a card table and folding chairs, and lots of U-Haul boxes still taped up tight.

Skyler looked around. "Uh…"

"I know. I still have a lot of unpacking to do."

"You've got nothing *but* unpacking to do."

"It hasn't been a priority. Look, I'm going to go in there and change, maybe take a really quick shower. That okay?"

"Sure."

"Make yourself at home. There's beer and some white wine in the fridge."

Alcohol!

Keith disappeared in the dim of a back bedroom and Skyler went into the small kitchen divided only from the living room carpet by a counter and the difference in flooring. He opened the fridge and snorted at the emptiness of it. The man seemed to live out of every fast food joint in town. Skyler opened a pizza box and saw two dried, curled pieces of pepperoni pizza. Closing the lid he grabbed some of the Chinese food cartons, opened one, sniffed it, and grimaced before putting it back. A six pack of beer was also in there along with a half drunk bottle of Chardonnay. He grabbed the Chard and closed the door. He picked a cabinet, opened it, but found only two coffee mugs. He picked another but it was empty.

"Jeez." He opted for a mug and poured the wine in. He drank and wiped his mouth. It was stale but better than nothing.

The shower came on in the other room and he wandered back

to the living room and settled into the recliner. It was all kinds of comfortable. "Man, if this wasn't so tacky…" He wiggled his ass in the seat and leaned back. "Oh." He moaned. This was *really* comfortable. Maybe Keith would get two, one for each of— Whoa. He sat up and clutched his mug. *I thought we were giving the boyfriend thing a break.* His brain thought it was a good idea but his ass didn't. At least when sitting on the recliner. Not for other things. Definitely not thinking about other things. Except the sounds of Keith in the shower in the next room were giving him ideas. Naked Keith ideas.

He swigged the wine and moved toward the boxes. They were stacked three high and were marked with a Sharpie with things like "kitchen," "bedroom," "living room." There were a couple of boxes scattered near the TV with their tape torn back and their lids sitting open. Skyler glanced over his shoulder toward the bedroom and with the sounds of the shower, was satisfied Keith was still busy.

He sidled over to the nearest one and leaned over, just casually glancing in. Books. On philosophy, biology, a few well-worn classics, like Henry James and Oscar Wilde. Skyler smiled. Well all right, then.

He wandered toward the other box marked "football" and saw a few trophies. He set the mug down on the floor and reached inside to bring one out. It was a high school trophy for Most Valuable Player, 1990. When he lifted it up it dislodged a picture in a silver frame. Skyler smiled upon beholding it and set the trophy down to pick it up. Young Keith Fletcher, maybe in his sophomore year of high school, in the typical football pose, wearing a jersey with oversized shoulder pads, arm cocked back with a football, ready to throw. His hair was a lot longer and even messier. His jaw was just as squared and no matter how you looked at it, he was a big guy, even at fifteen. "You were cute even then," he murmured.

He put it down and moved to the next box. Small tins full of loose items. One had fallen open and was spilling out a stack of cards. Skyler picked up the bundle with the idea in mind to put them back in the metal tin. But as he held them he kept staring at them, all thoughts of putting them away disappearing.

Driver's licenses. A lot of them. All for different states. But that wasn't unusual. Keith said he moved a lot.

But did he change his name each time?

On the one from Idaho he was Karl Miller. On the frayed one from North Dakota he was Thomas Sinclair. Another from Arizona where he was Sam Wallace. Three in California: Jeremy Stevens, Ross Falchon, and Steve Gaunt.

Skyler's pulse pounded, clamoring in his ears. A lump burned hot in his throat. He pushed aside a bar towel lying on top of the rest of the stuff in the box. It revealed a gun in a holster.

Skyler jumped back, knocking over the one lamp in the room. The light splashed against the wall, casting long, distorted shadows across the carpet.

Keith walked in, clean, wearing a T-shirt and jeans, with a towel slung over his shoulders. He was barefoot.

"Hey, what's going on in here? Skyler?"

Skyler stared at him, at the man he didn't know at all. He opened his hands and showed him the driver's licenses.

Keith's eyes widened. "Shit! What are you doing messing around in there?" He lunged toward Skyler and snatched the licenses out of his hand. He saw the exposed gun in the box and tried to hide it but Skyler snorted, amazed he was capable of speech.

"Don't bother. I've seen it. You keep a loaded gun in a box?"

"It's not loaded." He closed up the box and stood, facing Skyler. His face was blank and drawn.

Skyler's throat was still tight and he realized to his dismay that tears were streaming down his face. "So who are you? Is your name even Keith? Or Fletcher?"

"Yes. Both."

"Are you sure?" The incredible hurt he felt pierced his heart, throbbing it with an ache he'd never felt before. "Because it looks like you have a lot of names to choose from."

"Skyler, you have to believe me when I say—"

"*Believe* you? Believe *you*?" He wiped angrily at the tears on his face. "You are such a liar! You've lied to me at every step of the way. I really don't want to hear anything you have to say to me." Skyler turned and grabbed the doorknob but Keith closed his hand over his wrist. Skyler yanked it away and without looking back, screamed, "*Don't* touch me! I'm leaving."

"But—"

"I'm leaving and you're not stopping me."

"Skyler, wait!"

There was nothing more to say, nothing more to listen to. He yanked open the door and ran across the gallery to the nearest stairs. He took them two at a time and was running down the street back to the school. It didn't matter how far it was. He didn't really feel the pavement beneath his shoes. He just kept running, the cold slapping against his face, drying the tears.

Chapter Twenty-Four

He got home and took a hot, hot shower, as hot as he could stand. He wanted to be clean of everything, of all his choices and all the choices taken from him. When he finally shut off the water, he toweled quickly, rubbing hard until he was red all over. He stuffed himself into his fluffy robe and sat on the toilet seat staring at his bare feet.

What had he gotten into? Keith was some sort of criminal, running from the law. No wonder Sidney said there were holes in his record. It wasn't *his* record she was looking into. He dropped his head into his hands and rolled it back and forth. What was he going to do? Tell her? Don't tell her?

But wait. Couldn't there be other explanations for this? For having lots of names on different licenses? Ex-cop? That might also explain the gun. Witness protection maybe?

But wouldn't that mean keeping a low profile? Pulling a stunt like he did tonight did not constitute a low profile by any stretch.

But the thing that bothered him the most was that Skyler was becoming attached to him. He'd never given anyone else a chance before. Not Philip, not Jamie, not Rodolfo. No one. Just Keith Fletcher. If that was really his name.

"What have I gotten into?" he moaned. He didn't want to leave the bathroom let alone the apartment. But he had to go to the station and make a statement.

Reluctantly, he dragged himself to the bedroom, walking around the clothes he had dropped on the floor on his flight to the shower. He glanced at the phone on his bed where he tossed it. Messages. He opened it. Fifteen messages from Keith. He deleted them all without listening to them and turned off his phone.

He dressed slowly. Jeans, T-shirt, Boulder slip-ons, leather jacket.

Out the door and down the stairs he got into his car and took his time heading for the station.

Midnight. He meant to head straight there but he couldn't seem to face it just yet. Instead, he meandered his car down dark cramped streets crowded with post war bungalows divided from one another by dark oleanders. Eventually, he turned onto wide avenues shouldered by huge date palms, lording over the streets with their umbrella-like heads. No one was out on the sidewalks. Just pools of light under vintage light posts.

He slowed for a small white dog crossing the street, trotting swiftly over the cool asphalt as if he had somewhere important to be.

Without even thinking about it he switched on his player, and the slow strains of the Four Tops singing "Just Ask the Lonely" thrummed through his speakers and filled the lonesome places in his car.

He hadn't realized how lonely he *had* been. Yes, he had his friends. Sidney would come over at the drop of a hat. But now even *she* had someone. And it had been nice for him to have someone, too. But he needed to be able to trust that someone, to know who and what he was. And he had the awful feeling that it might be something bad.

When he glanced at the clock again he saw it was twelve-thirty. It was time to stop stalling and head over to the police station. He couldn't wait for this night to be over.

♫ ♫ ♫

He pulled into the station parking lot, passing a few black and whites in their parking spaces. He locked the car and walked across the pavement to the well lit front entrance. The rest of Redlands was asleep in their beds, but the police station was humming with activity, of people coming and going out of its lobby, where uncomfortable plastic chairs awaited.

When he walked up to the front counter, he asked for Detective Sidney Feldman and the female officer at the desk told him to take a seat while she called.

It took a few minutes but Sidney showed up. She ushered him past the security door and into the offices. She had a cubicle with walls no more than hip height and she gestured toward one of the chairs on the opposite side of her desk.

When she got comfortable in front of her laptop she stared at him. "Are you all right? You look awful."

"I'm okay. Let's just get this over with."

"Mike had to take him to the hospital. Your boyfriend did a number on him. Which I secretly cheer, by the way. No charges will be filed."

"He's not my boyfriend." And didn't that refrain finally sink home.

"He sure looked like that to me."

"Things change."

She seemed to sense his mood and became businesslike. "Okay, then. Tell me everything from your first encounter with James Fischer to what happened tonight."

Skyler raked his hand through his still damp hair and began to talk. He talked and talked, compartmentalizing it all in orderly fashion and explaining what he saw, what he did, and why, all in as cohesive a narrative as he could.

When he was finished and Sidney stopped tapping on the keyboard, she looked up. "Is that it?"

"Isn't that enough?"

"Pretty damned near. Mike called me from the hospital just before you arrived. Fallows confessed. Told a very interesting story about him and his pal Evan."

"So Fischer helped with the murder?"

"No, but he encouraged Fallows to get Evan to help with the pot growing. He thought he would be desperate enough to do it. But he wasn't interested in breaking the law. In fact, he got pretty vocal about it and threatened to turn them in. Fallows got scared and came back one evening to threaten or bribe him.

He said he came upon Evan just as he finished cleaning his gun. He wrestled it out of his hand and loaded the clip. He said he decided to make it look like a suicide and shoved it in his mouth, but Evan fought." She must have noticed the look on his face because she stopped and took a breath. "I'm sorry, hon. I keep forgetting. Anyway, Evan couldn't fight back because his other leg wasn't working very well and, well, you know the rest. When we got to the crime scene we found a perfect footprint of a boot sole. He must have been waiting for Jeff to leave. As soon as we got a lead on Fallows—thank you for that—we were able to get a warrant for his place and matched the boots. We were just about to go to the school anyway and arrest him when we got a call that something was up there."

"I wonder who that was."

"I don't know. It was a man and he said that there was a ruckus at the school. I imagine they meant your dancing with Keith."

"Oh."

"So do you want to tell me now why you look as if someone drowned your puppy?"

Skyler sat back in the chair and stared up at the drop ceiling, eyes following the pattern of holes in the tiles. "Tell me about these records you looked at, about Keith."

"Why? Skyler. Look at me. Why?"

He dropped his chin and leveled his gaze at her. "Because I don't think he can be trusted."

"Is this about the computer hacking? Because Fallows confessed that Wes Sherman Jr. was hired to do it. They changed the grades of all the football players so they could continue to play. That's going to mean that the whole season gets wiped. There are going to be a lot of angry parents when this news gets out."

"So it's not Keith?"

"No. Doesn't appear to be. Fallows doesn't know anything about Keith. At least he's not saying."

That almost made him feel better. But then those names and licenses kept creeping into his mind. "Sidney, would there be a reason for someone to…um."

"A reason for someone to…?"

"For someone to have more than one driver's license? With more than one name on it?"

"They legally changed their name either on their own or when they got married, or they're in the witness protection program, or they're an illegal alien, or undercover cop, or a criminal. Why?"

"I mean like a completely different name? First and last. And a lot of them. All different."

"Why, Skyler?"

"Because…because Keith has those. A lot of them. And he has a gun."

"What the fuck!" She leapt to her feet and came around the desk. "Did he hurt you? Are you okay?"

"I'm fine. I'm just a little shell-shocked."

"So what happened?"

He told her and he couldn't help wiping at his moist eyes again. She sat in the chair beside him and put her arm around his shoulders. Her expression warred between protectiveness and predator.

"Okay. Okay," she said once he'd stopped talking. "This is what we're going to do. You are going to go to my house. You aren't going to go home. You will not answer his calls. I'm going to clear this thing up once and for all."

"Okay."

"You're okay, Skyler. I won't let him hurt you. I won't let him near you. I want you to go to my house right now."

He rose. "Okay."

"And lock the door and don't open it unless it's me or Mike. Understand?"

"Yes. Thanks, Sidney."

"You don't have to worry." But her face was etched with concern.

He left the station and started driving, but when he got close to Jeff's house, he made a u-turn and headed there.

When his car came close he could see that lights were on, at least in the front part of the house. He checked his watch. Two am? Should he bother them? He pulled his car to the curb in front of the house and looked in through the window. People were moving around inside. He took a chance and shut off the engine and got out of the car.

He reached the front door and tentatively knocked. The door opened. Light spilled out onto the darkened porch. Jeff smiled upon seeing Skyler.

"God, Jeff. I'm sorry it's so late. I just…"

"Skyler." He pulled him into a hug. "Come in."

He followed his friend through the door and Jeff's sister Cindy was sitting on the sofa with a photo album opened on her lap. "Hi, Skyler," she said without getting up. She was wearing a soft sweater and tight blue jeans. Her feet were encased in fuzzy slippers.

"I'm sorry to interrupt, but I really couldn't wait to give you the good news." They looked at him expectantly. "You're in the clear, Jeff. They caught the guy. Well, *I* sort of caught the guy."

Jeff burst into tears and Skyler enclosed him in his arms. The photo album fell to the floor as Cindy joined them in a group hug. Eventually, she pulled them both to the sofa and urged them to sit.

She ran to the kitchen and returned with a glass of water and a paper towel, both of which she handed to her tear-streaked brother. He wiped his face and took a drink before setting the glass on the coffee table. She sat beside him with her hands curled around his arm. "Tell me, Sky," he said.

Skyler related all of it, and brother and sister both put hands to their mouths when Skyler told of his mortal struggle, though he tried to keep the drama out of it. Of course, he had to mention Keith, and his brittle emotions got the better of him, too. He wiped a few tears away. Fortunately, they took it for tears of joy at the outcome.

"Sidney said she sent the paperwork to the county and you should have a clean slate."

"Skyler, I can't tell you how grateful I am. I can't believe *you* solved the case. You're a regular Sherlock Holmes."

"I'm not, not really. I was just lucky."

"You're lucky you weren't killed. Good thing that boyfriend of yours was there to save the day."

"He's not my boyfriend. I don't know what he is."

For the first time, Jeff seemed to notice Skyler's distress. "Skyler. What's wrong?"

"I don't know. It's been a really long day and a lot of stuff has happened. I'd better get to bed."

He rose and went to the door. They trailed after him and hung in the doorway when he opened the front door.

"Oh, Skyler. I forgot to tell you. I actually heard from my Congressman. He called me! He said that LGBT concerns are one of his top priorities and he's taking my case. He said that he *will* get that dishonorable discharge re-evaluated to an honorable discharge. He said the wheels are already turning. I can at least get a decent job again."

"Jeff, I'm so glad to hear it. You deserve something good for a change."

"It was my good luck meeting up with you again. God bless you, Skyler. I hope…I hope everything works out for you."

"Me, too," he said softly.

♪ ♪ ♪

He finally made it to Sidney's apartment and as soon as he got in the door, Fishbreath, her enormous tabby cat, made for his legs and rubbed his head at his shins.

He crouched down and picked him up, holding him close, feeling comfort from the warmth and purring of the furry beast. He rubbed his cheek on his velvety head. "Hi, Fishbreath. Are you lonely? Me, too."

Just wanting the sound of something in the house, he flipped on the TV and sat with the cat on the sofa. The tabby was soon bored with sitting on his lap and wandered up to the top of the sofa back where he settled again, wrapping his long fluffy tail around Skyler's neck. Sklyer scooped up the remote and tuned in the old movie channel.

He grabbed a pillow and hugged it. Fishbreath softly purred by his head on the back of the sofa. He watched the images flicker in front of him, not really absorbing what his eyes were watching. His anxious mind jumped from here to there, never stopping, never resting. Briefly he thought about sleeping, but he didn't seem to feel tired enough.

The hours crawled by. When Fishbreath allowed it, he cuddled him, stroking down the soft fur between his ears. The cat head-butted him when his petting slowed. Sidney called and said that she would be there a little while longer. *She sure works late.* He looked at his watch again and saw, to his surprise, that it was five in the morning. He ran a hand over the sandpaper on his jaw and wondered how he looked. Probably had bags under his eyes. He sat for a while, listlessly watching the images on the television flicker by without really seeing them. What was Monday going to be like? Shit, it was going to be the longest weekend of his life.

Things were bad. He would bet anything that a special school board meeting got called. He might still lose his job, he certainly lost a boyfriend, and he might even be in danger from him. And what about the kids at school? Was Keith a hazard to them? He had saved Skyler a couple of times from trouble, but he had a pretty volatile personality. And did he carry his gun to school? Who knew what could happen? It was insane letting him come back to school to deal with kids. He couldn't let that happen. The whole grade fixing thing, one of the coaches turning out to be a murderer. Hell, maybe *Fallows* pushed Julia down the stairs. It would all come out in a few days or weeks.

But he couldn't in all good conscience let Keith back into the school. He had to talk to Mr. Sherman and he had to do it now.

♫ ♫ ♫

Skyler got in his car and headed to Mr. Sherman's house. He couldn't help but recall the last time he'd been to the man's house. It was with Sidney to tell him that his son was murdered. And this trip was no better. It was to tell him that one of his teachers—no—*two* of his teachers were dangerous. One was locked up but maybe the other one should also be.

The sky was still dark, with only the merest tinge of color at the horizon. Saturday commuters were beginning to hit the streets, but store fronts were still dark. So were most of the houses down the quiet neighborhood street where Mr. Sherman lived.

He remembered the way and parked across the street under a large date palm. Five o'clock on a Saturday morning was far too early to call on someone, but he couldn't wait till later. He had to tell Mr. Sherman, had to warn him.

A light went on upstairs and after a few minutes he could hear someone approaching the front door. It opened a crack behind a chain and an eye peered at him. The door closed again and opened to reveal Mr. Sherman clad in a bathrobe. His hair was mussed and he had a sleepy and perplexed look on his face. "Mr. Foxe? What are you doing here? What's wrong?"

"I know it's early. And I'm so sorry. Can I come in?"

"Certainly." He opened the door wider and Skyler slipped in. Mr. Sherman walked into the living room ahead of him and turned on a lamp. Skyler turned at the creak at the stair. He saw a pair of feet in slippers. "It's all right, Valerie," Sherman called up the stairs. "It's one of my teachers."

The footsteps retreated and Skyler ran his hand over his neck. It was still a little sore.

"I thought I'd be hearing from you, Mr. Foxe. Skyler. I got a call earlier in the evening from Alice Goodwin. And a school board member."

"It's such a mess. I'm so sorry, Mr. Sherman. I just don't know what happened."

"Young love," he said. It wasn't something he expected his stodgy principal to say but at least the man didn't seem that upset. "You and I both know it wouldn't have gotten the attention of the school board if it hadn't been two *gay* teachers dancing. But such is our present situation. You and I both can appreciate this particular case in this particular venue."

Boy, had he misjudged Wesley Sherman. He was a pretty savvy fellow after all. Skyler was liking him more and more. He only wished it hadn't taken these extreme circumstances to bring it out of him.

"Will they call for a special meeting of the school board and will I be required to attend?"

"I have no doubt there will be a special meeting called and that parents will wish to express their opinion on the matter."

"I'm doomed." He plunked his chin on his hand, his uncombed hair cascading over his eyes.

"Not so fast, Mr. Foxe. Though you are a new teacher, I'm certain there will be a gathering of the clan, so to speak. You have made a lot of friends among the faculty who will happily speak up for you."

"I...I didn't know that."

"Didn't you? I would be one of them."

"Thanks, Mr. Sherman. I appreciate that. But I hope you won't be in trouble. They've arrested one of the football coaches tonight. Last night, I guess. For murder."

He stiffened. "Yes, I'd heard that, too."

"A completely non-school related crime, though. However, he did confess that...well, that there was grade fixing going on."

Sherman nodded. This he also seemed to know. "By my son."

He swallowed, seeing the raw pain still in the man's eyes. "I'm afraid so."

He sighed. "Yes, well. I knew about the rumors. It had to come out, of course. It does create a very troubling problem for the students. The entire season will have to be scrapped. The football program will have to be suspended pending a complete investigation."

All he could think of was Alex. "But there are innocent kids involved, too, I'm sure of it."

"I know that, Skyler. You're thinking of young Mr. Ryan, aren't you? So am I. But it can't be helped. A lot more blood will be spilled before this is over. There will undoubtedly be some firings."

With a feral growl in his soul, he hoped one of them would be Scott Carson.

But the ache in his heart told him he needed to tell Sherman one last thing.

"There's more," he said, locking his gaze with his principal. "Keith Fletcher."

"I understand you two are probably close and—"

"No, it's not that. Mr. Sherman, something is going on at the school. Something unsavory and I don't know what it is. It's more than the grade fixing, I can feel it. Julia wasn't pushed down the stairs because of grades. I'm really scared, Mr. Sherman, and I think that Keith is part of some dangerous conspiracy at the school. I know it sounds crazy but—"

"Let me stop you right there, Mr. Foxe." His face lowered and he studied his hands, long fingers sliding one over the other. Finally, he looked up at Skyler with calm eyes and locked gazes. "Mr. Foxe, I know all about him."

"No, you don't. Mr. Sherman—"

He raised a hand to silence Skyler. "I assure you, Mr. Foxe, I do. You really have nothing to worry about. Keith Fletcher is definitely not a criminal. He's FBI."

To be concluded in OUT-FOXED.

We've come to the end of another Skyler Foxe Mystery and what do we get but a cliffhanger! Again! I hope you've been following the series and started with FOXE TAIL, because that would have explained more about what's going on. As I said in that Author's Afterword, I think of the first three books in the series as a sort of TV pilot to get you started into the rest of the books. Each of the first three books has its own mystery to solve but there is a greater mystery overarching the trilogy, sort of the Veronica Mars effect. I know it's a long time between each book but I hope you'll hang in there for the conclusion. I think you will find it worth the wait.

On another note, I wrote this book before Don't Ask Don't Tell was repealed. It was too much a part of the story to rewrite it, and besides, since we are moving along in a timeline, all these events happened *last* November, so we're okay.

People have asked me about my approach to writing the Skyler Foxe Mysteries, and I like to think of these as romantic comedies with a little bit of murder thrown in. I hope you find it as much fun reading it as I had in writing it. I know these guys. Been there done that. And maybe you know guys like that, too. Or, the greatest compliment of all, you *want* to know guys like that. I can totally see hanging out with them at the Taquito Grill and knocking back a margarita or two. In fact, I have!

In this book, the students start a Gay-Straight Alliance or GSA. This is a student organization *for* the students and run *by* the students. Anyone can start a GSA at a high school. They have to follow all the rules of that particular school when it comes to starting a club. In other words, they must find an adult advisor like a teacher, coach, or librarian. Sometimes they will be required to create and submit a constitution with their application. Students should check their school manuals for instructions on starting a club. If all the rules are followed, then the administration *has* to allow it. Forming a GSA club is protected under the Federal Equal Access Act. Under California law, AB 537, the school is legally responsible for protecting the students from harassment and discrimination. Any of my readers looking for more information on starting a GSA, should go to GSAnetwork.org.

As for the next Skyler Foxe Mystery, Skyler will finally get to the bottom of what is going on at James Polk High. Will he patch things up with Keith? Will Scott Carson prove to be a villain? What will happen between Alex and Rick? And what will Skyler's mom say? We'll have all the answers at last in the next book, OUT-FOXED. In the meantime, keep up with my writing news at the website http://SkylerFoxeMysteries.com where you can connect to my blog and join me on Facebook.

Cheers,

Haley Walsh

EXCERPT FROM
OUT-FOXED

CHAPTER ONE

Skyler Foxe stood for a long time in his principal's living room, the man's words about Keith Fletcher resonating in his brain.

Keith Fletcher. Gorgeous assistant football coach and biology teacher. Keith Fletcher, Skyler's lover for the past few weeks and then, very briefly, a boyfriend.

Keith Fletcher, the man who apparently stashed a number of fake driver's licenses in his apartment with different identities, alongside a gun.

And now Skyler was expected to let his emotions flip flop again—mistrust, trust, mistrust—into trust again?

For a long time, he had had his suspicions about the assistant football coach. First Skyler thought he was a homophobic jock, just trying to give Skyler a hard time in his first year as a brand new high school teacher. But then he discovered—most pleasantly indeed—that Keith was neither giving him a hard time nor was homophobic, being that he was a closeted teacher as well. They had been attracted to one another in a crazy dance of denial, and Skyler couldn't count the times Keith had been in his bed in the last few weeks, giving him a hard time of another sort. But then the old suspicions were back and the lies had surfaced. But *now*...

Skyler lowered to the sofa, his knees unable to hold him up anymore. "Are you sure, Mr. Sherman? Are you sure that Keith is with the...FBI?"

He couldn't believe it. All those lies were all just a cover-up to hide what Keith was really doing?

Wesley Sherman straightened his bathrobe. Skyler had quickly forgotten that he had barged into the man's house in the early hours of a Saturday morning.

Mr. Sherman, his school principal, was a throwback to an earlier era. Pushing fifty, his hair showed no gray but was instead a mousy brown and cut in a conservative above-the-ears style.

He wore suits to work and appeared to be a fairly straight-laced fellow, but Skyler knew that still waters ran deep, and they ran mighty deep in Mr. Sherman. He was more savvy than most people gave him credit for. And now there was a whole new level that Skyler was beginning to appreciate.

He sat next to Skyler and leaned back with a sigh. "Yes, I'm quite sure. There is a lot going on, Mr. Foxe, that I am not at liberty to discuss with you."

But Skyler jumped on all the things he needed to know and know now. "Is Keith Fletcher his real name?"

"As far as I know it is."

"Is he really a teacher?"

"I was assured by the FBI that he is indeed an accredited biology teacher and football coach."

"So...he is undercover?"

Mr. Sherman brushed back his mussed hair and folded his arms over his chest. "Yes. The FBI asked to place him. And that's really all I can tell you. Frankly, Mr. Foxe, because of the nature of your relationship with Mr. Fletcher, I thought he would have at least told you this much already."

Me, too. The fear was gone. Keith was a good guy, after all. No wonder Skyler's best friend Sidney, one of Redlands' finest, said that his record was clean except for suspicious holes.

Holes like all the time he spent at Quantico.

All the fear might have drained away but that left only anger. How dare he! How dare he fuck Skyler, make him care, and *use* him like this! What the hell! He couldn't tell the guy he supposedly cared about, the guy he was schtooping almost every night, that he was undercover at the school and could Skyler please keep it under his hat or someone could get hurt? He couldn't trust Skyler enough with that little tidbit of news?

He jumped to his feet. He didn't know which way to turn. He made a lunge for the front door but Mr. Sherman grabbed his wrist and pulled him back down to the sofa.

Skyler stared at the man. He had forgotten his principal was even in the room.

"Mr. Foxe, if anyone wears his heart on his sleeve it's certainly you. I could see everything you were thinking written plainly on your face. Please calm down and think this through."

"This is bullshit, Mr. Sherman! He lied to me. Everything he said was a lie."

"I very much doubt that. He assured me that he would try to maintain his cover by telling as few lies as possible, especially about his background and his other life experiences. And I have to believe, that whatever personal thing he shared with you about your…relationship…was also true. He didn't strike me as the type of man who would deceive in that manner."

Skyler was breathing hard and he tried to listen to Mr. Sherman's words and absorb them, but he couldn't help but feel hurt. Skyler hadn't been the world's most monogamous man. As a matter of fact, he was, by all accounts, a bit of a slut. But on meeting Keith, all that had changed. He hadn't been with anyone else once he began, well, dating him, something he had never done before either. And he hadn't wanted to be with anyone else. Keith was interesting and romantic and damned good in bed.

He hated to think that any of that was a lie.

"Well that's the thing, Mr. Sherman. I don't know any of that, do I?" He hated that his voice trembled and he wiped hard at the moisture at his eye.

"No, I suppose not. But just know this. What he's been doing has been very dangerous, but personally I have felt more at ease since he has come to the school. I would say that you might wish to give him a chance to explain himself at the very least. And don't forget. He will undoubtedly be your ally when the school board convenes, as I'm sure they will."

Oh shit! Skyler had nearly forgotten about that. And that was Keith's fault, too! He never would have outed himself in front of the school staff and students like that. Dancing together at a school dance! That had been insane. But Keith with his blue,

blue eyes and his sexy beard stubble, and his gentle plea, "Dance with me, babe," and Skyler had been putty in his hands. And now everything was a mess.

"I can see it all on your face again, Mr. Foxe. What can I do to help?"

"Have you got anything to drink?"

"I'm usually not a drinking man, but lately, there have been a few too many...events...in my life." He rose, and Skyler suddenly felt like shit watching him retreat to his darkened dining room. It was only a month or so ago that Skyler had found Sherman's murdered son outside a dance club. Maybe it was the fact that his son had been gay, too, or that Skyler had found the culprits, but the staid Mr. Sherman had taken Skyler under his wing and had even vowed to stand up for him when the school board meeting convened to see what to do about Keith and Skyler's stunt.

Had that only occurred just a few hours ago? God, so much had happened. The dance, another murderer apprehended, Skyler thinking Keith was a criminal, and now this.

He slumped on the sofa, easing himself with the fresh scent of lemon-waxed floors and shampooed upholstery. Mr. Sherman's house was as spic and span as the man himself. It was an orderly house but somehow hollow and had all the comfort of a model home.

Sherman returned with two glasses of something caramel-colored with ice. He handed one to Skyler and examined it himself through the cut crystal. Skyler sniffed it experimentally. Scotch.

"Well," said Mr. Sherman, solemn-faced as always. "As they say, bottoms up."

Skyler choked a laugh and raised it to his lips. He drank it down too fast for the burn to catch up to it. When it finally hit his throat, he expelled a fume-filled breath.

Mr. Sherman blinked his watery eyes a few times before setting the empty glass down on his thigh. "Yes. Well."

Skyler sat back, letting the alcohol warm his chest. But once it had started coursing through his system, he began to feel uncomfortable. Mr. Sherman was not the chummy type and this was bordering on sociable, sharing a drink in the middle of the night with one of his teachers. It was downright surreal.

Skyler turned his head to face the man. "Thanks. I think maybe I should go."

"Are you feeling a little calmer?"

"Yes. Yes, I am. Thanks for that. But I'm still going to have to talk to Keith about this."

"I understand." He rose and Skyler followed him to the door. Mr. Sherman unlocked it and opened it for Skyler. "Be careful driving, Mr. Foxe. I hope all is well enough that we can return to some semblance of order on Monday."

"Believe me, Mr. Sherman. I'd like that, too."

He shook the man's hand—Mr. Sherman in his bathrobe and Skyler in jeans and T-shirt—and walked slowly down the front pathway to the sidewalk.

Getting into his car, he watched the front door close and the porch light switch off. The living room light shut off and then another smaller one switched on upstairs.

He turned forward and stared at the steering wheel of his VW Bug. The horizon was beginning to glow from the impending sunrise. Trees and other objects were becoming clearer in the climbing light. He glanced at the clock and the green numbers showed him it was just six o'clock. What should he do first? Well, he supposed he should call Sidney and make sure she didn't shoot Keith.

He quickly grabbed his phone and clicked it on. He punched in Sidney's number and waited, tapping his hand impatiently on the steering wheel. "Come on, Sidney. Pick up!"

A click. "Skyler! Where the fuck are you? I told you to go to my apartment."

"I know. I did. But then I had to go over to Mr. Sherman's

house."

"What the hell are you doing there?"

"I wanted to warn him about Keith."

"You do know what a phone is, right?"

"Yes, detective, I know that. But I wanted to tell him, you know, in person."

"Well, get over here so I can lock you in. I have Mike going over to Keith's to bring him in for questioning."

"You don't have to do that. Keith is okay."

"Skyler, I am going to kill you. Were you lying to me about all that stuff?"

"No! Just call your partner back and tell him he doesn't have to do that. Jeez, I don't know how many people should know this but…I guess *you* should know. Mr. Sherman told me that Keith isn't a criminal. He works for the FBI. He's been undercover at the school all this time."

Silence.

"Sidney? Are you there?"

"You have *got* to be shitting me."

"No. No shit here."

"Jesus H. Christ. Couldn't the Feds bother to tell us this? Like we can't keep a fucking secret? What the hell? This isn't Mayberry. We have real law enforcement here."

"I know, Sidney."

There was more cursing. He didn't know where she picked it up but sometimes she could make a rapper blush. "So what is he investigating?" she asked when the diatribe had cooled. "At the school, no less?"

"Mr. Sherman couldn't tell me. The man's undercover. It's dangerous." But even as he said it, he began to feel a little proud of Special Agent Fletcher. So, not only an accomplished football coach and biology teacher, but G-man extraordinaire? It was kind of exciting.

"Oh that's nice. No one gets to know. I'll be calling the Feds first thing Monday morning."

"Shouldn't you be calling Mike de Guzman right now so he doesn't shoot Keith or something?"

"I guess so. This really pisses me off."

"What about me? It would have been nice to know some of this a while ago so I didn't freak out."

Sidney sighed long and deep. "I suppose it's make-up sex time for you, then."

Skyler hadn't thought of that, but now handcuffs were starting to creep into the picture. "I think I have some messages to return. Call Mike right now!"

"Yes, dear. Are you still staying at my place?"

"No need to. I'll be at home. I think. Bye." He clicked off and punched in Keith's number.

He picked up immediately. "Fuck, Skyler. I'm so glad to hear from you. You *have* to let me explain."

"You'd better come over to my place. The cops are heading over to yours."

"The cops?" And just then Skyler heard sirens in the background. "I think I gotta go. I'll be there in a few." The phone went dead. Skyler hoped that meant that Keith was just turning it off.

Skyler smiled for the first time that morning and started his car. Let Keith take the heat for a change.

He was only a few blocks from home so it took no time at all to pull in front of his apartment, one of Redlands' many old Victorian houses converted into multiple dwellings. The yard was filled with dwarf citrus trees and topiary hedges, while tall Washingtonia palm trees lined the streets, swaying their mysterious shadows above the vintage lamp posts.

Skyler's place was up an outside stair leading to a round tower covered in decorative gingerbread. And sitting on the top step of his landing was Keith Fletcher.

He certainly got there in record time. Skyler smiled again upon seeing him. He really was a gorgeous hunk of male flesh. Ice blue eyes, black mussed hair, square jaw covered in cultivated beard stubble, he was every gay man's underwear model dream.

He stood when Skyler got halfway up the stairs, all six foot six of him, and though he was a big broad-shouldered man, he meekly stepped aside for Skyler, looking for all the world like a puppy expecting to get smacked on the nose with a newspaper.

Skyler said nothing as he unlocked his door and left it open behind him so that Keith could follow. He switched on a light, closed the door, and then turned to face Keith, arms folded neatly over his chest.

He let the man stew for another moment more before he gave him a smirk. In his best Ricky Ricardo accent he said, "Lucy, you got some 'splaining to do."

About the Author

HALEY WALSH tried acting, but decided the actor's life was not for her. Instead, she became a successful graphic designer in Los Angeles, her hometown. After twelve years of burning money in the '80s and early '90s, she retired from the graphics industry and turned her interests toward writing novels. Under another name, she became a freelance newspaper reporter, wrote articles for quirky magazines, published award-winning short stories, and writes an acclaimed series of historical mysteries. She's lived all her life in southern California with a lot of gay friends dealing with a lot of gay issues. FOXE HUNT is the second in her Skyler Foxe Mystery series. Visit her website at http://SkylerFoxeMysteries.com

CPSIA information can be obtained at www.ICGtesting.com
Printed in the USA
LVOW13s2128050813

346448LV00001B/22/P